Praise for *Murder for Christmas*

"Fans of classic British mysteries will delight in this Christmas tale loaded with red herrings and cleverly planted clues."
—*Kirkus Reviews*

"Unexpected and accomplished twists to the cozy mystery formula add to the old-fashioned pleasures of this novel."
—*Publishers Weekly*

"Fans of Agatha Christie and Dorothy L. Sayers will enjoy Tremaine's exploits. Pair with Mavis Doriel Hay's *The Santa Klaus Murder* for a double shot of golden age yuletide mystery."
—*Library Journal*

"An old-fashioned mystery in the best possible way."
—*Tulsa World*

"There are hints of Agatha Christie's long-running play *The Mousetrap* here, as everyone at a multiday Christmas house party becomes a suspect when one of their number is found dead underneath the Christmas tree dressed in a Father Christmas robe... Dunca   he
murderer's identity unt

D0465319

Praise for *Murder Has a Motive*

"Fans of classic fair-play whodunits set in small English vil-
lages will find this just their cup of tea."

—*Publishers Weekly*

ALSO BY FRANCIS DUNCAN

In the Mordecai Tremaine Series

Murder Has a Motive

Murder for Christmas

In at the Death

Behold a Fair Woman

SO PRETTY
A
PROBLEM

WITHDRAWN

FRANCIS DUNCAN

sourcebooks
landmark

Published by Sourcebooks Landmark, an imprint of Sourcebooks, Inc.
P.O. Box 4410, Naperville, Illinois 60567-4410
(630) 961-3900
Fax: (630) 961-2168
sourcebooks.com

Originally published in 1947 in the United Kingdom by John Long. This edition issued based on the paperback edition published in 2016 in the United Kingdom by Vintage Books, an imprint of Penguin Random House UK.

Library of Congress Cataloging-in-Publication Data

Names: Duncan, Francis, author.
Title: So pretty a problem / Francis Duncan.
Description: Naperville, Illinois : Sourcebooks Landmark, [2018] | Series:
  Mordecai Tremaine mystery ; 3
Identifiers: LCCN 2017030615 | (softcover : acid-free
  paper)
Subjects: LCSH: Murder--Investigation--Fiction. | GSAFD: Mystery fiction.
Classification: LCC PR6007.U527 S67 2018 | DDC 823/.914--dc23 LC record
available at https://lccn.loc.gov/2017030615]

Printed and bound in the United States of America.
VP 10 9 8 7 6 5 4 3 2 1

PART ONE

QUERY: AT THE TIME OF THE CORPSE

1

It was a sharp sound that set the gulls wheeling with shrill, protesting cries.

Mordecai Tremaine opened his eyes. He saw only a yellow opaqueness hazily smudged with black. Reluctantly he lowered the newspaper from his face and peered sleepily around him, blinking in the sun.

Unless there was anyone concealed behind the scattered outcrops of rock running here and there down to the water's edge he had the beach to himself. There was no other human figure visible along its flat, sanded length.

He twisted awkwardly in his deck chair, staring up at the wall of cliff behind him. He could see no sign of movement on the path that zigzagged its way up to where the grass verge and the wooden palings at the cliff edge formed a border to the sky.

A little to the right he could see the bridge. Viewed from this angle its air of spidery unreality always sent a shiver through him. It looked as though the first wild wind from the sea would snatch it from its moorings and send it twisting impotently into space.

The bridge, too, was deserted.

Mordecai Tremaine looked at the gulls reproachfully. The instant of panic had passed. They were planing gracefully over the sand or skimming the lines of surf, oblivious to the fact that they had broken into what had been a pleasurable nap.

He replaced the newspaper over his face and leaned back. The sun was soothingly warm. The shrill chattering of the gulls and the surge of the waves along the beach merged into a muted background lullaby into which a vague buzzing sound intruded itself for a few moments before dying away. He drifted happily into the cozy world between sleeping and waking.

It did not occur to him to look at his watch—a lapse for which he afterward castigated himself bitterly—and he was never able to tell with accuracy how long it was before he became aware of the voice that was calling him back to active thought.

It was a woman's voice. It was a level voice and yet a voice that was terrible in its very calmness, for it was the unnatural calm of hysteria held on a tight rein. It was saying: "Please. Come quickly. Please. I've killed my husband."

In the moment before Mordecai Tremaine opened his eyes lethargy fell away from him and left him in a state of icy awareness. For he knew now what had been the cause of that earlier sound that had aroused him.

He looked up at Helen Carthallow. She brushed the falling lock of hair from her eyes. She said, tonelessly, "It was an accident. We were joking together. I pointed the gun at Adrian. It went off. I didn't know it was loaded. Adrian said that it wasn't."

Mordecai Tremaine said, "Have you told anyone else?"

She shook her head.

"No. I didn't know what to do. There's no one else in the house. And then I remembered you might be down here on the beach."

Mordecai Tremaine lifted himself from his deck chair.

"I think," he said, "we'd better go up."

They walked toward the cliffs. It was a fantastic walk that took them over yielding sands through a world that had suddenly become unreal. To Mordecai Tremaine it seemed that the warmth of the sun and the surge of the sea at his back belonged to another existence that he had known at some time that was incredibly remote.

He did not speak. He was watching Helen Carthallow, studying every movement of her slim, long-legged body. What he saw now might give him the secret of the tragedy that lay behind her presence even if she said no word.

She hurried toward the path. She kept a little in front of him, with her face averted as though she did not want to meet his eyes. He wondered whether her tenseness was the natural reaction of a woman who had encountered catastrophe and dared not give way to any kind of emotion lest it prove too much for her self-control or whether she was a woman who had something to hide and was fearful of making a slip that might betray her.

As he followed her slowly up the cliff steps Mordecai Tremaine found himself thinking that he had never been sure of Helen Carthallow. He had never been certain just what kind of person she was. And he had never been able to understand why she had married Adrian Carthallow or what was Carthallow's real attitude toward her.

Before they had gone a third of the way he was recognizing pantingly that he was no longer a young man. Besides, a tobacconist, which was what he had been before he had been able to retire and live upon a modest income, did not have much opportunity for exercise beyond an occasional climb to the higher shelves.

The distance between them increased, so that she reached the top of the steps some moments before him. He saw her glance hurriedly about her and then she turned, and the dark eyes, screened by the long lashes, looked down at him.

The lock of hair that was continually falling across her forehead served now to conceal her expression. She said, "There's no one here."

He wondered as he climbed the last few steps why she

had made that remark. She did not add to it, and her face told him nothing. She waited for him to draw level, and they crossed the cliff top and went down into the sheltered cutting in the rock in which lay the entrance to the bridge.

Helen Carthallow pushed open the iron gate. The bridge vibrated beneath their weight. Mordecai Tremaine glanced down. The beach, with its fringe of rocks, seemed a long way off. He was relieved when they reached the far side.

The bridge always affected him strangely. He knew, of course, that it was the result of an overactive imagination. But it always gave him the feeling that he was adventuring into realms where fantastic things might happen and that he was linked to the sober world in which law and policemen existed only by a gossamer structure that might vanish before he could return.

The house called Paradise had been built and named by a millionaire for his bride. Just what had happened there few men had learned, but there had been whispers that there had been a lover in the case, and it was an undoubted fact that the mistress of the house had been found lying with a broken neck at the foot of the cliffs whither she had apparently flung herself after leaving a despairing note that had not been made public.

Paradise had been closed, and the millionaire had gone away—to take an overdose of veronal two years later after his fortune had vanished in a financial crash that had brought down a continental government.

For many years the place had lain empty and neglected, with the thick mists and the driving rain closing in upon it in winter when the seas leaped in fury up the gray cliffs upon which it stood and with the summer sun beating down upon the rank wilderness of its gardens and peeling the paint from its doors and windows and the long, wooden veranda that looked out over the Atlantic.

It possessed so many obvious disadvantages. It was situated upon a great mass of cliff that must at one time have been joined to the mainland but that was now separated from it by a narrow but deep chasm through which when the tide was high the sea ran noisily. It could be reached only by the bridge, which was not wide enough to take a car.

And, inevitably, there was its reputation that made it a place to be avoided. The local people said that sometimes you could hear the thin, unhappy crying of a tortured soul that had been driven to self-destruction; only the skeptics sneered that it was odd that the sound was heard only when the wind was sighing over the cliffs and humming between the suspension wires of the bridge.

Adrian Carthallow had found the house by chance while driving in Cornwall and had bought it for the song for which such property was to be obtained in those days.

Whatever else might be said of Carthallow it was undeniable that he was an artist and that he possessed the gift of imagination. Paradise had appealed to his love of the flamboyant. Besides, to be the owner of a house with a history and literally perched in the Atlantic had offered an opportunity of valuable publicity to a painter who was still busily acquiring the reputation of a man whose work was worth cultivating.

As Mordecai Tremaine followed the woman who had startled him by her flat statement that she was now Carthallow's widow, his mind was projecting a series of vivid images, tracing the man's career from obscurity to the latest garish fame.

It *was* garish. Adrian Carthallow was not—*had* not been—the kind of man nor had he painted the kind of pictures to enable him to bask in the mellow light of a success that gave offense to none.

They were within sight now of the door of the house. The headland was larger than it appeared at first glance, and a long drive led from the bridge through an attractively planned garden.

Trees and shrubs had been planted to shield the house and break the force of the wind. A turn in the path had hidden the point at which they had crossed from the mainland, and the sense of remoteness and isolation was complete. Mordecai Tremaine looked up at the blue sky and saw himself ringed with trees that effectively blocked the rest of the world from his sight.

Helen Carthallow went into the house. She crossed the narrow hall, passing the open door of the lounge. And then, suddenly, she stopped and stood waiting by the long room overlooking the sea where a gap had been made in the sheltering trees and that her husband had used as a study and library.

Mordecai Tremaine stepped past her, and he drew in his breath at what he saw.

There was no doubt that she was a widow. Adrian Carthallow lay sprawled upon his face on the floor and the back of his head was a very unpleasant thing to see.

A desk stood in the center of the room and beside it there was an overturned chair. On the edge of the desk was a revolver. It was a heavy Webley of service pattern.

Mordecai Tremaine glanced at the woman who still stood in the doorway.

"Is this—?"

She nodded. "Yes. I put it there after—after—it happened."

He looked about the room. Apart from that overturned chair and the sprawled body there was no immediate sign of disturbance. On the right-hand side of the desk there were three drawers. There was a key in the lock of the center drawer, one of a bunch that dangled from a ring. He said, although he already knew the answer: "Did he always keep the gun in his desk?"

"Yes."

The scarlet lips that made a vivid gash in the whiteness of her face hardly seemed to quiver. He barely heard what she said.

"We shall have to notify the police, of course," he told her. He added quietly: "Before we do that is there anything you would like me to know?"

There was a flicker of fear in her eyes. He saw it before she could make the apparently innocent little movement of her head that brought down the concealing lock of hair.

"What do you mean?"

"I don't mean anything," he said. "If *you* don't. Will you show me the telephone?"

She took him into the hall. Lying on a table was a circular that had evidently come by the day's post. He glanced at it casually, noting that the envelope had not been opened.

He had known that the house possessed a telephone, but he was not aware of its exact location. She showed him the cabinet in which the instrument was concealed. He did not have to search for the number of the local police station.

It was the sergeant who answered.

"Is Inspector Penross there, Sergeant? He is? Ask him to speak to me please."

And when the inspector's strong voice came over the wire: "This is Tremaine, Inspector. I'm at Paradise. Mr. Carthallow is dead. Yes—dead. He's been shot. Mrs. Carthallow is with me."

The telephone crackled agitatedly for a few seconds. He said, "Yes. Of course. No. Of course."

He replaced the receiver.

"The inspector is coming out at once, He wants us to stay here until he arrives. He doesn't want us to touch anything."

"I understand," she said.

Her voice trembled, and he realized that her self-control was almost gone. He realized, too, that there had been antagonism in his own manner. He felt a twinge of conscience.

"There isn't anything we can do for the moment," he said, more gently. "Suppose we sit down somewhere until the inspector comes? This must have been a terrible shock for you."

She clutched at the word with an eagerness that surprised him with its sudden element of the pathetic. He thought of a small girl who was desperately anxious to be comforted.

"Yes," she said. "Yes, it was a great shock. When I saw Adrian—"

She broke off and turned away from him. He followed her into the lounge across the hall. She sat down in an easy chair facing the window. He said, "Perhaps a cigarette would help."

She took one with an unsteady hand from the case he held out. He lit it for her, and as she lay back against her cushion he chose a chair a little to her right so that he could study her without making her conscious of his scrutiny.

He was trying to analyze his thoughts; trying to discover

the reason for the mistrust that persisted in breaking the surface of his mind.

She was smoking her cigarette with quick, nervous puffs, without inhaling, so that the tobacco created a hazy screen, through which he could not be sure of her expression. Did she look and act like a woman who had just accidentally shot and killed her husband?

Mordecai Tremaine admitted that since his acquaintance with wives who had just killed their husbands was of the slightest he was hardly in a position to put forward a definite opinion. He wondered what his own reaction would be were he a wife who had just performed so untimely a deed. He thought he would be stunned and bewildered by what he had done. But he also thought that he would want to talk. He would want to repeat his story of what had happened over and over again. He would want to relieve the torment of his soul.

However, that was pure conjecture, after all. And in any case, no two people could be depended upon to react in just the same way.

A good deal, of course, would depend upon whether the wife had been in love with her husband. Some wives might secretly welcome the sudden removal of their partner from the sphere of the living.

He knew why his thoughts had traveled such a road. Lester Imleyson. Rather, Helen Carthallow and Lester Imleyson.

Deliberately he shut his mind upon any further wanderings in that direction. He must deal with facts. Sometimes preconceived theories had a habit of getting mixed up with the things that had really happened so that they produced results that were altogether false.

Helen Carthallow said, suddenly, through the smoke haze: "I'm terribly sorry for dragging you into all this."

"I wish I could do something to help," he told her. He took advantage of the opening she had given him. He said, "You came straight down to the beach? You didn't think of the telephone?"

He was expecting that she might hesitate, but she answered him immediately.

"No—I didn't think of the telephone. I suppose I was too confused. And I wanted to have someone with me. I—I couldn't stand being in the house alone. Then I thought *you* might still be on the beach. I noticed you there when I was crossing the bridge on the way in."

Mordecai Tremaine nodded. She did not offer to tell him any more, and he leaned back in his chair and wondered what Jonathan Boyce would say.

Jonathan Boyce was Chief Inspector Boyce, of Scotland Yard, now fishing somewhere out on the blue water of Falporth Bay and as yet unaware of the fact that his friend Mordecai Tremaine had managed to become involved with yet another body. Even as they had stood at Paddington Station before stepping into the train that had brought them on their Cornish holiday Boyce had said, "This really is going to be a rest cure, Mordecai. I doubt whether even you will be able to produce a body in Falporth."

Mordecai Tremaine shifted in his chair a little uneasily. There was no disputing the fact that even for an enthusiastic amateur criminologist he seemed to possess an uncanny habit of being in the near neighborhood whenever sudden death made its appearance.

Thinking of what Jonathan Boyce would say provided him with an explanation of Helen Carthallow's reluctance to talk to him. She knew that his reputation belied his mild countenance, and she was afraid of him.

Having reached that conclusion he was glad that Inspector Penross arrived so promptly. It was an uncomfortable feeling to know that a woman was afraid of him. His sentimental soul shrank from the admission.

He heard Penross coming up the drive and went to the door to meet him. The inspector headed a procession consisting of a sergeant, a constable, and a dumpy little man with a goatee who was carrying a bag and whom Tremaine knew to be Doctor Corbin, who acted as the police surgeon.

The inspector looked at him inquiringly. In his gruff voice

that was so oddly at variance with his slight frame he said, "It sounded a bad business, Mordecai. Just how bad is it?"

"That's *your* problem," said Mordecai Tremaine significantly. "Mrs. Carthallow is in the lounge." He added: "Would you like to see Carthallow's study first? That's where *he* is."

Penross nodded and followed him into the house. He stood in the doorway of the study and looked down at Adrian Carthallow's corpulent body.

"Very nasty," he said. "Very nasty indeed."

For a moment or two he stood surveying the room, and then he walked across to the dead man. Despite the apparent casualness of his manner Tremaine knew that his mind was photographing the scene so that afterward he would be able to recall every detail.

Doctor Corbin was still waiting in the doorway, bag in hand, a look of quivering professional eagerness on his puckered face. The sight of a man whose head had been distressingly treated by a revolver bullet of heavy caliber was not a new one to him, but this particular head had belonged to Adrian Carthallow.

Penross said, "Let me know what you think, Doc. You stay here with the doctor, Sergeant. Helsey can come with me."

Mordecai Tremaine did not think that he wanted to go on looking at the ugly thing on the floor anymore. His stomach was already moving protestingly.

He was close behind Penross and the constable as they went into the lounge and he saw Helen Carthallow turn to face them.

"Good afternoon, Inspector," she said quietly.

There was a certain tenseness in her attitude that betrayed that she had been nerving herself for this ordeal, but that was, after all, no more than natural.

"I'm afraid this is very painful for you, Mrs. Carthallow," Penross said, "but I'm sure you understand that there are formalities that have to be observed. I've just come from your husband's study. Perhaps you'd like to tell me in your own way how it happened."

"There isn't much to tell," she said. "Adrian and I were—well, we were playing the fool. We were joking together. You—you know how I mean. Then Adrian began to act as though he was afraid of me, and he unlocked his drawer and took out his revolver, saying that he needed something to protect himself with. He pointed it at me. I was rather scared. I told him to put it down in case it went off, and he laughed and said that it was quite harmless because it wasn't loaded. And then he said…"

Her voice trailed away. Tremaine saw her hands clench upon the arms of her chair. Penross did not make any comment. He waited for her to recover, and after an instant or two she went on: "He said, 'Go on, try it for yourself.'

He—he made me take the gun. I suppose I must have shown that I was frightened and didn't want to handle it because he laughed again and said something about William Tell shooting the apple from his son's head. Then he made some comment about my being a wealthy widow if anything went wrong. I can't remember exactly what happened after that. I suppose I must have pointed the revolver at him and pressed the trigger…"

She buried her face in her hands, as though to shut out the memory of it. Her slim shoulders were shaking.

"It was horrible," she said, through her fingers. "There was a flash and a bang. I saw Adrian fall. There was blood on his head and face. I didn't know what to do. I was too dazed even to think. At first I don't think I realized what had happened.

"Then I knew that I'd killed him. I knew that he was dead. There—there couldn't be any doubt about it. I put the gun on the desk. Everything was confused, like some dreadful nightmare. I felt I couldn't move. But I had to tell someone. I had to get help. I thought of Mr. Tremaine. I'd seen him on the beach when I came into the house, and I guessed he'd still be there. It didn't occur to me to use the telephone, although, of course, I should have known that the best thing to do was to get in touch with you. I told Mr. Tremaine what had happened, and we came back here together. He telephoned you at once."

She stopped. Penross nodded.

"I see. Thank you." His expression was quite blank. "I gather that you and your husband were alone? There were no servants in the house?"

"No. We employ a cook, a maid, and a general duty man who does any odd jobs that need to be done. Normally, the cook and the maid sleep in, but we'd been away for a couple of days and we'd given them the time off. They were to come back in time to prepare dinner for tonight."

"Ah, yes," said Penross. "The races at Wadestow. You've been staying over there, I believe, Mrs. Carthallow?"

"At the Polmurrion Hotel," she told him. "My husband had some business matters to attend to in the town and decided that it would be better to stay in Wadestow rather than make the journey back here each night."

"You returned together this afternoon?"

"Not together," she said. "I didn't expect Adrian back until later. He told me he had an appointment that would probably detain him a little while. He was using the car, so I came over by train."

"About what time would that be?"

"I caught the 1:10 from Wadestow. We must have been in Falporth about twenty minutes past two—it isn't much more than an hour's run. I took a taxi from the station, so I suppose I was here at some time between half past two and a quarter to three."

"And your husband?"

"Adrian was already here. I was surprised to see him because as I've said I hadn't expected him back until later. He told me that the business appointment he'd mentioned had had to be canceled at the last moment, so he'd decided to come straight here. Of course, he knew that I'd made my own arrangements thinking that he wouldn't be able to pick me up."

"He knew you were coming back by train?"

She moistened her lips.

"Yes," she said, after the merest of pauses. "I have a car of my own, but I didn't have it with me in Wadestow because Adrian drove us both there."

Penross appeared to be digesting what she had told him. Mordecai Tremaine, who'd had opportunities of studying him, knew that he was giving his impersonation of the guileless policeman who could be induced to believe anything by a person of average intelligence. It was a very useful part of his stock-in-trade.

"How long do you think it must have been," Penross said, "between the time of your return and the time when the revolver incident took place?"

Tremaine admired his use of the phrase "the revolver incident."

Helen Carthallow shook her head. She turned her dark

eyes upon Penross with a pathetic helplessness. With the lock of hair falling forward she made an appealing picture. It would obviously be unforgivable to attempt to force her memory at this moment.

"I'm sorry, Inspector," she said. "It would only be guess-work if I tried to tell you. I was too upset to give any thought to the time." She added: "But you know when I arrived here—the taxi driver will be able to confirm it—and you know the time when Mr. Tremaine telephoned you. Surely the rest isn't important?"

"Perhaps it isn't," agreed Penross. He rose to his feet. "I realize how painful this has been for you, Mrs. Carthallow. I'm afraid my men will have to look over the house—routine, you know. They'll be as unobtrusive as possible, of course. And I shall have to ask you to let me have all you've just told me in the form of a signed statement."

"I quite understand the position," she told him. "Adrian didn't die naturally. You will have to make a report."

"I'm glad you see it like that," Penross said, in the tone of one who was greatly relieved. "It makes a very unpleasant task a good deal lighter for me. I may have to ask you a few more questions later on, but I won't disturb you more than is absolutely necessary."

He was moving toward the door when he turned.

"If you'll pardon my taking the liberty," he said, "I'll ask

Doctor Corbin to come across. He's in the study. You've undergone a very great shock, and I'd feel happier if the doctor saw you."

"I'm perfectly all right, Inspector," she said, but Mordecai Tremaine saw that her lips were quivering.

Penross went over to the study, and Tremaine heard him speaking to the police surgeon. Discreetly he left the lounge as the doctor came briskly across the hall. The door closed upon the other's dapper little form, and a moment later Penross appeared again in the entrance to the study. The inspector caught his eye.

"It looks," he said, "as though you've done it again."

2

Mordecai Tremaine was annoyed to find himself beginning to feel embarrassed.

"Mrs. Carthallow told you what happened," he said, defensively. "I was on the beach. She saw me there and came down for help."

Penross was looking at him thoughtfully.

"You must have heard the shot," he said.

"I did. It woke me up. I didn't know what it was, of course. I looked around and couldn't see anything wrong, so I settled down in my chair again. The next thing I knew was that Mrs. Carthallow was standing in front of me saying that she'd killed her husband."

There was chagrin on Mordecai Tremaine's face.

"I know what you're going to ask," he said, "and I can't tell you. I didn't look at my watch. I don't know just how long it was after I heard the shot that Mrs. Carthallow came down to the beach."

Penross gave him a queer look, but all he said was, "There

was no reason why you should have noticed the time. You weren't to know what was happening."

Mordecai Tremaine was feeling like a star pupil who had let his master down in public. But the inspector did not seem to think that the matter was of any importance. He glanced about him. The sergeant and the constable were out of earshot. His gruff voice was lowered to a somewhat throaty whisper.

"I can talk to you more easily than I could to other people," he said. "Not just as a witness. Off the record. You knew Mr. and Mrs. Carthallow. Did they strike you as being a couple who were still in love with each other?"

"Not less so than dozens of other married couples I've met," said Tremaine carefully.

"But the first romantic bloom had worn off, eh?"

Mordecai Tremaine pushed his pince-nez back into position.

"Well—perhaps," he admitted.

Even his sentimental soul could not pretend that between Adrian Carthallow and his wife there had existed the perfect understanding born of a completely happy marriage. Not that it would have impressed Penross in any case, for there was plenty of outside evidence to show that the marriage had not been among the successes.

The inspector nodded. He did not make any comment, but no comment was necessary.

Mordecai Tremaine had experienced an unpleasant feeling of doubt when Helen Carthallow had been giving her version of how her husband had come to meet his death, and he knew what was in the inspector's mind. The picture of the happily married couple indulging in a youthful romp did not carry the stamp of truth. Still less did it seem likely that Adrian Carthallow would have compelled his wife, even more or less laughingly, to point a revolver at him and pull the trigger.

It did not follow, of course, that Helen Carthallow had lied. Tremaine knew from experience that some of the most fantastic of stories proved upon examination to be no more than sober fact. It was unbelievably easy for a person to become the victim of circumstances; sometimes the appearance of guilt was so overwhelming that innocence could be proved only after the most intensive of investigations.

The door of the lounge opened. Doctor Corbin came out. He said, "She's trying hard not to break down, but she's in a pretty overwrought state. I don't think it would be advisable for her to stay here on her own, and I've persuaded her to go over to Mrs. Eveland's. It's quite near. As soon as you've finished I'll drive her over—if you've no objection, of course."

Penross nodded.

"That's all right, Doc. As long as I know where she is so that I can handle all the formalities. And as long as she understands that I'll need to spend some time here yet."

Helen Carthallow seemed content to allow her immediate destiny to be arranged for her. Her face was white and drawn, and there was strain in her dark eyes and the pinched appearance of her nostrils. The rigidity that had marked her when she had been telling her story had vanished. She looked small and lonely and very pathetic.

She answered the further questions the inspector put to her, agreed to the accuracy of her statement when he went painstakingly through it with her, and agreed to sign the typewritten copy as soon as it was available.

"It will be necessary for me to keep my men on the premises, Mrs. Carthallow," he told her. "If you feel that you would prefer to be present…"

He left the opening for her. She said, "I know I can leave matters in your hands, Inspector. When the servants arrive perhaps you will arrange to send them over to me at Mrs. Eveland's so that I can see what will be the best thing to do."

"You don't propose to come back tonight?" he asked, and Mordecai Tremaine saw her shiver.

"Not unless I have to," she said, in a low voice. "I couldn't stay here alone. Not—not now. I'm sure that Hilda—Mrs. Eveland—will let me stay with her."

Tremaine knew Hilda Eveland. She lived about half a mile or so away on the outskirts of Falporth. She was middle-aged and one of those plump, cheerful people who never seem to lose their good humor. She lived permanently in the district, but she had seen a good deal of the Carthallows during their periodic visits to Paradise.

The doctor had had to leave his car on the mainland, since the bridge was too narrow to permit its passage. Mordecai Tremaine stood watching with Inspector Penross as he went down the drive with Helen Carthallow. She stumbled once, and he saw Corbin's hand go out to help her.

"Going over that bridge is the only way of getting to this place, isn't it?" Penross asked.

Tremaine nodded. The inspector said, as they went back inside the house: "Would it be possible for anyone to climb up from the beach and reach the grounds?"

"I don't think so. The cliff is too sheer for that."

"Did you see anyone else about when you went in with Mrs. Carthallow?"

"No."

"Hmm." It was a worried sound. Penross frowned. "I think," he said, "we'll take another look around."

Mordecai Tremaine was feeling worried, too. He was remembering how Helen Carthallow had gone up the cliff path ahead of him and how she had looked about her when she reached the top, as though she had half-expected to find someone there.

But he did not mention that fact. He felt that at this stage it would only serve to introduce an unnecessary complication.

Penross went back into the study where Adrian Carthallow's body lay.

"The photographers and fingerprint people ought to be here soon," he said. "They've got to come from Wadestow. In the meantime let's see what there is to see."

Mordecai Tremaine followed him gingerly, trying to tread lightly and avoid touching anything. A pair of sunglasses lay upon a chair by the bookcase that occupied part of one wall. They looked as though they might have been placed there carelessly by someone who had come in out of the sun to search for a book on the shelves.

Penross glanced reflectively at them for an instant or two as he passed. Suddenly he pursed his lips and went down on one knee.

"Hullo," he observed, "what's this?"

Tremaine looked over his shoulder at the metal object lying on the floorboards between the edge of the carpet and the skirting.

"Seems to be a pair of forceps," he remarked. "The kind surgeons use for holding arteries during operations. The Spencer Wells type, I think they call them."

"Funny sort of thing for an artist to have," Penross said.

He peered at them. Several tiny slivers of wood were adhering to the serrations, but otherwise they seemed to be unmarked.

"No sign of blood on them, anyway."

They left the study, and the inspector carried out a brief tour of the house. The place was not large, but it was expensively furnished.

"Must have spent a small fortune on it," Penross mused, as they glanced into the beautifully fitted bathroom adjoining the main bedroom. "Nice to be able to paint pictures that bring in that much money."

There was no sign of anything to arouse their suspicions, and they went back to the hall. The inspector noticed a door at the end.

"D'you know where this leads?"

"To Carthallow's studio," Tremaine told him. "It's built over the bedrooms, just under the roof. The stairs bypass the rest of the house."

They were awkward stairs, narrow and winding. Penross climbed them slowly and pushed open the door of the studio. He glanced about him, obviously intrigued by the thought that here amid this apparent confusion of materials so many works of art had been born. Carthallow had not been a tidy worker, and the studio was littered with tubes of pigment, charcoal sketches, palettes, and odds and ends of equipment.

Penross walked across to a big easel standing against the far wall and examined it casually. He gave a low whistle.

"Take a look at this," he said.

Mordecai Tremaine joined him. He looked at the canvas upon which Adrian Carthallow had been working. It presented a mass of startling color. Blue, red, and yellow had been smeared heavily across it so that the unfinished portrait beneath could barely be distinguished.

He adjusted his pince-nez to give himself time to think.

"Curious," he said, inadequately.

"The word 'curious,'" Penross remarked dryly, "seems somewhat of an understatement. It's Mrs. Carthallow's portrait, isn't it? You can just about tell that much."

"Yes. I knew he was painting her. But I haven't seen it until now. Carthallow was inclined to be touchy where portraits were concerned. He didn't like people to see them until they were completed."

"I see."

The inspector's tone was noncommittal, but Mordecai Tremaine did not feel very happy about it.

When they went downstairs again the fingerprint men and the photographers had arrived and were bringing their apparatus into the hall. Tremaine said, "I don't want to get in your way, and in any case I ought to be going back. You don't want me for anything?"

"I know where to find you if I do," said Penross. "I'll have to take an official statement from you for the record, of course. Possibly I'll drop in on you later, but I can't guarantee it. I've a feeling we're going to be here for some time."

Mordecai Tremaine knew what he meant. Inspector Penross was a long way from satisfied. He intended to have more than Helen Carthallow's unsupported story before he ruled a line under his report of Adrian Carthallow's death and regarded the matter as closed.

3

Jonathan Boyce had listened to the whole story, and to Mordecai Tremaine's relief he had made none of the expected comments on the subject of his own presence at the scene of the tragedy. To a Scotland Yard detective, even on holiday, a body is a matter for professional interest, and having, in addition, met the late occupant of the said body before his tenancy had been so abruptly terminated, Boyce was too thirsty for information to wish to start any red herrings, no matter how tempting.

"Did Charles say whether he was coming over?" he asked.

"When I left him," Mordecai Tremaine said, "the fingerprint men and the photographers had just arrived. He looked as though he was going to be busy."

It seemed strange now to hear Penross referred to as "Charles." Not, of course, that it was odd that Jonathan Boyce should have made use of the Christian name. But Inspector Penross engaged upon an official police investigation, with all the majesty of the law behind him, was not at all the same person as Charles Penross who had sat yarning with them in a deck chair until long after the sun had gone down.

Boyce and Penross were old friends. The Yard man's older sister and her husband had made their home in Falporth for some years, and Boyce had a standing invitation to spend his summer vacation with them. Which meant that it had been more or less inevitable that his acquaintance with Penross should have developed rapidly.

Their first meeting had been a chance encounter on a fishing trip. They had discovered that they were members of the same profession, and from then on the prospect of talking shop with Charles Penross had been an added attraction to bring Jonathan Boyce year by year to Cornwall.

On this occasion the annual invitation had been extended to include Mordecai Tremaine. Boyce had written a good deal in his letters to his sister about the retired tobacconist who had such an enthusiasm for crime detection, and in any case Arthur and Kate Tyning had read enough about him in the newspapers to make them eager to see him in the flesh.

For Mordecai Tremaine had found himself not long ago the center of a brief but violent blaze of publicity. The press had decided that it was a matter of no small interest that an elderly gentleman of mild appearance, whose pince-nez always seemed to be on the point of slipping off the end of his nose and who had a weakness for reading literature in which romance was depicted in colors more roseate than nature, should make a habit of solving murder mysteries in his spare time, and they had come to the conclusion that the public should know more about him.

It had all been very embarrassing. Being naturally rather a shy individual he had found it difficult to cope with his reputation as an astute detective. He possessed the perpetual feeling that he was not living up to what people expected of him.

This diffidence had been at the back of his mind when he had been with Penross during the afternoon. He had imagined that the inspector had been disappointed in him; that he had come to the conclusion that the idol was provided with feet of clay.

Jonathan Boyce was pulling at his chin.

"So Adrian Carthallow is dead," he said thoughtfully. "A lot of people are going to heave a sigh of relief over that."

"You mean because of his pictures?"

"I mean because of his pictures," agreed Boyce. "He was a clever devil. But a bit too clever. It made him plenty of enemies. Colonel Neale, for instance."

Mordecai Tremaine knew why Boyce had mentioned Colonel Neale. For Colonel Neale was in Falporth. He had arrived a day or two earlier. And Colonel Neale had publicly announced his intention of teaching Adrian Carthallow what he had described, with suitable military adjectives, as a much needed lesson.

The stir Adrian Carthallow's portrait of Christine Neale had caused had not quite died down, even now. It had been a very good portrait. Technically, indeed, it had been an excellent piece of work—one of the best things Carthallow had ever done.

But there was no doubt that it had also been a piece of sheer devilry that only Adrian Carthallow's twisted sense of humor could have devised. It was difficult to understand just why Christine Neale had allowed him to show it. Unless it was because she had been infatuated with him and had not realized what he had done until it had been too late.

He had painted the woman's soul. Or perhaps it would be kinder to say that he had painted the woman's soul as he had imagined it to be.

The hot, lustful eyes that had added the final touch of the wanton to the face of a woman whose sensuality was unmistakable had attracted the crowds all day when the picture had been shown, and columns of criticism on the rights and wrongs both of painting and of showing such a portrait had filled not only the art periodicals but the popular press—which was a proof of the news value of Carthallow's achievement.

Those who knew her could be in no doubt as to whom the portrait was intended to represent. Christine Neale's features had been lifelike, so much so that it seemed that it was the woman herself who stared boldly down from the canvas.

The devilish artistry of the thing lay in the fact that to the casual glance the portrait looked perfectly natural—just like any other well-executed likeness of a young and good-looking woman. It was only from certain angles that it seemed to come alive with that compelling sensuality.

Christine Neale had vanished when the storm of comment had broken. According to informed rumor she had been sent off to South Africa, where a brother was farming well up-country.

The colonel had gone raging to his lawyers, breathing threats and ready to sue, but the case had never reached the courts. His legal advisers had managed to impress upon him the unpalatable but indisputable fact that it would merely make matters worse, since it would prolong the publicity. And it was certain that Carthallow not only would make the most of his opportunity to provide the newspapers with fresh sensations but had plenty of material with which to do so.

Christine Neale had made no secret of the fact that she was in love with him. She had paraded her affections with the unthinking folly of a headstrong and spoiled young woman who had been allowed the use of too much money too early in life. Carthallow would have had little difficulty in convincing a jury that he had painted no more than the truth; that he had, in fact, displayed the consummate talent of a fine artist in bringing out the character of his sitter.

Mordecai Tremaine had often asked himself what it was that made a man like Adrian Carthallow attractive to women. Christine Neale had not been the only one to fall in love with him, although she had perhaps revealed her feelings more foolishly than some of the others.

Maybe it was because Carthallow treated them with such a contemptuous familiarity that they ran at his heels. Being a sentimentalist—and, moreover, a regular reader of *Romantic Stories*—Mordecai Tremaine was reluctant to admit that brutality toward a woman was the way to breed adoration. But whenever he thought of individuals of the Carthallow type he was aware of a disturbing feeling of uncertainty.

Jonathan Boyce said, suddenly, "Wasn't Carthallow painting his wife's portrait?"

"Yes," said Tremaine, and added: "It looks as though somebody didn't care for the idea."

"Meaning?"

"Meaning that even if Carthallow was still alive he wouldn't have been able to finish it. Somebody deliberately ruined it by daubing color all over the canvas."

Boyce pursed his lips. He looked disturbed.

"What did Mrs. Carthallow say about that?"

"She hasn't said anything," returned Mordecai Tremaine.

"Yet. She'd already gone to Mrs. Eveland's when Charles discovered it."

"Had anybody seen the portrait—as far as it had gone?"

"Mrs. Carthallow may have done so, but I don't think anybody else is likely to have seen it. Carthallow didn't like people viewing his unfinished portraits."

"So nobody knows…" said Boyce.

His voice trailed away. Tremaine said, "That's it. Nobody knows whether Carthallow was planning to put over another Christine Neale episode—with his wife in the role of the victim."

"Surely," said Boyce, "not his *wife*?"

Mordecai Tremaine was very uncomfortable. He felt that ever since that moment when he had looked upon Adrian Carthallow's extremely dead body the sentimental side of his nature had been forced to join issue with the criminologist whose duty it was to place truth above all else.

"Perhaps," he said, "especially his wife. In view of the latest developments. He didn't have affairs with other women despite the way they ran after him. So he may have been in love with her. The portrait may have been intended as his revenge for Imleyson."

"But I thought he didn't mind about Imleyson."

"He seldom showed that he did," agreed Tremaine. "But who can say what he really thought? On the other hand the portrait may have been intended as a genuine tribute. Perhaps he destroyed it himself because of something he found out."

Boyce was frowning.

"That story of hers. Suppose Carthallow gave her the gun, just as she said. But suppose he knew that it was loaded and gave it to her deliberately. *Because he wanted her to kill him.*"

"You mean he might have found out that things between his wife and Imleyson had gone further than he imagined? And that instead of going the orthodox way about it and shooting her first and then killing himself he arranged it so that *she* shot *him*?" Mordecai Tremaine shook his head. "It seems a clumsy way to commit suicide. And I can't see Adrian Carthallow wanting to kill himself in any case."

"Unless he was in trouble of some kind we don't yet know about," said Jonathan Boyce, and then he smiled. "But I'm wandering into the land of theory, Mordecai! Doing the kind of thing I've always told you a policeman can't afford. Maybe it's because I'm on holiday and it's someone else's pigeon!"

He thrust his hands into his pockets and stood, sucking on an empty pipe, staring out over the sea.

"Poor old Charles! She's an attractive woman. I've liked what I've seen of her—felt sorry for her, too. Sometimes, Mordecai, it's a damnable job being a detective."

Mordecai Tremaine regarded his friend in surprise. It was unlike Jonathan Boyce to give way to sentiment. It was, he thought, a sign that Helen Carthallow had unwittingly appealed to the sense of chivalry that lay dutifully buried beneath the Yard man's official dispassionate manner.

It recalled his own state of mind toward her, although his attitude had been more noncommittal. He had found it difficult to decide whether Helen Carthallow was the unfortunate victim of circumstances or whether she was a woman who possessed very little in the way of a heart and was therefore deserving of no special outpourings of sympathy. Whether, in fact, her slightly too made-up face was the mask with which a brave but lonely and tormented creature had determined to face the world in an attempt to pretend that all was well with her marriage or whether she was, in reality, no more than a shallow if physically attractive personality whose scarlet lips and painted nails betrayed her true nature.

The death of Adrian Carthallow was, naturally enough, the main topic at dinner.

"I suppose that by tomorrow there'll be swarms of reporters on the scene," remarked Arthur Tyning. "Falporth is going to be on the map. Fadeout of Famous Artist. Slain by Wife in Study, or Paradise Lost."

His wife looked at him reproachfully. She did not always approve of her husband's sense of humor.

"Poor Mrs. Carthallow. I feel sorry for her having to face all the questions and publicity. It's bad enough to have lost her husband in such a tragic fashion without having to bear the strain of all the police inquiries and reporters wanting to know everything as well."

"I trust that this solicitude on your part, my dear," Arthur Tyning said, "means that should you ever manage to shoot *me* by accident you'd display a suitable remorse!"

"Don't joke about it, Arthur. Poor soul—it must be terrible for her."

"Sorry, Kate," he told her. "But I can't shed any crocodile tears for Carthallow. I think she's well rid of him."

Tremaine noted that neither of them revealed any suspicion of Helen Carthallow, nor did they make any comment that was unfavorable to her. It seemed that only the naturally critical policemen, whose job it was not to take things at their face value, were at all doubtful as to the truth of her story.

It was significant, too, he thought, that whereas Jonathan Boyce had referred to "poor Charles" and Kate Tyning had spoken of "poor Mrs. Carthallow," nobody had shown any sympathy for the corpse. Adrian Carthallow seemed likely to be unwept and unhonored if not exactly unsung.

He smoked his routine after-dinner cigarette while they chatted over their coffee, and then he remarked, "I think I'll take a stroll up to Mrs. Eveland's. There may be something I can do."

The Tynings looked slightly eager, like schoolchildren

who had been secretly expecting to be invited to a treat but who had been afraid of having their optimism noticed in case the invitation didn't come. Jonathan Boyce said heartily, "Good idea, Mordecai. It looks as though Charles is going to be too busy to bring us any news himself."

Mordecai Tremaine instinctively pushed his pince-nez further back on his nose.

"After all, Jonathan," he said, somewhat distantly. "I *was* there. She may need my help."

He made what he prided himself was a dignified exit.

4

But when he was walking over the cliffs in the direction of Hilda Eveland's house he knew perfectly well that he was not going because of any belief that he might be able to help Helen Carthallow. He was going because he knew that the whole story had yet to be told, and anything in the nature of a mystery was something he had never yet been able to resist.

Besides, when he was honest with himself he admitted that Helen Carthallow had always fascinated him. Although he was a bachelor it was not because he was unmoved by the charm of a pretty woman. Her slim grace, her quick, eager movements, the toss of her head, the appeal of the childlike face with its delicate features—it *was* childlike in spite of those vivid lips and the eye shadow—had called to the sentimental part of him that lay behind the fact that he was an inveterate reader of *Romantic Stories*.

Mordecai Tremaine was simple enough to believe that all attractive young women should be in love and be loved. And he had not thought that Helen Carthallow's relations with her husband were as ideal as they should have been. He had felt sorry for her. He had wanted to do something about it. Which, of course, shows how fundamentally naive in such matters he really was.

His discovery of the existence of Lester Imleyson had been disturbing. His attitude toward marriage was soundly old-fashioned—as befitted a sentimentalist who had never experienced it—and the realization that Helen Carthallow might have turned for solace to a lover had been a shock.

He had not, as a matter of fact, quite recovered from it. To this very moment it had created in his mind a vague bias against her, and he was sufficiently aware of his own shortcomings to admit that he was still regarding her with a slightly distorted vision.

It was very pleasant on the footpath. Falporth was situated on one arm of a great bay that swept in rugged magnificence from the town to the white lighthouse guarding the rocks at the other extremity, and walking toward Hilda Eveland's house meant that all the way one faced that impressive coast-line with the blue water breaking white against the cliffs.

It was a view at which Mordecai Tremaine was never tired of looking. The firm golden sands that lay uncovered when the tide was out and the long white horses racing against the great gray cliffs when the sea was flooding in both had their irresistible appeal for him.

There were caves all along the bay, varying from shallow indentations scooped out in comparatively recent times to vast and ancient caverns tunneling back into the rock and in which the surge and boom of the sea formed a constant symphony of sound. Mordecai Tremaine's boyish imagination had peopled them with lusty Cornish smugglers, running in their illicit cargoes of silks and rum, but now, of course, they were empty apart from small boys and girls play-acting in those places the sea did not render inaccessible except by boat. These were much more sober days.

Or were they?

Maybe the world had not altered fundamentally, although there might no longer be skirmishes on the beaches between smugglers and excisemen. Thoughtfully he regarded the scattered houses that led fitfully toward the isolated spot where Paradise occupied its unique position. It all looked innocent enough, but who could tell? It wasn't until attention was focused on one particular spot that one realized just how many odd things could go on under the eyes of unsuspecting neighbors.

At that moment he saw a figure coming toward him. A tall figure, with hands deep in pockets. He recognized Lester Imleyson.

The other's normally good-humored face was morose and preoccupied. He did not notice Mordecai Tremaine until they had almost drawn level. Tremaine said, purely to open the conversation, "Nice evening."

Imleyson raised his eyes suddenly, as though he had been brought to an abrupt awareness of his surroundings.

"Oh—hullo," he said, ungraciously. "Didn't see you."

"I noticed," remarked Tremaine, "that you were deep in thought."

The significant note in his voice brought a flush to Imleyson's face.

"I don't have to tell *you* the reason."

"No," returned Mordecai Tremaine gently, "you don't." He added, "I'm on my way to see Mrs. Carthallow now. I thought there might be something I could do."

To his surprise, Imleyson took a step toward him and his hands grasped his shoulders.

"There *is* something you can do," he said tensely. "You can try and convince that wooden-headed inspector friend of yours that Carthallow's death was an accident. You can stop him continually worrying Helen and acting as though there was some mystery about it."

"Aren't you," said Tremaine, "being a little melodramatic?"

"Am I?" Imleyson's voice was bitter. "I've just come from her. She's been questioned and badgered so much that she doesn't know what she's doing or saying. Doesn't Penross recognize the truth when he hears it?"

His words held a note Tremaine found hard to define. He could not be certain whether it was the result of fear, hysteria, or nervous strain due to a natural anxiety for Helen Carthallow.

It rather surprised him. He had always thought of Imleyson as a well-balanced youngster who was unlikely to go to pieces in a crisis.

"Inspector Penross is only doing his duty," he observed. "It's inevitable that Mrs. Carthallow should be asked to answer questions and make statements. I'm sure she appreciates that. The law doesn't pay any regard to personalities, and the police have to carry out their instructions."

Imleyson seemed to have taken a grip on himself by now. The momentary wildness had died out of his eyes. He said, "Sorry. I'm a bit strung up. It was such a damnable thing to have happened."

They parted and Mordecai Tremaine went on his way. The situation appeared to be developing along unexpected lines. Judging by what had gone before, it would have been reasonable to suppose that Lester Imleyson would have been delighted to hear that Adrian Carthallow was dead, since it left him a clear field. One would not, of course, have expected him to give three hearty cheers and go around telling the world how pleased he was. But one would certainly not have imagined that he would display all the characteristics of a man who had temporarily lost his nerve.

Unless…

Unless he wasn't really in love with Helen Carthallow at all. Unless he had merely been amusing himself with her and now found himself trapped because her husband had inconsiderately managed to get himself shot.

Mordecai Tremaine didn't like it. He liked it even less the more he thought about it. He was glad when he reached Hilda Eveland's house and could no longer spare the time to think.

There seemed to be a lot of people on the premises. So much going and coming was in progress that it was difficult to sort out just who was present. He gathered that the news had spread effectively and that the genuinely concerned and the merely curious had converged upon the house.

Hilda Eveland greeted him with a smile of welcome that creased her plump face into its familiar lines.

"So there you are, Mordecai! We've been wondering when you were going to turn up!"

A friendly intimacy had grown up between them. Tremaine suspected her of a desire to mother him. He felt that secretly she regarded him as being in need of care and attention.

"Your friend Penross has just gone," she told him. "He's been going over things with Helen."

"Is she—?" he began, and she took him up before he could finish framing the question.

"Is she standing up to it? Don't worry, Mordecai. There's a good deal more in Helen than people imagine."

"I'm glad," said Tremaine. "After all, it was such a frightful shock. It might have produced a nasty reaction."

Hilda Eveland gave him a shrewd look.

"It did," she said. "She was beginning to show signs of it when she got here. It was as well that she came. Anything might have happened if she'd stayed in that house on her own."

Mordecai Tremaine could read the situation easily enough. As soon as Helen Carthallow had arrived, Hilda Eveland had taken her in hand. She had been allowed no time to sit and brood. With her bustling good humor and forceful personality the older woman had worked hard to take her mind off the tragedy—at least, as far as that was possible.

"I met young Imleyson on the way," he remarked. "He gave me the impression that Mrs. Carthallow was finding the strain rather too much for her. He seemed to think the police had been worrying her."

"Did he?"

A subtle change had affected Hilda Eveland's manner. Her tone had become guarded. She said, "He wasn't here long. As a matter of fact, I was surprised he didn't come before. In view of—everything."

Mordecai Tremaine was not altogether taken unawares by

the antagonism in her voice. He had always suspected that she did not greatly care for Lester Imleyson.

"*Has* Inspector Penross been very persistent?" he asked.

"Not more so than you might expect. After all, Adrian didn't exactly die from natural causes. Even if he hadn't been so much in the public eye the local police would have wanted to ask plenty of questions. And since it's obvious that there are going to be headlines in every newspaper in the country, Penross doesn't want to leave anything undone. When you're operating under a spotlight you aren't anxious to make any slips, so you do everything twice to make sure you haven't forgotten the very thing everybody else is sure to see first."

Even if Hilda's plump figure hadn't borne all the battle signs of a slightly ruffled hen determined to protect her brood, Tremaine would have accepted the logic of what she had said. It was, indeed, natural that Penross should move with caution. He said, "Have any reporters turned up yet?"

"So far only the local men. But the others will be here all right."

The door opened. Tremaine turned to see the bulky figure of Elton Steele. He was smoking the inevitable pipe, his big hand caressing the bowl.

"I think I'll push off, Hilda. Helen seems to be all right, and you've enough people on your hands without me."

"Thank you for coming, Elton. You're one of the few I was really glad to see."

"Wish I could have done something. Don't seem to have made any useful contribution at all."

"Just to look at you is enough to give her confidence," she told him. "I know your being here helped to steady Helen when she was most in need of it."

"You think so?" the big man said, as though eager to believe it and yet inwardly doubtful. "Nice of you, Hilda." He became aware of Mordecai Tremaine's presence. "Hullo, Tremaine. Pretty unpleasant business, eh?" He did not wait for a reply but addressed himself again to Hilda Eveland. "See you in the morning, Hilda. May need an errand boy or something."

"It's awfully good of you, Elton. I'll tell Helen."

Steele looked as though he was going to say something. He hesitated with his hand on the handle of the open door, his broad, tweed-clad shoulders almost blocking the entrance. Then he changed his mind, nodded, and went out.

When the door had closed behind him, Tremaine said, "I suppose it's only one of my romantic fancies, but you know, Hilda, sometimes I've found myself thinking that Steele's in love with Helen Carthallow."

"Of course he's in love with her," she said briskly. "You've only to see the way he watches her to realize that. Why do you suppose he came rushing over here the moment he heard what had happened?"

"Does she know?"

"She hasn't admitted it, if that's what you mean. But it's a very unusual woman who can't tell when a man's in love with her. It's a pity she didn't meet Elton before she married Adrian. And it's a pity Elton doesn't go in for a little less doglike devotion and a little more of the caveman tactics."

Elton Steele was a very near neighbor. He had an estate agent's business in Falporth that covered a wide area, and he was rumored to be comfortably off financially if he could not exactly be termed a rich man. He was one of those physically big men whose manner is gentle and who traditionally would not harm a fly. His pleasant, slow-speaking voice was rarely any other than calm. He was solid, inarticulate, dependable, with gray eyes that seemed to be perpetually surveying the world with a kind of amused tolerance—and yet the kind of man who *could* display a devastating wrath when he was aroused.

Mordecai Tremaine had never seen him give way to anger, but he had detected ominous rumblings, and he did not think that his judgment was at fault.

"This has certainly given Matilda something to talk about," Hilda Eveland observed, and he looked at her inquiringly.

Matilda Vickery was one of Hilda Eveland's good turns.

She had been a cook until rheumatoid arthritis had first attacked her legs and then crippled her hands so that she had become incapable of earning her own living. Unmarried, of strictly limited means, and with no near relatives to whom she could turn, her future would have been a bleak one, but Hilda had accepted responsibility for her. Apart from the fact that she appreciated a conscientious and loyal servant, her own good nature would not have allowed her to turn Matilda away.

She had installed her in a room of her own and had paid for medical treatment for her. There was no hope of a permanent cure, but she had determined to do what she could to make her declining years easier.

When Mordecai Tremaine had heard about it he had regarded Hilda Eveland with a much more understanding eye. At first he had thought of her as a cheerful, happy-go-lucky, but negative personality who was a pleasant companion but whose emotions seldom ran deep. Now he knew that beneath her plump jollity she possessed a brave and understanding soul.

"You know how much time she spends looking out of her window," Hilda went on. "There isn't much she misses. Whenever I want to bring myself up-to-date with the gossip of the neighborhood I sit down and chat to Matilda. People bring all their confidences to her, and naturally they tell her all they know about everybody else as well! She can see the bridge leading to Paradise, as you know. She saw you go in with Helen, and she saw Inspector Penross arrive. It was Matilda who gave me the first news that something was wrong."

"Has Penross had a talk with her?"

"Yes. He was interested in the fact that she can see the bridge from her room—" She broke off as the door opened. "Here's Helen now."

Helen Carthallow came into the room. Roberta Fairham was with her. Roberta was the mousy type, with straight hair strained back from her forehead and with nondescript features you couldn't recall a few moments after she had left you. Just recently she seemed to have been taking pains to improve her appearance. She had been experimenting with nail varnish, mascara, and lipstick. She had also been cultivating a bright manner. The results had not been entirely satisfactory. She had acquired the air of a half-finished portrait that the artist had had to leave because he wasn't quite certain how to go on.

Mordecai Tremaine addressed himself to a point midway between them. He said, "Good evening." And to Helen Carthallow he said, "I just thought I'd drop in and see whether I could be of any assistance to you, but it looks as though you've had an embarrassment of offers."

Helen Carthallow smiled.

"I didn't know I had so many friends. It was very good of you to come."

Her face was white, and there were contrasting patches of shadow under her eyes. He thought, too, that she had applied her lipstick with a slightly more prodigal hand than usual. But she had herself well under control; she was showing no sign that her nerves were reaching breaking point despite the questioning she had apparently undergone from Penross. She added, "There isn't really anything to do except wait. Inspector Penross has told me that his men will be staying at Paradise, and they've already been in touch with the servants and told them not to go back to the house for a day or two. The inspector said he'd see to all the formalities for me. He's been very kind."

There was no trace of irony in her voice. Tremaine gave her a quick, observant glance. If she was acting she was certainly playing a difficult part with extraordinary ability.

Deliberately he said, "I met Mr. Imleyson on my way over."

"I'm afraid Lester was rather perturbed by the way the inspector kept asking questions," she told him coolly. "Poor dear, I believe he thought I was going through some kind of third degree!"

She was fencing with him. Mordecai Tremaine was sure of it. She knew that he had told her about Imleyson in order to test her reaction, and she had met him on his own ground.

He realized then that in some subtle fashion she had changed since the afternoon. It was difficult to place the precise nature of the change, but her manner had grown harder. There was a bitterness in her eyes, a cynicism that had not been there before. She no longer appeared so fragile; the natural steel in her was nearer the surface.

He was not allowed to test her further. Hilda Eveland steered the conversation away from the subject of Adrian Carthallow's death, and in view of his self-announced reason for being present he had no option but to give her his support with every appearance of goodwill.

They were drinking coffee and Mordecai Tremaine was trying to think of a suitable exit line, since it was obvious that his visit was unlikely to produce any more information, when Lewis Haldean arrived. They heard the characteristic screech of brakes as his car pulled up outside the house with the usual breathtaking effect, and Hilda Eveland went out to meet him.

They heard his resonant voice in the hall.

"I didn't hear the news about poor Adrian until I got back this evening—been out fishing all day. Of course, I came straight over."

There was a vibrant, dramatic quality in his words. The whole man, in fact, was dramatic. With his distinguished appearance and his expressive voice he possessed all the outward characteristics of the successful actor.

Tremaine always thought of him in conjunction with Elton Steele. Partly because they were both big men, although there was slightly more solidity about Steele's build, and partly because Haldean's fair coloring and his short, carefully trimmed blond beard and his quick gesticulatory way of speaking contrasted so sharply with Steele's dark, clean-shaven features and slow-speaking deliberation.

Not that Steele's somber masculinity gave Haldean the appearance of softness. There was something of the Viking in the boldness of the blue eyes and the defiant thrust of that striking beard.

He was just outside the door by now. They heard him say, "What happened? All I heard was some garbled story about Adrian being dead. You know how people embroider any kind of rumor. Was it suicide?"

Hilda Eveland said, in a tone of warning, "I think you'd better come in, Lewis. Helen's inside."

Haldean's face appeared in the doorway. He saw Helen Carthallow and for a moment he looked disconcerted. Then he went toward her, his hand outstretched.

"Helen, my dear—I'm terribly sorry. I couldn't believe it when they told me. How did Adrian come to do it?"

"Adrian didn't," she told him. "*I* did it."

He stared at her, momentarily at a loss. Still holding her hand he turned back to Hilda.

"It was an accident," Hilda Eveland said. "Helen and Adrian were joking. Adrian took out his gun, and when she asked him to be careful because it naturally scared her, he gave it to her and said that it wasn't loaded and told her to try it for herself. It *was* loaded, after all."

Haldean turned back again, still with Helen Carthallow's hand in his own. An intuitive light flashed across Mordecai Tremaine's mind. Was he being romantic again, or was there something of particular significance in Haldean's manner?

Helen Carthallow said, "That's the story, Lewis. It's a very simple one, isn't it? I shot Adrian. I didn't mean to do it. I didn't know the revolver was loaded."

Lewis Haldean stood looking down at her. His face was grave. At last he said, "Is that how it happened?"

She inclined her head.

"Yes," she said. "That's how it happened."

The electric light was on now for it was beginning to grow dark. It was picking out the little golden lines in Haldean's beard. He looked very serious and somehow tense, poised over her like a blond statue.

"My dear," he said slowly. "My dear, you aren't—hiding anything?"

Mordecai Tremaine was watching Helen Carthallow, and he saw that the question had shaken her. For an instant there was a shadowy fear in her eyes. She moved her head and the lock of hair came down.

"I don't understand you, Lewis," she said.

Haldean said, "You aren't trying to protect Adrian? You're quite sure he didn't kill himself?"

"Of course," she said. Her voice rose. There was a shrillness in it. "Of course. I've told you how it happened. I've told the police. I shot him. Adrian gave me his gun, and I pointed it at him and fired. That's what he told me to do. He must have forgotten it was loaded—"

She broke off suddenly. She stared up at Haldean, and there was in her face the incredulous look of a person who had just become aware of a new and altogether unexpected possibility. "You mean," she whispered, "you mean that perhaps he *hadn't* forgotten? That he *wanted* me to kill him?"

Haldean did not make any comment. Roberta Fairham was leaning forward in her chair, her lips slightly parted. It was as though she was desperately anxious not to miss what Helen Carthallow might be going to say.

Mordecai Tremaine felt a sense of antagonism toward her. There seemed to be something of the ghoul in the pale eyes and the hard, peaked little face with its inexpert makeup. Why should she be displaying such a morbid curiosity?

But, of course, he already knew the answer. Roberta Fairham had been in love with Carthallow.

Carthallow hadn't given her much encouragement, or at least he hadn't appeared to. Which wasn't at all surprising, for even if he had been the kind of man to take all that infatuated women were ready to give him he would probably have drawn the line at Roberta. She was definitely not the type to cause men to lose their heads. The thought of being pursued by her, Mordecai Tremaine reflected unkindly, would be enough to cause the average man to shudder.

Still, that wouldn't affect her side of the story. She might have been nursing her passion against the day when the miracle might happen and it would be returned. To that extent, therefore, she would be interested in what Carthallow had had in his mind when he had handed that revolver to his wife. She had a kind of deferred share in the matter.

Helen Carthallow said, "No. It can't be true. It *can't*. Adrian *couldn't* have done that."

She seemed to be talking more to herself than to Haldean. It was as though her mind was somewhere else altogether.

Lewis Haldean's face still wore that expression of concern. It was clear that he wanted desperately to help her and didn't know quite how to approach her. At last he said, "You know, Helen, that if there's anything I can do, you can count on me."

She looked up at him, and then she began to laugh. Softly at first and then louder. It was a harsh, unnatural sound that had a metallic edge to it.

"It's so funny, Lewis. So awfully funny. Everybody wants to help me. And there isn't anything to be done. Adrian's dead and the police are in the house and there's nothing for anyone to do. That's what makes it so absurd—"

Hilda Eveland said, sharply, "Stop it, Helen!"

Helen Carthallow raised her hands to her face. She sat for a moment with her fingers pressed to her eyes, and when she took her hands away again there was no sign of the hysteria that had threatened to break her self-control.

"I'm sorry, Lewis," she said evenly. "You must think I'm an ungrateful beast. I'm not really. It's been rather a trying day."

"That's all right, my dear," he told her, "I understand."

Mordecai Tremaine was not certain, but he fancied there was chagrin in Roberta Fairham's face. He had the impression that she was disappointed that the incident had not been allowed to develop.

He found his eyes continually coming back to her. Fortunately she was too intent upon watching Helen Carthallow to be aware of his scrutiny.

He had once thought Roberta to be a rather negative person, incapable of strong emotion. He had believed that even her affection for Adrian Carthallow was of an ineffective type that was not banked by smoldering fires and was unlikely to achieve any climax.

But now he was by no means certain that the situation

was as simple as that. He had seen hate in her eyes when she had looked at Helen Carthallow. And it had been the hate of a soul that possessed the capacity for performing dark and violent deeds.

Altogether it was a stimulating evening. It didn't produce any startling facts, but it produced a great deal of atmosphere. Which, as far as Mordecai Tremaine was concerned, was equally as good. He thrived upon atmosphere. It was the best of all germinating influences for the seeds of theory that dwelt within him.

There was no doubt, he reflected, as he left Hilda Eveland's house, that he had plenty of scope for theorizing now. It was not altogether a comforting thought. Some of the theories seemed likely to lead to highly disturbing conclusions.

Two things stood sharply etched among the confusion of impressions the evening had brought him: the undisguised hate he had seen in Roberta Fairham's face and the hardness and the cynicism that had been in Helen Carthallow's eyes.

Mordecai Tremaine shook his head. He didn't like it. He didn't like it at all.

5

After breakfast Jonathan Boyce suggested a stroll along the cliffs. There were banks of clouds over the sea, but it looked as though they would pass and that it would be a fine day. Mordecai Tremaine said that he would be glad of the exercise. It was, of course, purely a coincidence that they walked toward Paradise.

At first they talked carefully about the view. Boyce puffed stolidly at his pipe and pointed out the fishing boats bobbing clear of the bay.

"Looks a bit rougher out there," he remarked. "The wind can be pretty fierce once you get around the headland. Glad I fixed my trip for yesterday. Even though," he added, "I missed the main event of the afternoon."

He looked at his companion. He said, "Did you learn anything last night, Mordecai?"

Mordecai Tremaine pushed his pince-nez back into position.

"I don't know," he said. "I've been hoping I didn't, but I don't know."

"There was a full house, wasn't there?"

"Yes. Steele, Haldean, Roberta Fairham, several people from the neighborhood—they all went over to see whether they could do anything to help."

"Or to see whether there was anything they could learn," interposed Boyce dryly.

"Not Steele," Tremaine returned. "Nor Haldean."

Boyce said, "Mrs. Carthallow appears to be popular. I'm not surprised. I like her myself. I'd be sorry to see anything go wrong."

There was a constable standing at the entrance to the bridge leading to Paradise. Boyce nodded a greeting to him but did not attempt to approach him. It was a strange feeling to know that a police investigation was in progress and yet to have no right of entry, but he knew that the constable was aware of his identity, and he did not wish to put the man in a difficult position. At the moment he was merely a civilian vacationer. He had no official standing.

Fortunately Penross arrived a few minutes later, and the inspector had decided upon his course of action.

"I'd like you to come into the house with me," he said. "I'll take a chance with the chief constable. Although I don't think he's likely to raise objections seeing who you both are."

Mordecai Tremaine followed him over the bridge with a chest inflated with pride. He began to feel that maybe it wasn't at all a bad thing to have earned a reputation as a crime investigator.

When they reached the house: "I've asked Mrs. Carthallow to come over," said Penross. "I told her I'd appreciate her help in checking one or two details."

They went with him into the study. Mordecai Tremaine found it difficult to recall that not many hours ago he had been in this same room with the body of a man who had died violently. The said body had, of course, been removed. There was only the still overturned chair to add a slightly jarring note to what was otherwise a perfectly ordinary scene.

"You've been here before, Mordecai," Penross said. "Before yesterday, I mean. Is there anything different about the appearance of this room?"

Mordecai Tremaine looked carefully around him, although he had already impressed every detail upon his memory.

"Only the desk," he said. "Usually it stood over there."

He indicated a position against the outer wall of the study. Penross nodded.

"That's what I thought," he said. "You can see the marks in the carpet as though it was resting there for a long time. I wonder what made him move it?"

He was looking expectantly at Mordecai Tremaine, but that gentleman shook his head.

"Sorry, Charles. No suggestions."

Jonathan Boyce had been surveying the room, his stocky form pivoting slowly, his sharp eyes peering intently about him.

"Where did you find the sun spectacles?" he asked.

Penross smiled.

"I thought maybe you'd have all the details by now," he observed. "That's why I didn't go over them again." He indicated a chair standing against the bookcase. "They were here."

"Folded or open?"

"Open. As though they'd just been placed there while somebody looked for a book."

Boyce nodded.

"And the forceps?"

"Not quite so obvious," said Penross. "They were lying on the floor against the edge of the carpet just behind this leather cushion."

"And Mrs. Carthallow," remarked Tremaine, "says that the spectacles are hers and that she must have left them there several days ago but that she can't explain the forceps. She thinks they must have belonged to her husband. He was always dabbling with pills and medicines and various medical gadgets."

Boyce nodded again.

"What about the picture?" he said. "I take it that it's in the studio?"

"I'll show you," said Penross.

He took them up the narrow stairway. Boyce glanced around at the untidy litter Adrian Carthallow had left behind him. He took up one or two of the charcoal sketches.

"Not bad," he said. "He's got the sweep of the coast even in this rough drawing. He had talent all right."

"I wonder," said Penross, "what he was preparing to do with it?"

He went up to the big easel and swung it around so that Boyce could see the canvas. Jonathan Boyce whistled.

"So somebody *didn't* like it," he said.

He stepped closer to the portrait. The thick streaks of yellow ocher, cadmium red, and cobalt blue that had been daubed across it by a vicious hand effectively prevented any detailed examination of the original painting. It was still possible to tell that the sitter was Helen Carthallow, but it was hopeless to attempt to judge the expression her husband had given her. The eyes, which would have betrayed the rest of the painting, had been obliterated with great patches of blue as though the tube had been squeezed out against the canvas and rubbed in with savage force.

"Was it going to be the Mona Lisa?" said Mordecai Tremaine. "Or Circe?"

From outside the house, through the open window of the studio, they heard the heavy tones of the constable stationed at the door and then a woman's voice.

"That sounds like Mrs. Carthallow now," said Penross.

When they reached the lounge she was already there waiting for them. She was wearing a gray costume with a flared skirt that was tailored to her slim figure. She wore no hat; her dark hair was brushed back from her forehead to fall gracefully to her shoulders. It was fine, silky hair that glimmered in the light from the window behind her. Her lips were not their usual vivid scarlet; she seemed, indeed, to be wearing very little makeup this morning.

There was tragedy in her face but there was a dignity as well. Mordecai Tremaine felt something catch at his throat. The hardness had gone from her, and she looked very sad and very beautiful.

"Good morning," she said, as they came in. "You wanted to see me, Inspector?"

"Yes," said Penross. "Thank you for coming over, Mrs. Carthallow. There are just one or two things I'd like to clear up, and I thought it would be easier to deal with them on the spot."

She looked at him with a puzzled air.

"But I told you all I could, Inspector. I thought I went over everything. It was all in my statement."

Penross said, as though he was unaware of the question in her voice, "You know these two gentlemen, of course?"

"Yes, of course."

"You have no objection to their being here?"

There was a touch of asperity in her voice.

"I don't understand you, Inspector. Why should I object?"

"What I meant, Mrs. Carthallow," said Penross, "was that they aren't here in any official capacity. If you would rather not answer any questions or make any statements in their presence there is no reason why you should do so. As a matter of fact," he added, "you aren't compelled to answer questions in any case, although I shall naturally appreciate any help you are able to give me."

She gave him a steady, speculative glance.

"You aren't—cautioning me, Inspector?"

"What gave you that impression, Mrs. Carthallow?" he asked. "No, I'm just anxious that you should be aware of your rights. That's part of my job, you know, to make sure that people understand all the rules that are laid down for their protection. Now," he said, "I wonder if you'll be good enough to come across to your husband's study?"

She sat very still.

"Is it—necessary?" she said, in a low voice.

"I'm afraid it is," he told her gravely.

They crossed the hall and went into the room where Adrian Carthallow had died. She looked instinctively at the desk. The faint color that had been in her cheeks when she had arrived had vanished.

"What is it you want me to do?"

"I'd like you to show me," said Penross, "exactly where you were standing when your husband was shot."

She hesitated for a second or two, as though recollecting, and then walked across the room.

"I was here," she said steadily.

Penross began to move slowly toward her.

"Tell me to stop," he said, "when I'm just about where your husband was standing."

She watched him. When Penross drew level with the desk she made a little gesture. Penross stopped.

"Here?"

"I'm not sure," she said slowly. "I think—I think it must have been more to the left."

Penross shifted his position.

"About here?"

"Yes," she said. "About there. Adrian was sitting at his desk when he took the revolver out of the drawer. He got up and gave it to me. I think I must have backed away from him. That's when he laughed and said that there wasn't anything to worry about because it wasn't loaded."

Penross appeared to be thinking hard. He said, "When you fired, did you hold your arm straight out in front of you, or did you bend it slightly?"

She frowned.

"I don't think," she said, "it could have been straight. I'm not certain—it's all rather hazy. But the revolver was heavy. It wasn't easy for me to hold."

"I see. So when you actually fired the shot, if what you've just said is correct, you must have been about two or three yards away from your husband. Is that right?"

It was obvious that she was troubled. There was a watchfulness in her manner, and it seemed that there was fear in it, too.

"Yes," she said unwillingly. "Yes, that's right."

Penross looked at her. He shook his head.

"I'm afraid, Mrs. Carthallow," he said, "it won't do."

She tried to conceal her agitation, but she did not quite succeed. Her breathing had become hurried.

"What do you mean?" she said.

"I mean that it didn't happen like that," Penross said quietly.

"The doctor says that the shot that killed your husband was fired at close quarters. *Very* close quarters. Why don't you tell me the truth, Mrs. Carthallow?"

She tried to speak, but although her lips shaped words no sound came out of them. Penross watched her. His manner was gentle, but there was something inflexible behind it. Mordecai Tremaine knew that he wasn't going to let go.

And at last Helen Carthallow said, "All right, Inspector. I'll tell you the truth. I'll tell you what really happened."

Penross pulled forward one of the easy chairs. He was utterly noncommittal.

"I think," he said, "that will be much more satisfactory." He motioned to her to sit down. "I don't want you to regard this as an ordeal, and I don't want you to say anything until you're quite sure what you want to tell me. There's no hurry at all. The only thing that matters," he said, and now there was a trace of significance in his voice, "is that we should get at the truth."

She sat down. Her hand went up to her forehead with an instinctive gesture that conveyed despair and helplessness.

"I've been very foolish," she said. "I realize that. I'm sorry, Inspector. I should have known better than to try to tell you such a story. It was obvious yesterday that you didn't believe me. I knew myself how thin it sounded. I knew that I ought to tell you the truth, but it was too late then to go back on what I'd said. And I wanted to avoid the scandal. Adrian was a well-known figure. His death would make a stir. The newspapers would be searching out all they could about him.

"I thought that if I could cover up what had really happened it would be passed over more easily and there wouldn't be so much fear of the newspaper reporters making a sensation out of it. If I'd only stopped to think clearly I'd have realized how much worse I was making things by not telling the truth, but at the time I was too flustered, too shocked by what I'd done to see the wisest course to adopt."

She looked Penross full in the face, without flinching.

"I told you that Adrian and I were joking," she said. "It wasn't true. We weren't joking. We were quarreling."

"What," said Penross, "was the subject of the quarrel?"

"Can't you guess?" she said, and there was a bitter twist to her lips. "It was over Lester—Mr. Imleyson. I thought everybody in Falporth knew about Lester and me. That's why I tried to hush things up. I knew what the busybodies would say as soon as they heard that Adrian had been shot."

Penross said, "I'm sorry if I'm treading on delicate ground, Mrs. Carthallow, but had there been any other quarrels with your husband over the same cause?"

"Oh, yes," she said, with the bitterness echoed in her voice, "there'd been other quarrels. People sometimes thought Adrian was a mild-tempered, tolerant person, but he wasn't really like that at all. Sometimes he would get into a violent temper when he wouldn't be responsible for what he was doing.

"When I came back yesterday he started asking me questions about Mr. Imleyson. He considered that I'd been seeing too much of him. He didn't like what he called the fact that everybody was talking about us. In moods like those he was beyond reason. He'd just go on and on, becoming more violent, as though he was deliberately driving himself into a fury."

She was staring in front of her now, her arms clutching the chair.

"I suppose I should have been sensible enough to act differently, knowing Adrian as I did. I should have known that he was making such a scene because he knew that there were no servants in the house to overhear him. But I didn't stop to think. He was so—so abusive. I just couldn't stand it. I tried to argue with him, tried to make him see how he was exaggerating everything, and naturally it only made him angrier than ever.

"He suddenly turned to his desk and took out his revolver. I think he only meant to frighten me, but at the time he looked as though he really intended to do me some harm. I caught at his arm and tried to take the gun away. We struggled for several seconds, Adrian trying to wrench his arm free while I did my best to hold on to him, hoping he'd realize what he was doing and become calmer."

"Just where," interposed Penross, "did this struggle take place?"

"We were both by the desk," she said. "In fact, we were half across it." She closed her eyes as though in an effort to reconstruct the scene and call back the details to her mind. Her sentences came jerkily. "Adrian was leaning forward. My weight was preventing him from getting up. His left elbow was resting on the desk so that he could support himself. The gun must have been underneath us somehow. I remember Adrian making a movement to twist out of my grasp, and then the gun went off.

"It was horrible. He didn't make a sound. When I bent over him I saw his head. I felt sick. I believe I almost fainted. I was still stunned by the sound of the revolver going off, and I can't remember clearly what I did then. I know I put the gun back on the desk and then sat down in a chair. The next thing I can recall is trying to think out what I ought to do.

"I suppose it was then that I realized how it would look to people outside. Every little incident would be twisted to make it seem as black as possible. All the scandalmongers would be busy. Perhaps I was frightened for myself, too. There was no one else in the house. I knew they might even say that it wasn't an accident; that I'd shot Adrian deliberately..."

She lowered her head, and the concealing lock of hair came down.

"I told you I didn't think of the telephone, Inspector. I did think of it. But I knew that Mr. Tremaine was down on the beach, and I thought that if I could get him into the house before the police came he would be able to act as a witness. His evidence might help to show that Adrian's death was an accident, so that there mightn't be too many questions asked after all."

She looked up at Penross again, and there was a desperate, pleading note in her voice.

"Please believe me, Inspector. That's the whole story. I haven't kept anything back this time."

"You're prepared to sign another statement setting down what you've just told me?" Penross asked.

She nodded.

"Yes. Of course. You've every right to be suspicious of me, Inspector. But you won't need any more statements after this one."

Penross was looking at her reflectively. He said, "There's something I'd like you to see, Mrs. Carthallow."

Immediately she was on her guard. It seemed to Mordecai Tremaine, watching her for every sign, that he could see her mental defenses go up.

"Yes, Inspector?"

"I've been looking around your husband's studio," he said and waited.

It did not seem to convey anything to her.

"Adrian did a great deal of work down here," she said, almost disinterestedly. "He thought the setting of this house gave him inspiration."

It sounded as though she might have intended to be

ironic, but there was nothing in either her face or her voice to confirm it.

"Have you been to the studio lately?" said Penross.

"You mean since I came back yesterday?" she shook her head. "No. As a matter of fact I don't think I've been anywhere except here and in the lounge."

"I'd be glad if you'd come with me now."

She rose obediently to her feet. Once more a little procession made its way up the narrow stairs. Penross said, over his shoulder, "I believe your husband was doing a portrait of you, Mrs. Carthallow."

"Yes." she added, after a pause. "It isn't unusual, you know, for an artist to wish to paint his wife."

"No," said Penross. "I wasn't thinking there was anything unusual in *that*."

He walked across the room to where the easel stood and swung it quickly around. Helen Carthallow had just come through the door, and she stared full at the canvas.

Her eyes dilated. She gave a gasp, and her hand went to her lips. She said, whisperingly, "When—when did it happen?"

"I don't know," said Penross. "Do you?"

"No," she said. "No." There was a piteous note in her voice. She looked as though she was going to fall. Jonathan Boyce moved instinctively toward her. But she remained on her feet, staring at the portrait, and after a moment or two she said, "It must have been Adrian. He must have done it before I came back. I didn't know—I didn't realize he would have taken it so hard."

"You said," remarked Penross, "that sometimes your husband displayed a violent temper. Was it usual for him to destroy his work if he felt dissatisfied with it?"

"You mean would he lose his control like—like this?" she hesitated. "It didn't happen often," she said. "Adrian used to say that the artistic temperament was all nonsense and that if he didn't turn out a good picture it was because his workmanship was faulty."

"But you think he did *this*?"

Penross indicated the portrait. Again she hesitated.

"Yes," she said at last. "Although he was much more balanced about things as a rule I *have* known him to act like it before. Besides," she added ingenuously, "who else *could* have done it?"

Penross ignored the question. He said, "That was what I wanted you to see. I was hoping you'd be able to help me clear it up. It's only a small point, of course, but I like to feel that everything's nicely explained. Now, if you'll be good enough to come with me we can have your statement typed out ready for you to sign."

He led the way out of the room, and she followed him without further comment. Mordecai Tremaine watched them go with troubled eyes.

He was quite certain that whatever Adrian Carthallow might have thought about that portrait he would never have desecrated it so savagely with those vicious slashes of color.

6

There were three deck chairs on the terrace in front of Arthur Tyning's house overlooking the sea. In the right-hand chair Jonathan Boyce sat chewing thoughtfully at an empty pipe. In the left-hand chair Mordecai Tremaine was puffing out unnecessary clouds of tobacco smoke and struggling so hard against a desire to cough that he was going red in the face. After much tribulation he had schooled his stomach to take to a pipe without bringing public disgrace upon him, but there were still times when rebellious nature took a delight in making his role of the Great Detective, smoking his way to a solution of the latest mystery, an extremely difficult one to maintain in comfort.

The center chair was empty. Its very emptiness lent to it an air of expectancy and importance. I, it seemed to be saying, am the set piece of the evening. Without me there can be nothing.

A shadow fell across it. Boyce said, "Sit down, Charles. Mordecai's been jumping up and down like a jack-in-the-box the whole evening looking to see if you were in sight."

Tremaine lowered his pipe—not without a certain secret thankfulness.

"What," he said indignantly, "about you?"

Jonathan Boyce grinned.

"All right," he said. "We've *both* been waiting for you. What goes on, Charles?"

Penross sat down in the vacant chair. He took out his pipe and began to fill it carefully.

"That's why I'm here," he said. "To talk it over with you. It ought to be simple. Adrian Carthallow, the famous artist, is accidentally shot. There are obituaries in all the newspapers, there's an inquest in which the coroner says how sorry he is for the widow, the verdict is death by misadventure, and that's that. I *don't* think."

Mordecai Tremaine said, "Are you doing anything about Helen Carthallow?"

Penross paused in the act of lighting his pipe.

"Meaning?"

"She made a statement yesterday telling you just how it happened. You found out that it couldn't have happened that way at all. So today she made another statement. The real one this time. The one that didn't leave any ends untied. I don't doubt that you've already discovered that the second statement is just as much a fairy tale as the first."

"What," said Penross, "makes you think so?"

"I'll save my theory," returned Tremaine. "*You* tell *me*."

"You're right, anyway," said Penross gloomily. "And I'm damned if I like it. I've a feeling that if I was doing my duty I'd be asking for a warrant for her arrest on a charge of murder. But I can't do it. I don't *want* her to be guilty. I'm hoping that you'll be able to see something I've missed."

Jonathan Boyce said, "It won't do, Charles. You're a policeman. You can't afford to start being sentimental. If she killed him she'll have to pay for it, and that's the end of it."

But his voice betrayed him. Mordecai Tremaine said, soberly:

"You're as bad as any of us, Jonathan. Because she has a pretty face neither of us wants to see the truth even if it stares at us. But how do we know that she's as attractive inside as she is outside? I've seen more of her than either of you, and *I* can't make up my mind about her. Loveliness can be ugly when you probe deep into it. But suppose you bring us up-to-date, Charles. You mentioned this morning that Carthallow was killed by a bullet fired at close quarters."

"You saw the results," said Penross. "According to the doc the gun must have been held against his temple. You know just what kind of mess it made. The bullet finished up in the picture rail of the wall behind him. Which," he added, "is where things start to go wrong."

"You did all you could, Charles," observed Mordecai Tremaine, "to get her to tell you a story that would hold together."

The inspector gave him a shrewd glance.

"You're on the right track," he said. "I've been over the photographs a dozen times, and I've checked them in the study itself. But I can't do anything about it. If you draw a straight line from the point where Helen Carthallow said she was standing when she was struggling with her husband through the place where she said his head must have been when the gun went off it ends somewhere in the ceiling."

Jonathan Boyce grunted sympathetically.

"I see what you mean, Charles. It's the sort of thing you can't ignore."

Mordecai Tremaine said, "At a time like that she wouldn't have been too certain of what was going on. Imagine it for yourself. The two of them struggling over the desk and with Carthallow holding the gun. Suddenly there's a flash and an explosion. She looks down to see that her husband is dead, and since he's been hit at close range with a heavy caliber weapon it's a sight to unnerve any woman. Surely it's reasonable to suppose that she might have made a mistake over what actually happened in those awful moments?"

Penross nodded.

"Yes," he said. "It's reasonable. That's why I gave her a

chance to explain. I've done all I could. More, in fact, than I should have done."

Boyce was drawing away on his pipe now, his brow creased frowningly.

"There's no possibility," he asked, "that she *was* mistaken? After all, it must have been a terrifying experience for her."

"You were there," said Penross, "when she was telling me how it happened. Did she look as though she was confused and uncertain?"

"No," admitted Boyce reluctantly.

"I've tested it all ways," said Penross, "and to get a line to that bullet hole you've got to imagine the gun placed against Carthallow's head in such a manner that it's obvious that it must have been held there deliberately. It's impossible to reconstruct the same situation in the course of the kind of struggle that Mrs. Carthallow described. Besides, she said that her husband took the gun out of the drawer and that he was holding it while she was trying to prevent him using it. The gun's been checked, of course. *And the only fingerprints on it belong to her.*"

There was a long silence. Mordecai Tremaine was the first to break it. He said, "I don't think, Charles, that it can end there."

"It looks," Penross said, "all too much like the end to me."

Mordecai Tremaine pushed his pince-nez back from their precarious balancing point on the end of his nose. There was a light in his eyes as though he was straining after an idea that had floated across his mind, exciting him with its possibilities, but that he had not been able to persuade to adopt a definite form.

"Helen Carthallow is an intelligent woman. If she killed her husband why didn't she make up a story that would sound convincing? Why, for instance, didn't she say in the beginning that there'd been a struggle and that the gun had gone off accidentally? It would have aroused less suspicion than the story she did tell about Carthallow giving her the gun and getting her to pull the trigger."

"She was scared," said Penross. "She was speaking the truth when she said that she didn't want to admit that there'd been a quarrel—and a violent one—because she didn't think anybody would believe it had been an accident. She probably argued that there would be less chance of suspicion against her if she made out that she'd been joking with her husband and had merely done what he told her to do, even if it did sound an odd sort of thing for him to have said, than if she used the story of a quarrel and the gun going off during the struggle. After all, Carthallow had the reputation of being a queer sort of chap. It wouldn't be out of keeping with his character.

"But she overlooked the fact that it would be plain that the shot must have been fired at close quarters. When I showed her that her story wasn't going to carry her over *that* hurdle, she knew that the only thing she could do was to try the quarrel version, after all, and take a chance on getting away with it."

Mordecai Tremaine was not satisfied. He shifted restlessly in his chair, and the wooden frame creaked protestingly.

"Do you think she *did* overlook it, Charles? Is it possible that Carthallow shot himself?"

"If you're asking whether the wound could have been self-inflicted in the sense that it would have been physically possible for Carthallow to have held the gun to his head in just that position, the answer is yes. The bullet went in at the right temple, and the right temple is the favorite spot for suicides. But," said Penross, "if Carthallow did shoot himself his fingerprints would have been on the gun."

"If he *did* kill himself," persevered Tremaine, "would Helen Carthallow have any reason for wanting to hide the fact?"

Jonathan Boyce inserted himself into the conversation.

"I can think of two possibilities," he said. "The idealistic angle that she wanted to protect her husband's memory, and the cynical one that she wanted to collect his insurance money. Maybe the company will pay out for accidental death, but suicide is a different proposition."

"You mean," said Penross, "that she might have wiped his fingerprints off the gun and left her own? It seems to me to be a pretty frightful risk for a woman to take." He gave each of his companions a long, searching look. "This case," he said, "is difficult enough already."

"It's a pleasant thought," Boyce remarked, "that I'm on holiday and that this is *your* worry."

Mordecai Tremaine was staring out over the cliffs.

"I don't suppose," he said casually, "there was anyone else at Paradise yesterday afternoon?"

"I've tried it," said Penross briefly. "I went up to Mrs. Eveland's and had a word with Matilda Vickery. I dare say you know that she can see the bridge leading to Paradise from her bedroom window. It's one of her occupations, poor soul, to watch the people who go up to the house. Since the place had been empty for a day or two there wasn't much doing yesterday. She didn't have much difficulty in recollecting who'd been across the bridge.

"Up to the moment when you went into the house with Mrs. Carthallow only four people used it. The postman, who called twice, on the early morning round and then with the second delivery; the milkman—he crosses the bridge and leaves the milk in a box affair on the far side from which the servants collect it—and Mr. and Mrs. Carthallow. She saw the postman and the milkman cross over and return, and she saw Carthallow and his wife arrive."

"Together?"

"No. Carthallow was first by a quarter of an hour or so. His wife came alone. That much at least bears out her story."

"It doesn't seem," said Mordecai Tremaine, "to be particularly convincing evidence. Miss Vickery may easily have been mistaken. Someone could have gone in without her knowledge."

Penross leaned back in his chair. His attitude was that of a man who had already found the answers to all the possible questions.

"She had a bad day yesterday—was in pain most of the time. She couldn't concentrate on reading, so she just lay in bed and watched from her window. She's positive that she didn't doze off at all and that she saw everything that went on. Her memory's remarkably good—probably because she's compelled to spend so much time looking at the world instead of playing an active part in it—and I don't think there's much escapes her. Even if she did nod for a moment or two and miss someone going in it's unlikely that she would have missed the same person coming out as well."

"I can't swear," said Mordecai Tremaine, "that there wasn't anyone else in the house when I went back with Mrs. Carthallow. I didn't search the premises, and it would have been simple enough for a person who had been in hiding to have got away during the time we were waiting for you to turn up."

"But only," said Penross, "across the bridge. There's only

one way into that house. Miss Vickery says that she was watching the bridge the whole time. She's positive that no one left the house between the time you crossed over with Mrs. Carthallow and the time when I got there after your telephone message.

"I questioned her pretty thoroughly, and from what she told me about other things she'd seen and that I could check for myself I'm convinced she's right. And I can vouch for the fact that nobody who hasn't been accounted for left after that. I put one of my men at the entrance to the bridge, and if anybody had tried to pass him I'd have known about it."

He stopped. And then he said, with deliberate emphasis, "There were only two people in that house. One was Mrs. Carthallow, and the other was her husband."

"I take it," said Boyce, "that as a matter of routine you've looked into one or two people's alibis?"

Penross took out a notebook from his pocket and thumbed through the pages.

"I've made a list of the people who seem to have had most to do with Carthallow. I haven't had time to break down any of their stories so far, of course, but they all claim to have been a long way from Paradise when he was killed. Ah— here we are. Roberta Fairham. Was at a tennis party at the other end of the town. Says she was there before two thirty, although she can't be certain of the actual time, and didn't leave until after five. It should be easy enough to check. She can't have been the only person there.

"Lewis Haldean was over at St. Mawgan—didn't get back until last night. He wasn't due until today but says he came straight here when he heard the news."

"I happened to be at Mrs. Eveland's when he arrived," said Mordecai Tremaine. "He'd found out that Mrs. Carthallow was there."

Penross was studying his notes.

"I wonder what brought him back in such a hurry?" he said thoughtfully.

He left the question in the air, but he glanced suggestively at Mordecai Tremaine, and that gentleman understood what he meant.

"There isn't anything between them—as far as I know," he said defensively. "Haldean's more or less one of the family circle, and I suppose it was natural for him to come back to see whether there was anything he could do. As a matter of fact, I always had the impression that he was on better terms with Adrian Carthallow than with his wife. So I don't think, Charles, you'll get very far with trying to bring him into an eternal triangle."

"*I* haven't said anything about an eternal triangle," Penross remarked. "But since you've raised the subject I thought the most likely candidate for one side of the triangle was Lester Imleyson."

"All right," said Boyce, "where was Imleyson at the vital time?"

"On the road between Wadestow and Falporth," returned the other. "His car broke down—one of the leads managed to become disconnected, and it took him a little while to locate the trouble. He was coming back from the race meeting."

"So his car broke down," said Boyce. "After all, it might have happened to anybody. I wonder where he would have been if he hadn't been delayed?"

"If we knew the answer I don't see that it would prove anything." There was a note of disappointment in the inspector's voice. "The important thing is that he wasn't at Paradise."

Mordecai Tremaine's face was grave. He was thinking that Penross was going to find it difficult not to make up his mind about Helen Carthallow one way or the other. Falporth had already produced a blossoming of reporters who would not be slow at hunting out the facts of the situation, and the chief constable would have studied the reports and would be expecting something to be done.

And it was no good trying to oppose unpalatable evidence with mere sentiment.

He went over in his mind all the points Penross had brought forward, and it was undeniable that they added up to a damning indictment.

Adrian Carthallow had been killed with a gun that carried

only his wife's fingerprints. The two of them had been alone in the house at the time. Helen Carthallow was known to be in love with Lester Imleyson. She had admitted that it had been the cause of a violent quarrel between her husband and herself. She had already given two versions of the way in which Adrian Carthallow had died, and neither of them was the correct one.

There were, he thought, four possible explanations.

One. Adrian Carthallow had killed himself for some reason yet to be ascertained. In which case why had there been no fingerprints of his on the gun?

Two. Helen Carthallow had killed him but accidentally. In which case why had she not told a straightforward story instead of making two statements the police had easily proved to be untrue?

Three. Helen Carthallow was a murderess and had killed her husband with malice aforethought. In which case why had she not made at least an intelligent attempt to protect herself?

Four. Some third person, at present unknown, had been responsible. In which case how had he or she managed to come and go unseen?

He realized then that he had not, after all, covered all the possibilities. There was a fifth. One that Jonathan Boyce had raised.

Adrian Carthallow had wanted his wife to kill him and

had lied deliberately in telling her that the gun was not loaded. But in that case why had he chosen such a clumsy method of committing suicide, and why hadn't she told the truth about where she had been standing when she had fired?

He recalled the first time he had met Adrian Carthallow and his wife, probing into his memory to find some clue that would help him now, searching for the link with that dreadful scene in the study at Paradise that must exist in the background of their lives. He could see Helen Carthallow's face; could see the dark eyes and the overvivid lips; could see them and could not be certain of what they meant.

Inspector Penross dug his hands deep into his pockets. He heaved a long and heavy sigh.

"The question is," he said, "where do we go from here? Instead of a nice, neat little accident it looks like being as pretty a problem as I've struck."

Mordecai Tremaine said, "Yes. She is, isn't she?"

Part Two

BACKGROUND:

BEFORE THE CORPSE

1

Mordecai Tremaine was thinking that it was a very good party. There were a lot of people present, and he liked meeting people.

It was true, of course, that he had brought a dangerous enthusiasm to the task of passing judgment on Anita Lane's latest capture from her wine merchant. If he was not exactly wearing rosy-colored glasses the pince-nez through which he was beaming happily were temporarily possessed of a quality that had invested the scene with a mellowness slightly larger than life.

As a stage and film critic Anita's circle of acquaintances was a wide one, and all kinds of guests were likely to be found at her Kensington flat. Tonight it was Adrian Carthallow who was the social lion.

Carthallow's latest picture, *The Triumphal March of the Nations*, had just been exhibited, and the art world was still being torn violently in opposite directions by those who considered that it was worthy to hang alongside the masters and those who contended that such depths of bitterness and cyn-icism would have been best left untouched.

Tremaine had not seen the painting, but he had read the criticisms of both sides, and he was inclined to support Carthallow, for if it was bitter and cynical it was at least founded upon truth.

It was intended to represent evolution and showed the growth of man from the primeval apes to the flowering of the modern nations. For a comparatively small canvas it was a remarkable achievement.

Carthallow had made clever use of impressionism with-out falling into the error of exaggeration, and the eye was carried from left to right and upward in a bold sweep of color that showed mankind pressing on to fulfillment, the figures crowding one upon the other beneath the irresistible impetus of the life force. The whole point of the picture lay in the fact that the triumphant nations at the summit of the evolutionary tree bore the faces of war, famine, pestilence, and greed. From a distance they appeared to be figures of nobility, but when one approached closer to the canvas they were revealed as grimacing skeletons, with evil eyes burning from fleshless sockets.

It produced a sensation of physical shock to stand near to it and see the whole thing change so sickeningly to some-thing that conjured up the horrible odor of the charnel house. Carthallow had been asked to reveal the technique that had produced that telling effect, but he had refused to gratify his questioners.

"Rembrandt had his secrets," he had said grandly. "I have mine."

Anita Lane introduced Mordecai Tremaine early in the proceedings.

"He's been dying to add you to his collection, Adrian," she said.

Carthallow was puzzled at first and then a look of understanding came into his face.

"Tremaine? Are you the Mordecai Tremaine who goes around solving murders?"

Mordecai Tremaine assumed an air of modesty.

"I have been in the neighborhood once or twice when the police have been working on a case," he admitted, "and the newspapers have given me rather a lot of publicity."

"So," Carthallow observed, "I've noticed."

"It wasn't altogether welcome," said Tremaine hastily, thinking his modesty had been overdone and was in danger of becoming suspect. "There was a tendency to neglect the part played by the police, and after all they did most of the real work."

"Any time," Carthallow said, "you feel you're getting too much publicity, just let *me* know. I thrive on it."

He had the air of the sublime egotist. Tremaine felt the beginnings of dislike stirring regretfully within him. But he told himself that it was shortsighted to leap to conclusions. First impressions were sometimes a long way from the truth.

He looked at his companion reflectively, taking in the long, rather pinched nose, the thinning hair, the hint of the paunch of the successful man that was pushing insidiously at Carthallow's waistline. Although the artist was a man who liked to live in the limelight and be the center of attraction, it did not follow that he was fundamentally unsound. It might very well be the natural exuberance of the creative artist that drove him to take the center of the stage.

And as the evening progressed Tremaine found that initial resentment dying away.

"Even the cleverest of criminals," he said, in response to a question the other had put to him concerning his hobby, "slips up sooner or later. And once the police have had their suspicions aroused there's no escaping them."

"So you don't," said Carthallow, "believe in the perfect crime?"

"The perfect crime," returned Tremaine, "isn't likely ever to be analyzed because once the police know about it the perfection's gone. The essence of it is that no one should suspect that there *has* been a crime."

"I see your point," Carthallow observed, and there was a note almost of regret in his voice. "It must be depressing to commit the perfect murder and then not be able to take the credit for it just because you've done the job so well. I wonder how many unsuspected murderers are walking around now," he said reflectively, "just aching to tell the world how clever they've been!"

"I hope there aren't many," said Mordecai Tremaine hastily. Carthallow eyed him with a hint of amusement. He said, "You'd better keep an eye on *me*."

Tremaine peered doubtfully over his pince-nez.

"You don't mean," he said, "that *you're* contemplating committing what you hope is going to be the perfect murder?"

Carthallow grinned.

"Not exactly. But you never know when I might be called upon to play a leading part in one of your detective problems. The part of the corpse. A lot of people don't like me at all, and some of them have told me how delighted they'd be to have an opportunity of laying me out. I'd like to think that I was going to be revenged by someone who really knew his stuff!"

The words were bantering, but somehow they impacted upon Mordecai Tremaine's mind with an odd sense of chill. He felt for an instant or two that he was walking over a grave. And then he said, "I suppose an artist is bound to make enemies. Especially if he paints exactly what he sees. But words aren't deeds. A lot of things are said that aren't meant."

"Maybe," said Carthallow, and he grinned and turned to look for another whiskey.

There was no opportunity of continuing the discussion for Carthallow was in constant demand. There was no doubt that he enjoyed the role.

Mordecai Tremaine would probably have finished the evening with an active dislike for him but for one circumstance. And the circumstance was Carthallow's attitude toward his wife.

He never forgot that she was present. He took pains to see that she was not neglected. His concern for her was understandable, for Helen Carthallow was an attractive woman. Mordecai Tremaine thought that he would have preferred it if she had been a little less vivacious and if her laugh had been slightly more subdued. But he was aware of his own limitations and was prepared to admit that in some respects he was old-fashioned.

Besides, when he talked to her he did not feel that he was speaking to a hard and unsympathetic person. Despite the boldness of her makeup he was conscious of something essentially feminine in her.

Searching for a common ground for conversation he mentioned a musical play he had seen the previous week, and when she spoke of the theatre her face took on an enthusiasm that told him he had found a subject in which she had a genuine interest. Her slim, graceful body seemed to develop a new vitality: the dark eyes acquired a natural eagerness, the color came into the whiteness of her cheeks, and by contrast the harsh scarlet of her lips was toned down so that it was barely noticeable.

For a brief space of time she became a different person, and the result was that by the end of the evening Mordecai Tremaine's feelings had become so mixed that he was incapable of making up his mind about her.

If he had not seen her in that mood, displaying the spontaneous pleasure of a child with no adult inhibitions to guard her speech, he would have dismissed her as a rather metallic, empty creature who moved in a bohemian world, continually acting the gay wife of a successful artist, smiling without meaning and uttering flatteries that were false. Now he was wondering which of the two women he had seen was the real Helen Carthallow. He was wondering whether the lipstick and the overbright manner were symbols of defense.

As the wife of Adrian Carthallow it was inevitable that she should move in the limelight and that she would be called upon to act the hostess with or to meet people with whom she would otherwise have had nothing in common. Was she inwardly a little afraid of it all, and was this her instinctive reaction?

He cried a halt before he could become too involved with theorizing. At any rate it was gratifying to his sense of the romantic to see that Adrian Carthallow displayed such consideration toward her. In times when the sanctity of marriage seemed to be going the downhill way of all the other moral standards it was reassuring to find a man who paid court to his wife in public.

Later, and before he bade good night to Anita, he said as much to her. Unaccustomed wine had mellowed him. He was prepared to take an exaggeratedly sentimental view of the universe.

Anita Lane gave him a curious look. She said, dryly, "Do you still read *Romantic Stories*, Mordecai?"

Despite his mood he sensed the critical note in her voice.

"What do you mean?" he asked her.

"Let it pass, Mordecai," she told him. "Sometimes it's better to have your head in the clouds."

He wanted to question her further, but she turned to attend to others of her departing guests, and in his state of exaltation it seemed in any case to be of no importance.

8

Possibly it was merely because Adrian Carthallow's name had moved up a step or two in his subconscious mind that he noticed it more, but it seemed that in the course of the following weeks it came to his notice with a frequency that had all the marks of being ordained by fate.

There were reports of speeches Adrian Carthallow had made at various functions. Usually they were caustic and calculated to produce feelings of antagonism in some section of the community, which meant that they received due publicity and was no doubt why they had been made. There were photographs in the society periodicals of Adrian Carthallow attending this affair or that in company with his attractive wife.

He began to take an interest in the man. He found himself reading up as much as was known of his career, tracing his rise painting by painting from the time, some eight years previously, when he had arrived unknown with a bundle of canvases under his arm and had proceeded to barnstorm the Royal Academy.

Adrian Carthallow could not be ignored. That was the fundamental fact about him. His paintings might call down a torrent of argument, but their technical excellence was never in doubt, and it was the knowledge that he knew how to hold a brush and could hold his own in any discussion on the methods of the masters that enabled him to overcome the initial antagonism that greets a new performer trying to break into the circle of the elect without first having starved in a garret or died unrecognized.

At least, he would never admit to having starved, although it was certain enough that only years of patient endeavor could have developed his skill to such a point, and even a genius must feed his body while his mind is flowering and his hand is learning its cunning.

What he had been and where he had lived before the boat train from Paris had deposited him in a London he had been determined to conquer was obscure. He was reported variously to have lived in Buenos Aires, Chicago, and Boston. He himself was stated to have declared that he had learned his art in Rome, from an old man, unknown to the world at large, who was possessed of secrets handed down from Michelangelo and Titian and who had passed them on, so Carthallow claimed, because he had befriended the old man in his last, poverty-stricken years and had paid to send his daughter to a Swiss sanatorium.

It was all very expansive, typically Carthallow, and highly suspect. Nobody could prove it, but neither, so far, had anybody been able to deny it.

Piece by piece Mordecai Tremaine assembled the scanty fragments of the puzzle that had made up Carthallow's life since his arrival in England. But there was nothing at this time to tell him that there was a drama in the making in which he himself was to play no small part. He thought merely that he was exercising his intense curiosity. He liked to tabulate people. Having met them he liked to know exactly who they were and what they did.

His interest extended to all matters connected with art. He found himself, for instance, paying unexpected attention to such news items as the arrival in England of Warren Belmont. Normally, a rich American visitor would have meant nothing to him, but Belmont, it seemed, had come over in order to invest a not inconsiderable number of dollars in various art treasures, including paintings. Tremaine wondered whether he would consider Adrian Carthallow's work worth buying with an eye on posterity, or whether Carthallow would convince him in spite of himself.

And then there came the Christine Neale affair.

The controversy over *The Triumphal March of the Nations* was just beginning to subside, which meant that it was the psychological moment for a new brick to be flung into the

calming waters. Adrian Carthallow undoubtedly knew when
to make the next move.

For a week or more the newspapers were busy exploring
new angles to the story. Christine Neale's disappearance from
the scene, her father's threat-breathing visit to Carthallow's
club, the speech Carthallow made the following day all made
the headlines.

Strangely enough Carthallow received a certain amount
of sympathy from his male acquaintances, although they
regarded him generally as a *poseur*. Christine Neale had been
making herself a nuisance. She had been throwing herself at
Carthallow's head and had only herself to blame if he had
painted what he had seen.

Adrian Carthallow, Mordecai Tremaine learned—it was
a discovery that left him with mixed feelings—was one of
those men who fascinate women. They fell over themselves
to win his favors, particularly the spoiled, empty-headed
Christine Neale variety.

So far, of course, it was just the old story over again. The
creative artist, possessed of an irresistible power over women
and treading his careless way undeterred by broken hearts
or irate husbands, was one of the most familiar of the lus-
cious novelist's stock figures. But Adrian Carthallow did
not run true to type. He was by no means attracted by the
women who were so eager to fling themselves at his feet. His

reputation was of the purest. No breath of that kind of scandal attached to his name.

Mordecai Tremaine, whose opinion of him went up and down daily according to the latest news item, regarded this particular revelation with satisfaction. He remembered Carthallow's attitude toward his wife and was pleasantly tolerant about him and even prepared to like him a little.

Winter rained its way into a period of frost and a bright, crisp March. On a certain sunny day that made London look shabby and begrimed by contrast, Mordecai Tremaine decided to visit the Tower of London.

The visit, in itself, was without significance. He enjoyed himself as always, for his mind was receptive to atmosphere and to stand on Raleigh's Walk or to look out across the green turf where the private scaffold had been erected was to absorb the history of the gray stones around him. He passed the Traitors' Gate with his usual shudder at the thought of all the unfortunates who had entered under its wide span, turned up by the Bloody Tower, and spent an hour browsing among the armor in the main keep of the White Tower.

He came away with the intention of walking through to St. Paul's, and it was as he was traversing the crowded, narrow streets in the region of the Monument that he saw Adrian Carthallow.

The artist was standing at the entrance to an alley that lost itself in a maze of ramshackle property that looked as though it might house a dozen dens of iniquity but was probably perfectly innocuous. He was talking to a shabbily dressed individual. Mordecai Tremaine, ever ready to add to his collection of human oddities, studied him with interest. He was short, squat, and with a bald head that was peculiarly flat. He looked, in fact, as though he was one of the porters who perform such feats of balancing in the markets and had developed the perfect platform for the carrying on of his trade.

The shabby one must have sensed his scrutiny, for he looked up suddenly. Tremaine saw him nudge Carthallow, and the artist turned sharply and looked in his direction.

It was difficult to be certain of what actually happened. To Mordecai Tremaine it seemed that Carthallow made a startled and hasty gesture to his companion and that the shabby one vanished promptly in the depths of the alley. But it might well have been that their conversation had finished and that the whole thing was perfectly spontaneous.

Tremaine wondered at first whether Carthallow would remember their meeting, for it had, after all, taken place some time before and the artist must encounter many new faces. It was unlikely that his own interest in the other had been reciprocated.

But Carthallow's recognition was open enough. He came forward, his hand outstretched.

"Why," he said, "isn't it the sleuth? What are *you* doing in these wild parts?"

"I'm studying the natives," Mordecai Tremaine returned, entering into the spirit of the thing. "But I might put the same question to you!"

"You'd receive the same answer," Carthallow said. There was no trace of embarrassment in his manner. "I'm in search of copy. I often take a stroll down this way. Have to see how everybody else is living, you know, if you aren't to become stale. But, of course, *you* know all about that."

"Yes," said Mordecai Tremaine, "I know all about that."

They made their way along the busy pavement, thronged with a diverse assortment of human beings. Carthallow swung confidently along, nothing furtive about him, no sign visible that he resented having been detected in conversation with the shabby individual at the end of the alley. He seemed, indeed, in a highly jovial mood. He took a delight in pointing out people and places, displaying a keen knowledge both of humanity and of the neighborhood through which they were passing.

Their progress was enlivened with his comments.

"That fellow over there by the pub," he said. "You see him? What a study he'd make! Big ears, low forehead, the ape written all over him. I wish I'd had *him* as a model!"

And a few yards further on: "Have a look at that restaurant," he said, indicating it with a lordly sweep of his arm that earned a scowl of resentment from the wayfarer it all but decapitated. "The tiny place on the corner. If you want to see life in the raw that's the place to find it. A Spaniard who calls himself Pedro runs it, and a more villainous-looking scoundrel I've yet to see. Nobody ever hears his real name although Scotland Yard probably know it. I'd use him if I wasn't afraid of having my throat cut when he found out! If ever you go in there take my advice and sit tight like Brer Rabbit!"

Mordecai Tremaine said, "You seem to know your way about."

Carthallow accepted it as a compliment and beamed expansively.

"You can't just sit in a studio and paint indefinitely," he returned. "You've got to get out and see what the world is doing and what kind of people are making it happen."

An egotist Adrian Carthallow might be, but to walk alongside him was a stimulating experience, although it was inclined to be like a parade along the footlights with the audience staring from all parts of the house. Even in a city in which the unusual was the ordinary he stood out from the multitude. Curious stares followed them, and when at length they parted Mordecai Tremaine felt a trifle breathless and like an exhibit in a glass case.

"We must see more of you," Carthallow said. "I'll tell Helen to ask you along when we're holding court. We'll be in town some while yet. By the way," he added, "are you going to the Allied Arts Ball next week?"

And when Mordecai Tremaine, not daring to confess that he had no idea that the Allied Arts—whoever they might be—were arranging such a function or where it was taking place, admitted hesitantly that he was not: "No? I'll send you a couple of tickets. You mustn't miss it, my dear fellow. The maddest thing of the year!"

In a slight daze Mordecai Tremaine found himself handing over his card so that there would be no mistake about his address.

"It's extraordinarily kind of you," he began.

"Nonsense! You'll be doing *me* a favor. You're just the sort of man I want to cultivate. Perhaps I'll be only too glad of your professional services one day!"

Mordecai Tremaine judged that their acquaintanceship had ripened sufficiently to enable him to take a chance. He said, "You mean because of Christine Neale?"

To his relief Carthallow displayed no rancor.

"So you read about that storm in a teacup," he said, with a modesty that rang loudly false. "Women," he added, "are the devil."

Mordecai Tremaine's sentimental soul caused him to add certain mental reservations to the statement, but he could understand the other's attitude. Man, the hunter, does not take kindly to the role of the hunted.

9

The next day, after sleep had erected a barrier from the far side of which he could see the incident in a more normal perspective, Tremaine came to the conclusion that it had been no more than a chance encounter that had ended where it had begun. He had caught the artist in an ebullient mood, in the full sweep of his creative vision; by now Carthallow had forgotten all about him. The date of the Allied Arts Ball—he had looked it up in the meantime and had discovered that it was expected to be one of Chelsea's liveliest efforts—could be safely crossed from his diary.

But in this he was mistaken. Two days later the promised tickets arrived. There was a brief note from Carthallow to say that he was looking forward to seeing him and that his wife was inviting a few friends to their house on the evening of the following Wednesday and would be delighted if he could come.

Mordecai Tremaine, who had not danced for longer than he was willing to recall, practiced awkward steps in front of his dressing-table mirror and then rang up Anita Lane.

Her voice revealed her surprise.

"Why, Mordecai! You're becoming quite the gallant cavalier. I'm not doing anything, and of course I'd love to come. If only," she added wickedly, "to see you dance the polka!"

"At one time," said Mordecai Tremaine stiffly, "I was considered an excellent dancer."

Her laugh came over the wire, and he could imagine the amusement in her gray eyes.

"Seriously, Mordecai," she said, for he had told her the source of the tickets, "you seem to have made a hit with Adrian. I thought he only went after people like Belmont."

The name was vaguely familiar to him.

"Belmont?"

"Warren Belmont," she explained. "The American millionaire. He's over here to buy pictures, and Adrian isn't the man to lose an opportunity."

Oddly there crept into his mind then a faint memory of what she had said to him when he had been leaving her flat on the night the Carthallows had been there. He said, "Nita, you were going to tell me something once about Adrian Carthallow. I'd just spoken to you about how much he seemed to be in love with his wife, and you said something about keeping my head in the clouds. Remember?"

"Yes," she said quietly, and her voice had lost its note of humor. "I remember. But whatever it was I was going to say,

Mordecai, is better left unsaid." She was silent for a moment or two. And then: "You aren't—up to anything, Mordecai?" she asked.

"Up to anything?" he said, genuinely surprised.

"I mean with the Carthallows."

"Of course not," he told her. "What should I be up to?"

"Nothing," she said. "Nothing at all. Goodbye, Mordecai. It was very sweet of you to think of asking me."

He heard the click as the receiver went down, and he sat staring at the instrument in his hand, a puzzled frown on his face. It was unlike Anita to be mysterious. He wondered what was going on. It was frustrating to have something waved in front of him and then whisked away again before he could see it properly. He would have to tell Anita so.

But when he saw her again there were many other things to think about. The Allied Arts Ball was a fancy dress affair. What, he said to Anita, did she think of going as Elizabeth and Essex?

Essex, said Anita practically, would look rather odd in pince-nez. She had been thinking of something a little more subdued, like Pierrot and Pierette. Tremaine abandoned his vision of himself as the dashing if unfortunate earl with a sigh of regret, but he realized the soundness of Anita's objections. She had mentioned only his pince-nez, but it was also extremely doubtful whether his attenuated shanks would have shown to the best advantage in the costume of an Elizabethan gallant; it would be safer if they were to be decently concealed by the baggy trousers of Pierrot.

Adrian Carthallow had spoken of the ball as the maddest affair of the year, and when Mordecai Tremaine ushered his partner into the vast hall where the festivities were already in full swing he realized that for once the artist had not been exaggerating.

Gypsies, admirals, and field marshals; ballet dancers, peddlers, and princes were whirling together under flying paper streamers and falling balloons. Around the edge of the floor moved a procession out of the fantastic deeps of an inebriate's nightmare. Enormously tall men with faces of a moonlike roundness and painted grotesquely moved stiffly among an assortment of weird creatures most of whom looked like the freakish results of trying to cross a dragon with a dinosaur.

Mordecai Tremaine began to enjoy himself. He responded to the atmosphere like a tropical flower in the sun. It seemed unlikely that he would encounter Adrian Carthallow in such a wild entanglement of humanity disguised with wood and canvas and dresses of many hues, but there was no reason why he should not make the most of the opportunity the other had given him.

Two hours later, uttering a silent prayer of thanks that there was more room for relaxation in Pierrot's ample folds than would have been provided by the unyielding garments of the earl of Essex, he found himself trying to make his perilous way back to Anita with the soft drink for which she had asked. A balloon rebounded gently from his pince-nez, leaving them even more precariously poised than usual. A huge face loomed over him; he met the fixed stare of a painted eye and wondered vaguely why it looked so human.

He sidestepped skillfully out of danger, and in that moment a corpulent jester with a flaunting red nose and bells jingling on his cap flourished a rattle in front of him.

"What have you done with it?" hissed a conspiratorial voice in his ear.

Mordecai Tremaine looked startled.

"Done with what?" he asked.

"The body!" said the jester dramatically, and he realized that it was Carthallow.

The artist grasped him by the arm.

"Come along, we've been searching everywhere for you!"

"My partner—" Mordecai Tremaine managed to gasp before Carthallow could drag him off his course and cause him to lose his bearings completely.

Fortunately Anita was near enough at hand to have witnessed the scene.

"I thought it was you, Adrian," she said. "Nobody else could look quite such a dervish!"

Carthallow's exuberance cleared a way for them through the dancers. In a few moments he had guided them across the floor to his wife's side.

"I've found him," he announced and stood aside to reveal his prize with the air of a magician who produces the final wonder from the inevitable top hat.

Breathless and damply perspiring Mordecai Tremaine restored his pince-nez and tried to look dignified, suddenly aware that he was getting too old to go capering around as Pierrot. But Helen Carthallow did not seem to find anything incongruous in his appearance.

"I hope Adrian didn't tear you away from your friends," she said, with a smile. "He's in one of his buoyant moods tonight."

"On such a night," said Mordecai Tremaine, "all can be forgiven. In any case, Nita and I were hoping we might find you."

He thought that she was looking very beautiful. She was wearing a dark dress of some velvet material that shone under the light and that flowed gracefully about her as she moved. A tiny black silken mask concealed the upper part of her features; only the redness of her lips and the whiteness of her skin offered a contrast to the dress and the mask.

Carthallow noticed his admiration.

"Who is she?" he demanded. "Let *me* play the Fool, but for Helen, she whose face once launched a thousand ships, there is another title!"

Mordecai Tremaine searched hazily in a mind too limp with the excitements and exertions of the past two hours to enable him to recall the character whom Helen Carthallow was supposed to represent. The only name that would come to him was that of Helen of Troy, which seemed too obvious.

"The clue, my dear fellow," said Carthallow. "I gave you the clue!"

And then, as Mordecai Tremaine still stared blankly, he capered triumphantly.

"The Dark Lady of the sonnets," he announced.

The red lips under the silken mask parted in a smile.

"You mustn't mind Adrian," said Helen Carthallow. "His cap and bells have licensed him for the evening."

"Shakespeare's lady of mystery," Carthallow was saying, more as if he was declaiming to the air because he loved the sound of the words than with any idea of addressing his companions. "The dark lady from nowhere who inspired the poet to touch the heights. Who can say her name or what were her thoughts—or who were her lovers?"

For a fleeting, unreal moment Mordecai Tremaine experienced the sensation of gazing upon impossible things. It seemed that the face of the jester was a satirical mask, that Helen Carthallow's somber beauty was possessed of the taut quality of a woman who stood on guard, and that there was an anguish of waiting in the dark eyes that looked out from the silken strip.

But it was absurd, of course, because her husband had taken her arm and she was smiling, and they were standing together like a pair of young lovers.

Anita Lane and Helen Carthallow knew each other well, and it was only a moment or two before they had gone instinctively into the conversational clinch that develops inevitably when two women who need no introduction to each other get together. Carthallow glanced at them with exaggerated resignation and proceeded to escort Mordecai Tremaine to the bar. Thereafter to that gentleman the evening was a rosy blur, punctuated by vaguely arduous intervals during which he endeavored to dance in a crush that had become even more reminiscent of a victory night celebration.

When he climbed wearily into bed after having deposited at her flat an Anita shuddering at the thought of the early film show awaiting her only a few hours ahead, the whole thing had resolved itself into a mixture of waving streamers, dancing balloons, and colorful, whirling bodies. Only an odd incident here and there still detached itself from the general background.

Adrian Carthallow, in cap and bells, prancing like an excited schoolboy; Anita Lane's flushed and eager face; Roberta Fairham showering paper streamers over them from her mailbag.

Carthallow had introduced her—a fair-haired girl whose

features it was difficult to keep in mind since they possessed so little personality. She was dressed as a postman and the bag was intended to represent her collection of letters.

It was doubtful whether Mordecai Tremaine would have retained any clear impression of her among so much that was blurred had it not been for the adoration in her pale eyes when she had looked up at Carthallow. Her attitude had been that of a worshipper at a shrine; the artist had glanced across at him and shrugged significantly.

So Roberta Fairham was among the women who were eager to fall for Adrian Carthallow. Tremaine, having witnessed the phenomenon for himself, could sympathize with him. It must be extremely embarrassing, even for a man so ready for adulation, to be pursued with such public constancy.

Not that Roberta Fairham belonged to the obvious huntress type. She was not of the alluring race of sirens who can be depended upon to sweep the susceptible male off his feet and away from the arms of his lawful wife on an irresistible tide of glamour. Her adoration was of the self-effacing kind. She admired from a distance; she was content to build her dreams upon any stray glances that might be sent in her direction by her god in his wisdom.

Helen Carthallow could not have failed to be aware of the situation, but she gave no sign of it. Her manner toward the other woman was natural and friendly and with no suggestion that she had invested the title with significant capitals. No doubt she was resigned to the knowledge that her husband was a target for her sex and was accustomed to the necessity for treating philosophically what could not be mended. And, after all, a wife who is confident of her husband's regard can afford to be tolerant where less fortunate females are concerned.

With thoughts of Helen Carthallow occupying his mind it was, perhaps, inevitable that the last incident to drift cameo-like out of the evening's happy blur should have concerned her.

It had happened when Adrian Carthallow had been dancing with Anita Lane. His wife had asked to be excused from being hurled into the maelstrom occupying the dance floor, and Tremaine had been sitting out with her. And in the midst of their conversation he had seen the dark eyes looking out from the mask become suddenly vitalized, and he had known that she was no longer listening to him.

A gypsy had been going by. A tall, handsome gypsy, who moved with a muscular ease among the packed dancers. He had been looking over his partner's shoulder full in their direction.

Mordecai Tremaine had seen them staring at each other across the floor for just that instant that had yet seemed so long a time. Two young people facing each other with the world between them. The woman with the vivid contrasts of her white skin and dark gown and the red of her lips, and the man with his good looks and the virile confidence of youth.

And that, he thought, would be enough of that. *Romantic Stories* could supply all the color he needed.

10

A day or two later a pleasantly worded note from Helen Carthallow invited him to a party she and her husband were giving for a few of their friends. With the feeling that he was developing into a gay dog Tremaine sent off an acceptance. Gazing into his mirror he found himself wondering whether this was indeed the same man who not so very long ago had been standing for many hours a day behind the counter of his shop dispensing cigarettes and pipe tobacco to his customers and not suspecting how much there was of interest in the larger world outside.

But he knew that in that he was not being fair to his old self. It had been because he had known that there were more things in life than were bounded by ounces of empire mixture and packets of twenty that he had developed into an amateur criminologist. And it was as a direct result of his dabblings in crime that he was tonight bound for Adrian Carthallow's house, for he had an instinctive feeling that if it had not been for his reputation as a solver of murder mysteries he would never have attracted the artist's attention.

In these last few weeks murder seemed to have receded into the background of his life. He had paid little heed to the latest examples of man's propensity for removing his fellow man—or woman—by such refinements as shooting, poisoning, or the wielding of a blunt instrument. He was rather glad that it had been so. There had been a time when the thought of being engaged upon a real murder case instead of merely reading about it had exhilarated him and quickened his pulses; now he knew that there was more to such an investigation than the excitement of solving a fascinating puzzle. When you faced such a problem in the flesh instead of in the pages of a book it took on a different and more terrible aspect.

There was a victim who was a reality instead of a name. There was a murderer one might know intimately and even grow to like before one discovered the truth and realized that this was a human soul that had to be branded with the red stigma of guilt. When you reached the truth you had to hurry over it and then do your utmost to forget it before the horror of it could overwhelm you.

It was a relief not to have to hound someone; not to have to work with the knowledge that someone knew what you were trying to do and was waiting, with fear and hate in his heart, to see whether you were near the truth or not. It was pleasant to be able to go to the Allied Arts Ball and to Adrian Carthallow's house and not have the eternal thought that these things were only a means to an end and that sooner or later you would have to strip away the pretense and stand forth as the accuser, invoking the awesome paraphernalia of the law.

There were a lot of people present whom he did not know, and at first he was doubtful whether, from his personal point of view, the evening was going to be a success. But he need not have worried. Carthallow went out of his way to make sure that he did not feel neglected.

The artist's house was expensively furnished. His income, Mordecai Tremaine reflected, must be a considerable one; it must be very pleasant to be a successful artist.

Several of Carthallow's own studies were on the walls. They were chiefly Cornish scenes, and Tremaine, who loved Cornwall, remarked upon them.

"Most of them are of the coast near Falporth," said Carthallow. "Helen and I usually spend a few months there during the summer. We've a house just outside the town."

He waited, as though he expected some comment, but Mordecai Tremaine, who had not at that time heard of the house called Paradise, was unsatisfyingly silent.

Possibly because of Tremaine's genuine interest in his

work, possibly for obscure reasons of his own, Carthallow tended to become confidential. He slipped away from the rest of his guests for a few moments to lead the way to his studio, a big room occupying almost the whole of the top floor.

Tremaine gazed around at the stacked canvases, the easel, and the various tools of the artist's profession—brushes, palettes, pigments, oils, varnishes. Crayon sketches lay untidily upon a raised table under the window. At one end of the room was a model's throne.

He sighed.

"It must be satisfying to be able to create something," he said. "Something that wouldn't have existed if you hadn't given your mind and your talent to it."

"It doesn't always work out like that," said Carthallow. "There are occasions when you ask yourself whether it wouldn't have been better if you hadn't started it!"

But there was no ring of truth in his voice. There was, rather, a queer triumph.

Mordecai Tremaine was wandering about the studio, gazing at the canvases standing against the wall, some finished, some obviously needing a considerable amount of work to complete them.

He was thinking about the portrait of Christine Neale that had come out of this studio not so long ago and was wondering how best to phrase his question. At last he said,

"When you decide upon a subject—a portrait, say—how do you approach the actual painting? Do you start with a definite plan in mind of what you're going to do, or do you wait until the sittings begin and then paint exactly what you see?"

Carthallow stood under the bright light in the center of the room, his brow creased in thought, as though he was posing for one of his own portraits.

"I try," he said, "to paint something I think is typical of the person who is sitting for me. Different people create in me the impression of different moods. I try to catch the mood I think is the dominant one and paint it against a background that serves to emphasize that particular facet of the sitter's personality."

Mordecai Tremaine nodded learnedly. He was trying to translate it into simpler language and apply it to Christine Neale. Carthallow had painted that portrait for a reason. He might, conceivably, have believed that he was painting truth as he saw it, but he had seen a certain kind of truth because he was a certain kind of man.

"I see," he said. "You don't paint merely to reproduce what a camera might capture, but to paint a living individual?"

"I paint," said Carthallow, "always with the desire to find the soul that lies behind the eyes and pin it to the canvas." The phrase seemed to please him. He repeated it with savor. "To pin the soul to the canvas. There is the true vocation of the artist!"

"I envy you," said Tremaine, momentarily fired by the same tendency to embark upon the purple passage, "because you possess the gift of immortality. After you have passed your creations will live on!"

Instead of arousing Carthallow to further lyric heights his speech had the opposite effect.

"You sound damned morbid!" the artist said. "Anyway, painting with oils on wood and canvas—or on anything else for that matter—is no way to win immortality. Pictures don't last—not when you're thinking in terms of centuries. If Reynolds, for instance, could have seen how many of his were going to crack or melt in less than two hundred years he'd have been more careful with the varnish!"

"At least," observed Tremaine, trying to regain lost ground, "you've had the satisfaction of being recognized in your lifetime. You've been able to taste your success."

There was a strange, shadowed look in Adrian Carthallow's face; the look of a man who was hugging a secret to his inner soul.

"I'm not like your perfect murderer, eh?" he said, with a sudden smile. "I don't have to keep quiet about the wonders I've performed!"

They went out of the studio, and as they walked down the stairs the artist went on: "I've always felt sorry for people like Chatterton. He put his heart into the job of writing poetry and then couldn't claim it as his own because he'd have betrayed himself as a fake. Poor little devil, starving in a garret when he ought to have been hailed as a genius!"

Mordecai Tremaine found himself at a loss. There was something wrong with Adrian Carthallow's argument, and yet for the moment he could not tell definitely what that something was. He experienced the same kind of frustration he had known when Anita Lane had hung up her telephone receiver. Perhaps it was linked in some subtle fashion with the peculiar note he had detected in Carthallow's voice.

Before he could straighten out his thoughts they had reached the floor where the party was being held. As they entered the room he became aware that something unexpected was in progress. Instead of the hum of conversation, the clink of glasses, and the strumming of a piano that he had left behind when he had gone out with Carthallow, there was an unnatural silence. Everybody was looking in Helen Carthallow's direction. She was talking to a gray-haired man whose shoulders still carried a military squareness and whose form was still upright despite his years.

At their entrance Helen Carthallow made an involuntary movement. The gray-haired man saw it and turned quickly.

Helen Carthallow said, "Adrian…"

There was distress in her voice. Carthallow stepped into

the room. His face bore a sardonic expression. He said, coolly, "I wasn't expecting this pleasure, Colonel."

The gray-haired man was already moving. No one had time to stop him.

"You damned scoundrel!"

His fist landed against Carthallow's jaw. The artist staggered under the blow and went back against the wall. A thin trickle of blood showed on his lips.

The other clearly intended to go after him, but before he could aim another blow, two of the male members of the party had gripped him by the arms. Carthallow took out his handkerchief and wiped the blood carefully from his face. He said, "Let him go."

A little dubiously the two released their captive. Tremaine half expected that he would spring forward again, but he merely stood facing Carthallow with a deadly hate in his eyes.

"You're being very foolish, Colonel," said Carthallow. "This kind of thing doesn't do any good."

"I suppose," the gray-haired man said icily, "that it's too much to expect that you'll settle this as man to man?"

"Pistols for two?" said Carthallow, and his lip curled. "Don't be absurd. This isn't the eighteenth century, nor is it France. And if it's fists you mean I could beat you to a pulp. I've done a fair amount of boxing in my time, and I'm a younger man than you."

Mordecai Tremaine stood looking at Christine Neale's

father. There was nothing he could do. This was purely Adrian Carthallow's affair.

He felt sorry for the gray-haired man. It was easy to understand the motive that had driven him to invade the house of the man who had pilloried his daughter, foolish though the action had been.

Carthallow said, "You realize, Colonel, that by assaulting me in this fashion you've laid yourself open to legal proceedings on my part. But I've no wish to make capital out of it. If you'll leave at once I'm quite prepared to overlook it."

Colonel Neale did not speak. The hate in his face was undiminished, but he had the look now of a man who realized that he was in a false position and that any further attempt to get to grips with the object of his hatred would merely result in an undignified scuffle.

He turned at last, his eyes searching for Carthallow's wife.

"My apologies to *you*, Mrs. Carthallow," he said.

There was a silence as he went out. It lasted for several moments. It was broken only when Adrian Carthallow stepped smilingly across the floor as if nothing had happened.

"Why don't you play for us, Helen?"

She moved toward the piano. The color was in her cheeks, but otherwise she gave no sign that the incident had affected her. Her long, slim fingers caressed the keys. Chopin, Mozart, and, finally, the elfin melancholy of Grieg.

Mordecai Tremaine could have gone on listening to her and was annoyed when the steadily rising hum of conversation caused her to stop. He wanted to stand up and condemn such an exhibition of bad manners, but he knew nevertheless that she was not displeased. She had at least succeeded in doing what her husband had desired and had removed the awkwardness that had followed the scene with Colonel Neale.

But the atmosphere that had existed before that jarring note had intruded was never quite regained. Despite Carthallow's efforts to obliterate it his guests were finding it too intriguing to be forgotten, and it was a fruitful source of conversation for the small groups of conscious bohemians into which the party tended to disintegrate.

Mordecai Tremaine searched in his mind for some topic that would be safe.

"I wonder what makes some people buy pictures?" he observed. "Warren Belmont, for instance, the millionaire who's just come over here. I wonder whether he buys them because he really appreciates them or because he feels that having made several million dollars he's expected to have a few art treasures in his home?"

But Adrian Carthallow was not inclined to be talkative.

"Belmont? Don't know the fellow," he said shortly.

He moved away, and Mordecai Tremaine was left with

the impression that he had somehow managed to say the wrong thing.

Mingled with a sense of pity for Neale, behaving, after all, only as a father might have been expected to act, there was a feeling that Adrian Carthallow had come out of it rather well. That blow had been a heavy one, and the artist would have been justified in retaliating. His growing corpulence did not disguise the fact that he was a much more powerfully built man than the elderly colonel and would have had no difficulty in knocking him down.

He had displayed a magnanimity that gave the lie to those who had decried him when Christine Neale's portrait had been exhibited and had said that he was seeking only to achieve notoriety. If he had chosen to make capital out of Neale's assault he could have been sure of publicity; the newspapers would have attended to that. Instead of seizing his opportunity he had allowed the incident to be forgotten.

He spoke of this altruism to Anita Lane when he saw her on the following day and was surprised by her cynicism.

"Maybe," she said, "he did it because he was quite sure it *wouldn't* pass unnoticed and he was clever enough to put himself in a good light by pretending to turn the other cheek."

Mordecai Tremaine stared at her in dismay. Rebuffs and disappointments in a hard world had not yet convinced him that human nature possessed such tortuous depths.

"You don't mean," he protested, "that Carthallow intended all the time to tell the newspapers?"

"Why should he?" said Anita practically. "There were plenty of people at last night's party who'll be only too willing to see that the story gets into print. And Adrian Carthallow, not being by any means a fool, is well aware of that."

Tremaine tried to convince himself that long experience as a critic had tended to make Anita oversuspicious, but he was unable to banish the tiny, carping doubt. *Had* Carthallow been acting? Had he been keeping one eye on the newspapers all the time?

He thought of something that had been puzzling him.

"By the way, Nita," he said, "you did tell me that Carthallow would be certain to try and contact Warren Belmont, didn't you?"

"It won't be Adrian if he doesn't. I don't think they've met publicly, but you can bet he knows all about Belmont and is moving heaven and earth to get acquainted."

"You're sure?"

"Of course I'm sure. What are you being so mysterious about?"

Mordecai Tremaine said, "Oh—nothing."

But in this he was not strictly truthful. He knew that it was a trivial incident. Adrian Carthallow, preoccupied with thoughts of his brush with Colonel Neale, had been in no mood for confidences. He had been paying small attention and might even have misheard what had been said. Tremaine was aware that there could be a dozen simple explanations for the artist's unwillingness to discuss Belmont.

And yet it puzzled him.

11

It was two days after the party at Adrian Carthallow's house that Mordecai Tremaine heard from Jonathan Boyce. Although his meetings with the Scotland Yard detective were irregular—Boyce had now been confirmed in the rank of chief inspector and was seldom free from official duties—they kept in touch with each other, and knowing his friend's absorbing interest in all things criminal, Boyce often gave him an outline of the cases upon which he was engaged.

They understood each other. Between the stocky, brusquely spoken Yard man and the mild-looking, elderly retired tobacconist there was a bond based upon mutual trust. With Boyce to guide him Tremaine had found his way among the strange places of the underworld. His knowledge and his appetite had grown rapidly, and it would have surprised those casual acquaintances who knew him only as a benevolent, rather garrulous, and romantic elderly gentleman to learn of the store of criminal matters that lay within his mind.

Boyce, it seemed, was engaged upon an investigation that required him to visit a house in the West End where a considerable amount of gambling was rumored to take place. He was not going in his official capacity, and would Mordecai Tremaine care to accompany him?

Mordecai Tremaine, of course, would be delighted. He had always wanted to visit a gambling hell, and accordingly, although inwardly a little tremulous at the thought of the haunt of iniquity in which he might find himself, he met the Yard man at the appointed rendezvous.

His first reaction was one of intense disappointment. He had been expecting a basement room, approached by a series of guarded doors and filled with tough-looking individuals scrutinizing every stranger. Instead, he was admitted to a well-furnished, impeccably decorated house by a dignified servant whom it was impossible to associate with anything not done in the best circles.

If there was any check upon the people who were given entrance it was one with which Jonathan Boyce evidently knew how to deal, for no questions were asked. The only concession to convention was that it was necessary to pass another door before arriving at the room in which the serious business was carried on, and here stood a custodian who made a more careful examination, although he did it with the polite air of a sales clerk attending to the wants of a valued customer. Boyce produced a card, and the door was opened for them.

Mordecai Tremaine said, under his breath, "I take it that they don't know who you really are?"

"I hope not," the inspector returned grimly. "I went to a great deal of trouble to make sure there wouldn't be any rough stuff."

Tremaine could not repress a suspicion that his companion was exaggerating. It was difficult to imagine anything untoward taking place in this long, quiet chamber that was like a room in a highly exclusive club.

The gathering was an all-male one. Groups of men were dotted about the room, some seated, some standing, and all of them behaving with a decorum that contrasted violently with Mordecai Tremaine's preconceived ideas.

The biggest group was centered upon a large table, and when he drew closer he saw that it carried a roulette wheel. Judging by the chips near the elbows of several of the players there were considerable amounts being wagered.

Mordecai Tremaine's curious eyes wandered from face to face, eager to observe what type of man it was who was prepared to commit his financial destiny to the laws of chance—assuming, of course, that there was no skillfully balanced wheel to enable the croupier to exercise a nice judgment as to who should declare a profit on the evening's entertainment.

And it was then that he saw Adrian Carthallow.

The artist's attention was fixed upon the spinning wheel. There was a small heap of counters in front of him. Tremaine guessed from his strained expression that it was smaller than it had been when he had started to play.

The wheel stopped. Tremaine was not close enough to hear the croupier's words, but it was clear from Carthallow's face that the worst had happened.

With a savage gesture he pushed the remaining counters from him on to another number. His companion said something to him. Carthallow looked blackly thunderous for an instant or two, and then he seemed to become aware that he was betraying himself and managed to smile. The other pushed his own pile of counters toward him.

Evidently the two were on intimate terms. The man who was with Adrian Carthallow had not acted like a stranger, performing a diffident deed of generosity, but like an old friend who was familiar enough to be able to do such things without the need for explanations.

Tremaine scrutinized him carefully. He was not a man likely to be either overlooked or forgotten. He was a big man, wide-shouldered, with fair coloring and with a carefully trimmed beard that gleamed silkily under the light. His voice was resonant. Tremaine heard him laugh and set him down as a man who both enjoyed life and lived it hard.

So far Carthallow, intent upon his game, had not looked

in his direction. But now, as the wheel spun again, he glanced across and their eyes met.

Mordecai Tremaine began to make a smiling recognition, for it was obvious that the artist must have seen him and he was expecting the other to acknowledge him with a friendly gesture.

But the smile died away, for the gesture did not come. Carthallow looked at him as if he was looking at a stranger. Or perhaps with more significance than he would have employed with someone he did not know. Almost there was a hostile resentment in his eyes.

It was only for a second or two that their glances held across the room. And then Adrian Carthallow's eyes dropped, and he began to speak to the blond man at his side.

Jonathan Boyce said, "Someone you know?"

Mordecai Tremaine nodded.

"Someone I thought I knew," he amended.

Boyce gave him a curious glance but did not question him. He had his own inquiries to make, and in any case he knew that if there was anything of real interest in the air Mordecai Tremaine would tell him sooner or later what it was.

The Yard man purchased a handful of chips and joined the players around the roulette table. Tremaine stood just behind him watching the spinning wheel that carried so much of hope and fear in its whirling numbers. He guessed that Jonathan Boyce was merely making a show in order to lend credence to his presence.

He did not want to give Adrian Carthallow the impression that he was being spied upon, and he deliberately refrained from looking across to the other side of the table. When at last he risked a glance, the artist had gone and so had the fair-haired man with him. They must have left the table almost as soon as Jonathan Boyce and himself had joined it.

Following upon Carthallow's refusal to acknowledge him, it seemed a little odd. But maybe, he reflected, the other had been chagrined at being discovered in such a place; it had been his way of indicating that he did not wish the matter to be remarked upon.

Boyce did not spend long at the table. After ten minutes or so he glanced at his watch and then gave an exclamation and gathered up the chips remaining to him. Mordecai Tremaine took the hint and waited discreetly in the background as Boyce obtained cash in exchange and then walked with him toward the door.

The custodian regarded them with what Mordecai Tremaine felt to be a suspicious eye.

"Leaving already, sir?" he said, casually enough.

"Must, unfortunately," returned Boyce. "Just remembered an appointment. Damned nuisance."

Mordecai Tremaine pushed his pince-nez back into

position and hoped his hand wasn't shaking. His throat felt dry. He was thinking that the more robust aspects of a crime investigator's life were by no means in his line.

When they were outside in the cool night air and the house was a block behind them, Boyce said, "Well, Mordecai, what did you think of it?"

"I'm glad to be out," Mordecai Tremaine said. "But perhaps it's because I was scaring myself before we went in with lurid thoughts of the kind of place it was going to turn out to be. It didn't look any more dangerous really than a friendly society meeting."

"Provided you spend your money and don't make trouble it's friendly enough," said the inspector. "It has to be. Otherwise the customers wouldn't come. By the way," he added curiously, "who was your friend?"

Mordecai Tremaine said, slowly:

"Adrian Carthallow. The artist. He didn't seem very pleased to see me."

"No?" Boyce seemed unimpressed. "Carthallow, eh? Half the people in there tonight are respectable members of society who'd hate to think their names were going to appear in the newspapers. It's surprising how the desire to appear to lead a moral life in the eyes of the neighbors still clings. Carthallow's probably like the rest of them—didn't like to be caught out doing what most of his friends already know he does anyway."

Mordecai Tremaine went to bed trying to convince himself that Jonathan Boyce was right and that that had indeed been the reason for Carthallow's attitude. But somehow his mind refused to accept such a soothing explanation. The incident persisted in linking itself with Carthallow's refusal to talk about Warren Belmont. It stirred vague doubts. It made him wonder what it was the artist wanted to hide.

He told himself that his imagination was getting the better of him again and picked up *Romantic Stories*. He settled down to read the latest sugared offering from his favorite author.

It was an excellent story—well written and with an original plot—and it should have calmed him into a state of pleasure in which sleep should have been easy. But the formula refused to work. He placed the magazine on the bedside table with *So Come Kiss Me, Sweet and Twenty* only half read and switched off the light.

He lay back on the pillows and stared into the darkness. He was absorbed by the thought that when he had mentioned Warren Belmont to Adrian Carthallow the artist had been afraid.

Which, of course, regarded soberly, was absurd.

Mordecai Tremaine sighed, turned over, and applied himself grimly to the business of going to sleep.

12

It was another coincidence that the morning newspapers should have carried a further reference to Warren Belmont. The millionaire had just reached New York. He had given the reporters an interview and had boasted of his purchases.

A tapestry from Paris, a marble from Rome, a rare example of the goldsmith's art in the shape of a gold christening cup from Florence, and from England he had been successful in obtaining a Gainsborough from the earl of Harsley's collection. There was also a hitherto unsuspected painting by Reynolds that he had bought after protracted negotiations with its owner, an impoverished peer, who had requested as a condition of the sale that his name should not be made public.

Although no longer of first-rank importance, impoverished peers still possessed a certain news value, and, of course, the new Reynolds was of passing interest. The New York correspondents of the London dailies who ran semi-gossip columns in their home journals had considered the item worthy of being cabled across the Atlantic.

Mordecai Tremaine folded his newspaper, observed the spring sunshine, and decided that he would pay a visit to the National Gallery. It was a long time since he had been to the gallery, and in view of his present interest in things artistic it would, he considered, be an excellent plan if he were to renew his acquaintance with it.

He did not dream that there was anything of particular significance in his sudden decision, nor that fate was once more guiding his footsteps.

He wandered through the galleries, studying the exhibits with a painstaking thoroughness. He prided himself that he was giving a convincing impersonation of an expert.

The Italians, with their curves and their insistence upon religious backgrounds, were inclined to weary him, but he was genuinely stirred by the clear lines of the Dutch school. He stood before Jan Van Eyck's *Arnolfini and His Wife*, admiring the detailed perfection of the image in the mirror on the wall behind the two subjects of the portrait.

The Rembrandts, too, stirred his pulses. He was fascinated by the cunning use by that master of his craft of dark masses and the concentration of light upon a single point.

At the far end of one wall was a Rubens—the *Portrait of a Doctor*. Tremaine studied the wise old man, a twinkle in his eye, his face highlighted by the ruff, and wondered how much shrewdness and knowledge had lain behind that wide brow in his lifetime. He moved on, past the vivid purple splendor of El Greco's *Agony in the Garden*, toward the center of the room, where hung the vast achievement of sir Anthony Van Dyck's *Charles I*. Looking at the armored figure seated so proudly on his horse, Tremaine found himself reflecting upon the bloody end to which that ill-starred monarch had come. Little sign here of what destiny had in store; no warning shadow of the scaffold.

He stepped back so that he could observe the general effect more easily, and it was then that he saw Helen Carthallow.

She was a yard or two away from him, occupying one of the wooden seats running down the center of the gallery. There was someone with her. Mordecai Tremaine frowned, stared, and then knew that he had not been mistaken. It was the gypsy of the Allied Arts Ball.

Even if his sentimental soul had not been always ready to thrust forward romantic ideas, he would have known that here were two people in love. It was in their faces, in their eyes, in the way they sat so closely, oblivious of the paintings and of the people about them.

Helen Carthallow was wearing a gray costume with a white blouse that was gathered softly feminine at her throat, and a gray fur hat perched attractively upon her dark hair. She was beautiful with an air of appeal he had not observed in her before. It was as though she had lowered the defensive barrier she normally erected against the world. No doubt, Mordecai Tremaine's mind said, it was because she was with her lover.

He could not stifle the bitterness. He had old-fashioned ideas on the sanctity of marriage; *Romantic Stories* did not always allow the course of true love to run smooth, but its code did not approve of the eternal triangle, and Mordecai Tremaine had been raised on a diet whose basic ingredient was a belief in the permanency of the marriage vows.

He turned his attention to her companion. He was not so young as he had at first imagined. Tremaine put him at somewhere near thirty. He was well built, with broad features and thick, curling hair. He had an easy charm of manner, and he was looking at Helen Carthallow in a way that would have flattered any woman.

Mordecai Tremaine took an instinctive dislike to him. Here, he decided, was the gigolo type, able to attract women and quite ready to make the most of it.

All the enjoyment had gone out of him. He felt that he was peeping through a window at a sordid intrigue. He saw that next to *Charles I* there hung the *Rokeby Venus* of Velasquez. There was something ironic in the nude study.

So far he did not think that Helen Carthallow had seen him. He took a step backward and then went slowly out of the gallery, as though he had noticed nothing beyond the pictures on the wall.

He was remembering the inflection in Anita Lane's voice when she had told him that sometimes it was better to have one's head in the clouds; was recalling her evasiveness when he had asked her later what she had meant. She had, of course, known all about this.

Quite suddenly he was feeling sorry for Adrian Carthallow. It was the first time his emotions concerning the artist had been so clear. Until now his state of mind had been confused; he had not known whether to like him moderately or dislike him intensely. Now, his sympathy for him as one who was being deceived bathed him in a mellow light. Carthallow was a much injured man and could therefore be forgiven many things.

He reached the exit door and stepped into Trafalgar Square with the sensation that one of the pillars supporting a world he had thought stable had been swept away. He wished he had never decided to visit the National Gallery; wished he had not seen Helen Carthallow.

But that would not have altered one single fact. It would not have canceled out the truth.

He tried not to meet Adrian Carthallow again. Carthallow's circle and his own touched only at such points as Anita Lane, and all it was necessary for him to do was to make sure that he did not accept any invitations from her when there was a danger of the artist being present.

Not that he ceased to have news of him. The newspapers continued to feature his activities. An exhibition of his paintings was held at a famous private gallery—an exhibition to which Mordecai Tremaine carefully avoided going—and it seemed that his reputation was steadily climbing.

There were, of course, other events. For instance, Jonathan Boyce, after spending days in pursuit of the evidence that would enable him to bring home a conviction, went down with pneumonia. At first it was touch and go. Mordecai Tremaine went to the nursing home on the day of the crisis, and for a time he was afraid. But the Yard man's tough constitution pulled him through, and it was not long before he was obstinately convalescent.

Adrian Carthallow had gone to Cornwall. Tremaine saw the announcement on the morning after he had learned that Jonathan Boyce was not, after all, going to die and had heaved a sigh of relief at the thought that he could now walk abroad without the fear of a chance encounter with Helen Carthallow or her husband. The item stated that the artist was spending a few months at Falporth, where, of course, he owned the house called Paradise, built entrancingly out over the Atlantic and joined to the mainland only by an iron bridge. He intended to spend his time in a pleasant mixture of painting and relaxation.

Three weeks later a pale and shaky Jonathan Boyce called

upon Mordecai Tremaine with the news that the commissioner was insisting upon his taking extended sick leave. The commissioner did not, he had stated, want a chief detective inspector whose legs were liable to fold under him.

"I'm going to Cornwall," said Boyce. "The old man swears he won't let me back until I've a cast iron bill of health." He looked at Mordecai Tremaine. "How, Mordecai," he went on, "would you like to come with me?"

Mordecai Tremaine pursed his lips.

"I haven't been thinking," he said, "of spending a holiday in Cornwall. What's in your mind, Jonathan?"

"As a matter of fact," said Jonathan Boyce, with a smile, "I'm hoping to take you on tour. I'm staying with my sister and her husband. I've told them a lot about you, and they're anxious to see what a great detective really looks like. I thought you might act as my meal ticket!"

There was a twinkle in Boyce's eye, and Mordecai Tremaine, who knew the real Jonathan now, was aware that despite his apparent cynicism the invitation was kindly meant.

"Maybe," he said, "it mightn't be a bad idea. Whereabouts in Cornwall does your sister live?"

"Falporth," said Jonathan Boyce, and behind his pince-nez Mordecai Tremaine's eyes were suddenly bright.

"Falporth!" he whispered.

This was the final gesture from fate, the ultimate sign that it was written that his own path and Adrian Carthallow's were destined to meet.

"Well, Mordecai," said Jonathan Boyce, "what do you say? Will you come?"

"Yes, Jonathan," said Mordecai Tremaine. "I'll come."

He knew that there was no other answer he could make.

13

Falporth was big enough to contain an adequate and attractive shopping center and several cinemas and theaters, and yet it was not a victim of that peculiarly seaside adiposity that produces a bulging waistline composed of artificial promenades, amusement arcades, and overcrowded beaches.

It was far enough from the main railway line to make development expensive and difficult but not frankly impossible, and it had retained much of its natural beauty. A line of hotels and boarding houses ran along the steep cliffs and dipped into the old town, which lay clustered around the tiny harbor sheltered by Falporth Headland. The cliffs on the far side of the headland carried only a scattering of houses, mainly purely residential and occupied by people who had discovered the advantages Falporth had to offer and had decided that they could do no better than find a house overlooking the rugged splendor of that magnificent coast.

Kate and Arthur Tyning, who were Jonathan Boyce's sister and brother-in-law, lived in a detached house that stood near the edge of the cliff on the outskirts of the town. As soon as Mordecai Tremaine saw the neat, carefully tended garden and the green shutters and the sun terrace, he knew that he was going to enjoy his stay.

Kate Tyning was a mellow edition of her brother, like him in features but without the occasional brusqueness that crept into Jonathan Boyce's manner and was the result of his official duties. Her husband was a gray-haired, quietly speaking man, with a pair of blue eyes twinkling out of a weather-beaten face that had evidently been tanned by many a Cornish wind. A sniper's bullet in the first of the world's all-in wars had left him with a permanent limp, but it had not warped his sense of humor.

Both of them welcomed the visitors with genuine enthusiasm. No mention was made of Mordecai Tremaine's reputation, but he sensed a certain reserve, as though they were not quite certain of what his reaction would be if they spoke of his connection with Chief Detective Inspector Boyce, of Scotland Yard.

But Mordecai Tremaine was already sure that he was among friends.

"I'm not really," he said.

Arthur Tyning looked at him inquiringly but with the twinkle in his eyes already revealing that he thought he understood. Tremaine smiled.

"A real Sherlock Holmes," he explained. "If Jonathan's been telling you that I'm so good that it's a wonder they go on keeping any policemen at all at Scotland Yard then he's been exaggerating. I've done my best to act up to the part, of course. I've even forced myself to get used to a pipe to build up the right atmosphere. But it's only bluff—I'm quite harmless."

The ice was soon completely broken, and after dinner that evening they sat on the terrace outside the house watching a red sun dip into a steel-blue sea. Arthur Tyning was pointing out features of interest around the bay, for it was a wonderful vantage point, emphasizing his remarks with a stabbing pipe stem.

"That's Roscastle Point," he said, with a gesture toward the long arm of rock that formed one side of the great bay on which Falporth was set. "You can see the lighthouse guarding the submerged rocks. On this side of it is Trecarne Head. The cliffs are three hundred feet high just there, and there's a sheer fall down to the sea. There are caves in the cliff face. Smugglers are supposed to have used them, and there are stories that they had a secret entrance a mile or so inland. If it's true the entrance must have been blocked long ago because there's no sign of it.

"The caves aren't used now. Even at low tide the rocks make it a nasty stretch of coast, and most people like to keep clear of it. If you go for a stroll up that way," he added, "Watch your step. The cliff edge isn't guarded, and it's liable to crumble. There were one or two heavy falls of rock last winter. No one was hurt, fortunately, but there's no telling when the next slide will come."

He turned in his chair, and his pipe described a semicircle and came to rest pointing up the coast in the opposite direction.

"On the other side of the headland there," he went on, "is St. Mawgan. It isn't much more than a fishing village, although just lately it's been developed quite a bit. It's about twenty miles by car because you've got to go so far inland to reach the main road, but if the weather's good you can take a boat around the coast and be there in half the time."

"Do you happen to know," said Mordecai Tremaine, lighting a pipe that, as usual, was going out with monotonous frequency, "a house called Paradise near here?"

Arthur Tyning chuckled.

"Everybody knows Paradise. It's the local showpiece. Adrian Carthallow lives there—the artist. You've heard of him, of course."

"Yes," said Mordecai Tremaine, "I've heard of him."

"You must take a walk up that way," Tyning went on. "It's only a mile or so up the coast. You can't mistake it. The house is built on a headland that's broken away from the main cliff. You can only reach it by an iron bridge."

"Sounds a depressing place to live in during the winter," observed Tremaine.

"In the winter," said Tyning, "no one does live there. Carthallow usually spends part of the summer there, but the rest of the year it's closed."

Mordecai Tremaine had managed to get his pipe going by now. He settled back in his chair and blew out a smoke cloud with a certain boastfulness.

"A house like that," he said, "built out over the sea, must have a history."

"The locals have all kinds of tales about it," said Tyning. "They say that during the winter it isn't empty at all but that all the lonely, tormented spirits on this part of the coast come back there for shelter. They say that it's a doomed house and that sooner or later tragedy will come to anyone who lives there. It's all nonsense, of course. It springs from the fact that the man who built it didn't enjoy any happiness there."

"No?" said Mordecai Tremaine hopefully, and thus encouraged Arthur Tyning told him the story of the millionaire who had built Paradise.

As he listened he felt again the premonitory stirrings within him that had their birth in his imagination and that he yet knew he could not entirely ignore. Perhaps the tragedy of Paradise had not been fully played out; perhaps there was another tale of violence and unhappiness to be told. In his mind he saw the house, gray and bleak, shuttered against the storms, with the wind driving the white seas up the cliff face, a fitting background for a tale of darkness.

Determinedly he drove the image from him. He said, "Do you see much of Carthallow?"

Arthur Tyning shook his head.

"I've met him occasionally—sometimes he goes sketching along the cliffs—but we're not exactly acquaintances. Not that he's standoffish. As a matter of fact, he's usually ready to pass the time of day. But Kate and I don't lead what you could call a social life."

"What," said Mordecai Tremaine carefully, "do they think in the district about having a famous artist for a neighbor?"

"Oh, people are used to it now," Tyning returned. "Carthallow's been coming here for several years. Everybody follows his career, of course. He's looked upon as a kind of local possession."

Mordecai Tremaine's ears, trained to detect the false note, conveyed a subtle warning to his mind. He looked at Arthur Tyning. Did the weathered face seem to be disconcerted?

But he did not make any comment. He tried, indeed, to tell himself that he had been mistaken.

For what had he seen and heard of Adrian Carthallow and his wife to lead him to the belief that they were anything other than a happily married couple, enjoying Carthallow's increasing success as an artist?

A word or two he might have invested with more significance than they had really possessed; an impression here and there that might have been over-colored in his mind; the fact that he had seen Helen Carthallow in the National Gallery with the gypsy who had been at the Allied Arts Ball. Did those things really form a reasonable basis for the vague suspicions within him?

Viewed at this distance of time even the incident in the gallery had lost the sharp quality with which it had at first impacted upon him. He knew his own weakness. He was aware that his leanings toward romanticism had more than once led him astray. It was quite possible that Helen Carthallow had met a chance acquaintance and had merely stayed to exchange a friendly word. There might have been no more than that for his imagination to falsify.

And yet, despite his newly arisen doubts, he could not banish that first reaction. He could not forget the look he had seen in Helen Carthallow's eyes. The look of a woman in love.

14

―――――――――――

The next morning, with Jonathan Boyce as his guide, he set out to explore Falporth.

The task was easily accomplished. There was very little depth to the town; most of it lay behind the road that ran along the top of the cliffs for a couple of miles or so before turning sharp inland. They ended their tour with a coffee at one of the numerous cafés and finished the morning with an hour's laze on the firm sands of the main beach before going back to lunch.

Mordecai Tremaine was highly satisfied with what he had seen. There were enough visitors to bring the color and vitality he enjoyed but not so many of them that life became a series of queues. He watched the children scrambling among the rock pools and was very glad that he had accepted Jonathan Boyce's invitation. For a while he even forgot to think about Helen Carthallow.

The afternoon took them further afield. It took them, in fact, to Trecarne Head, the precipitous cliff Arthur Tyning had pointed out to them on the previous evening. The warning he had given them about the crumbling nature of the rock had been amply justified. They could see where a great section of the cliff face had fallen into the sea comparatively recently, and at one point a small headland had been almost completely separated from the main cliff; only a narrow path remained.

Far below them they could see a tumble of jagged rocks among which the sea was swirling angrily, although the day was calm. Mordecai Tremaine watched the waves come surging in, saw them rolling up out of the blue sea, gathering strength until the moment when their crests began to break and they flung themselves against the cliffs in a wild fury of cascading waters, only to recoil defeated in a white, frustrated foam.

He counted them, held by their constant assault against a black pinnacle of rock thrusting itself sullenly in their path. Sometimes as early as the sixth, sometimes as late as the ninth, but bitterly inevitable, a wave would come larger than the others. It would lift itself out of the ocean as it neared the land, racing forward in a long green line that would hammer against the rock as if it would hurl it back into the waiting cliffs, and then in that moment disintegrate into a hissing mass of spray beneath which the pinnacle would vanish for an instant before rearing unbeaten shoulders, shrugging off the flatly falling water from which the life seemed to have been drained.

There was fascination in that turmoil of rock and foam and spray, but there was cruelty, too. Instinctively Mordecai Tremaine drew back from the treacherous edge a yard or two away. There would be no chance for anyone who lost his footing on the shaly lip of rock that marked the beginning of that sheer drop, and to slip would be unpleasantly easy. He wondered how many men had gone to their deaths at this point in the dark of a winter's night when they could not see how near they had strayed and when the wind perhaps was tearing with greedy shrillness.

He envied Carthallow the gift that enabled him to capture such a scene and preserve it in oils or watercolor if he chose. Odd that Carthallow should have come into his mind. He tried and failed to retrace the manner in which the thought had come.

As they were walking back over the cliff path Jonathan Boyce said, "Don't forget I'm supposed to be an invalid, Mordecai. I'm proposing to take things easily. So don't worry about me while we're down here. Go ahead with your own plans." He added: "I imagine you *have* one or two plans?"

He gave his companion a significant glance. Mordecai Tremaine said, "Well—perhaps."

"All I hope," went on Boyce, "is that you aren't contemplating getting mixed up with any more bodies."

Mordecai Tremaine looked shocked.

"Oh, no," he said. "Dear me, no."

It was a direct result of this conversation that, on the following morning, he set out alone, leaving the Yard man happily settled in a deck chair with his pipe and a book. This time he walked in the opposite direction to Trecarne Head. He tried to tell himself that it was because he was anxious to explore a fresh part of the coast, but he knew that the real reason was that it would take him toward the house called Paradise.

There was no mistaking the place, as Arthur Tyning had said. When he was still some distance off he saw the island of rock upon which it was built, and a few moments later the bridge that was its only connection with the mainland also came into view.

It was not possible to see much of the building on account of the screening trees, but it was somehow not what he had expected to find. He had pictured something invested with gloom and set amid a grim desolation; instead he found himself looking upon a very pleasant scene, with the house perched upon its rocky eminence with a happy picturesqueness, the greenery with which it was surrounded contrasting with the blue sea beyond. It was easy to understand the appeal the place had made to Adrian Carthallow. It seemed to have been created for an artist.

The island was much larger than he had imagined. It was a long headland that had been cut off at its base where the sea had worn a steep channel from either side as it had come swirling in for century after century, until at last the two-pronged attack had split away the rock. The headland's surface appeared surprisingly even, so that the house must possess quite an extensive garden.

He had come by way of the cliff path, and he decided to make the return journey by striking inland and then coming into the town from behind. The map had shown him that there was a public path across the fields at the rear of Falporth: it was apparently a popular walk to go out by the cliffs and home by the fields.

He had left the last of the houses behind and had turned to go in the direction of the town again when he saw a figure ahead of him. It was that of a man, seated at an easel on one side of the path. He knew that it was Adrian Carthallow even before the sound of his approach caused the other to turn and he saw the artist's rather flabby features.

Momentarily he felt uncomfortable. Not having seen Carthallow since the incident in London when the other had refused to acknowledge him he was dubious of the reception he might receive. However, it was too late to draw back.

Adrian Carthallow gave him a long look and then, to his relief, broke into a smile.

"It is!" he said. "The sleuth in person! What brings you to Falporth?"

"I've friends in the district," said Mordecai Tremaine hesitantly. He added, with a glance at the easel at which

Carthallow had been working: "Don't let me disturb you. I see you're busy."

"Only having a busman's holiday," said Carthallow. He began to put away his tubes and fold the easel. "I was about to pack up, anyway. As a matter of fact, when I heard you coming along the path I thought you might be Helen. That's why I turned. If you're staying down this way you must come along and see us. Why not come back with me to lunch?"

"I'm afraid I can't manage that," returned Tremaine.

"All right then, make it dinner tonight," said Carthallow. He seemed to take it for granted that his invitation would be accepted. "About seven. You know the place, of course. Paradise—on the headland back there." He gestured awkwardly with the hand in which he carried the easel. "The door to the bridge is always open."

Mordecai Tremaine pushed his pince-nez into their orthodox position on the bridge of his nose and tried to think of an excuse. He was not at all keen on the idea of going to dinner at Paradise. It would mean meeting Helen Carthallow, and he shrank from that ordeal.

But the excuse would not come, and before he could exercise any control over the situation, he found himself continuing on his way while Adrian Carthallow, paint box tucked under his arm and easel draped over his shoulder, was striding in the opposite direction.

15

On his return Mordecai Tremaine discovered that Jonathan Boyce had also renewed an old acquaintance. Charles Penross had learned that he was in the neighborhood and had called to see him. Penross was Inspector Penross, of the local constabulary.

"I've told Charles all about you, Mordecai," Boyce said. "You should get on together."

"As an amateur," said Mordecai Tremaine, "I'm always delighted to meet a working professional. Is there anything interesting in the way of crime in Falporth, Inspector?"

Penross smiled. He was a small man for a policeman, thin of features. But there was an air of alertness and vitality about him that revealed that he was a man who knew his job.

"If you mean have there been any good murders lately," he observed, "I'm happy to say there haven't. Falporth must be one of the most law-abiding spots in the country. I dare say," he added, slyly, "that it's because we can all make as much money as we need out of the city visitors who come here during the season!"

It was a surprise to hear him speak. His voice was gruff and resonant. It was the kind of voice that should properly have belonged to a big, hearty man with a round red face and the shoulders of an ox.

He proved an entertaining companion. At the end of an hour or two Mordecai Tremaine felt that he was an old friend. He had a rich fund of stories acquired during twenty years of police experience, and there seemed nothing he did not know concerning the district.

Several times Tremaine was possessed of the urge to mention Adrian Carthallow, but on each occasion he restrained himself. He did not wish to find himself in the position of being called upon to explain something for which he did not have any sort of explanation at all.

After Penross had gone he spoke of his meeting with the artist and of the dinner invitation he had received—somewhat diffidently, for he did not wish his host and hostess to think that already he was running away from them.

They did their best to set him at his ease.

"We want you to do just as you like as long as you're here," Kate Tyning told him. "Besides, Adrian Carthallow is a local celebrity. Think what it will do for my standing in the town when it's known that you're a visitor to his house!"

Mordecai Tremaine set out in a taxi just before seven that evening with feelings resembling those that normally attend the visitor to a dentist's waiting room who is unhappily certain that trouble is in store for him. Carefully he rehearsed a little set speech to Helen Carthallow; he hoped that he would be able to complete it without betraying himself.

The entrance to the bridge lay in a cutting in the cliff. As Carthallow had told him, the iron door was unlocked. He pushed it open and stepped onto the bridge.

The tide was well out now, and the sands below him had been dried firm by the afternoon's sun. He could see the ribbed sides of the rock pools where the water had slowly drained away and the gulls holding conference around them or aimlessly skimming the beach. A lazy line of surf was creaming the sands and licking at the end of the headland upon which the house was built.

The bridge vibrated under his step. It seemed very frail, although he knew that it could not be, otherwise it would never have withstood so many winter storms. He hurried forward and it seemed that he was cutting himself adrift from the comforting world to which the taxi belonged and was crossing into an existence that was suspended in space.

It was an illusion, of course, born of the fact that the bridge gave beneath him so that he felt that it had no contact with the solid ground, but it brought him on to the headland with quickened pulses and the sense of being face to face with a crisis.

The house was some distance from the bridge. A drive

led toward it through the trees, and as he walked Mordecai Tremaine applied himself to the task of bringing his imagination under proper control. By the time the maid admitted him, he had managed to regain a condition approaching normal.

Helen Carthallow greeted him with a smile.

"I'm so glad you were able to come," she said.

The dark eyes met his own calmly. There was no trace of discomfiture in them. There was, in fact, an odd flicker of something very like amusement.

"Damn it," thought Mordecai Tremaine, with a sudden surge of irritation, "I believe she's laughing at me!"

Strangely, it set him at his ease with her because it put him on his mettle. Instead of having to take the initiative without quite knowing the best thing to do, he was able to react naturally to her own attitude toward him.

There was a further cause for relief in that it was not the private dinner party he had been fearing with himself as the only guest. Several other people were already there. He experienced the usual breathless introductions, with Carthallow throwing names at him that he tried to catch like a juggler catching coins on a plate. It left him bewildered, nursing a grim determination to sort them out as soon as he had an opportunity of studying them at leisure.

Fortunately, there was one familiar name to serve as a starting point.

"We've met before, Miss Fairham," he said, as he came face-to-face with Roberta Fairham's mousiness.

She nodded.

"Of course. At the Allied Arts Ball, wasn't it? I remember seeing you there with Adrian." She added, hastily, as though she thought he might ask questions and was anxious to prevent him: "Are you enjoying your stay in Falporth, Mr. Tremaine? Adrian told me you have friends here."

"I love Cornwall," he said, "and this seems to me to be one of the most perfect parts of it."

It was at this moment that another guest arrived.

Helen Carthallow led the newcomer toward him. At first he thought that it had been done with a deliberate emphasis, but he realized later that it was merely because he was the only stranger present.

"I don't believe," she said, "you've met Lester Imleyson. Lester, this is Mordecai Tremaine."

There was the briefest of pauses while Mordecai Tremaine recovered his self-possession. It was true that he had not been introduced to the tall young man at Helen Carthallow's side, but he had undoubtedly seen him before. At the Allied Arts Ball and at the National Gallery.

He said, levelly, "How do you do, Mr. Imleyson. Are you in Falporth on holiday like myself?"

"I'm one of the local fittings," Imleyson told him.

He had a pleasant voice, firm and friendly. It suited his fresh, open countenance.

Rather to his annoyance Mordecai Tremaine found himself liking him. Imleyson possessed a charm of manner that was neither forced nor feminine. He was good-looking, and he had the build of a man who would be good at games. It was impossible to dismiss him purely as a gigolo or a philanderer.

Helen Carthallow was regarding them both quizzically. Her dark eyes held a challenge. Mordecai Tremaine saw that her lips had been heavily crimsoned and that she possessed traces of that overbright air he had noticed at their first meeting at Anita Lane's flat. He had the sudden impression that she was waiting for him to throw down the gauntlet and was tensed to fling it back in his face as if she did not care.

For an instant or two an air of crisis hung over them. And then Adrian Carthallow's hand had come down boisterously upon Imleyson's shoulder, and his jovial voice was saying:

"Hullo, Lester! You've heard of our friend Tremaine, of course. He's the Mordecai Tremaine who's always getting himself in the news for solving murder cases."

A shadow darkened Imleyson's face. He said, slowly, "I hadn't realized that."

"We'll have to watch ourselves as long as he's here, eh?" Carthallow boomed. "Don't want to find all our secrets uncovered!" He turned toward his wife. "Will you excuse me a moment, my dear? I want to take Lewis up to the studio. There's just time before dinner, and I'm sure you'll be able to look after Lester and the others."

"Of course, Adrian," she said.

Tremaine watched him cross the room and go out with Lewis Haldean. He had already been introduced to the big, blond man with the Viking beard and the face of a sea rover. Carthallow had made no mention of the fact that he must have seen Haldean that night at the gambling house in London.

Haldean, too, had been silent on the subject, and Mordecai Tremaine, always an apostle of tact, had suffered himself to be introduced as a stranger to a stranger.

He wondered just why Adrian Carthallow had been so reticent about the incident. He wondered, too, whether he was aware of what was going on beneath his nose. From his attitude toward Lester Imleyson it did not seem that he had any suspicions of that young man. Was he being cuckolded under his own roof?

He was relieved to see Hilda Eveland's plump figure coming toward him, so that he was saved from the necessity of trying to make conversation with Helen Carthallow and Imleyson. He had decided that he was going to like happily rounded, jolly-looking Hilda, with her unashamed middle-aged spread and her rich, good-tempered chuckle.

"Hullo, Lester," she said. "Why haven't you been along for the last two or three days? Matilda's been asking about you."

"I'm sorry, Hilda," he returned contritely. "I've been pretty busy, and I haven't been able to get over. But tell her I'll be along tomorrow whatever happens."

The conversation became general then. Both Roberta Fairham and Elton Steele joined them. Steele was a quietly spoken man, grave-faced but with amusement in the depths of his gray eyes. Like Haldean he was a big man, but he did not have Haldean's dramatic air and quickness of movement. He looked the solid, dependable type. He was the kind of man you could imagine unperturbed amid the earthquake, refusing to be impressed by the wildest tremors.

Adrian Carthallow and Haldean came back from the studio just as dinner was announced. The meal was a pleasant one. Everybody seemed to be on the friendliest of terms. Mordecai Tremaine's sentimental soul expanded happily. He beamed over his pince-nez.

Several times he glanced at Helen Carthallow, wondering yet again whether he had seen what was not there. It was only the occasional still amused look he fancied she bestowed upon himself that kept his suspicions alive. Carthallow, as always, was especially attentive toward her; he seemed, in fact, to be that rare thing: the perfect husband.

After dinner the artist took him by the arm.

"Let me show you around, Tremaine. The others will excuse us. They're practically members of the family, anyway!"

Roberta Fairham said quickly, "Do you mind if I come with you, Adrian?"

Her pale eyes blinked nervously behind her spectacles. Mordecai Tremaine felt sorry for her. She was so pathetically eager. He did not really want her to come with them, but he hoped in spite of himself that Carthallow would not refuse.

"Mind?" the artist's voice was rich with well-being. "My dear Roberta, of course I don't mind. You know how delighted I always am to display my possessions!"

There was another of those moments that left Mordecai Tremaine wondering whether he was imagining things or whether there really were mysterious and not very pleasant undercurrents beneath the surface of tranquility. It seemed to him that as he spoke Adrian Carthallow's sardonic eyes met those of his wife and that Helen Carthallow's face held an expression that was part resentment, part tragic, and part dislike. It seemed, too, that the words had been intended to convey more than their apparent meaning.

And then, as though a film that had been running smoothly and had then been stilled for an instant had started up again, everybody seemed to move and Mordecai Tremaine found himself in the hall outside the door of the drawing room.

Adrian Carthallow said, "Let's make a start with the gardens."

For the first time Mordecai Tremaine saw the full extent of the grounds in which the house was set, and he was surprised at the rock terraces, lawns, and flower beds, all carefully tended, that lay about it. They went through the iron gate set in the low boundary wall enclosing the lawn and walked out upon the springy turf of the headland. In a few moments they had reached the rocky edge, and there was nothing in front of them but the blue water, flecked here and there with white where the evening breeze fanned over it, stretching back to the horizon.

Carthallow flung back his shoulders.

"Ah, that's what I like! Pure air straight from the Atlantic, with no smoke and grime from belching cities!"

Mordecai Tremaine turned slowly, savoring that marvelous view. Out here between the sea and the sky it was possible to see the whole proud sweep of Falporth Bay, for owing to the outward surge of the coast the headland guarding Falporth no longer formed a complete barrier and beyond it the cliffs and the beaches lay visible.

His gaze passed along the great rim of sea, touched already by the first reddening lights of the setting sun, that ran from the white fingerpost of the lighthouse that marked the right-hand extremity of the bay to the far headland on the left beyond which lay St. Mawgan. There were times, he knew, when there would be only a wild darkness of tumultuous seas out of which would come an icy spray on the chill breath of a shrieking wind, but now it was restful and soothing to the senses.

He came around to face the house. Here again trees and shrubs had been skillfully placed to screen it, stunted and deformed these, shaped under the winds it was their task to defy. Only in one place, where the gate was set in the wall, could they see a gap through which part of the building was exposed.

"It's a perfect spot for an artist. You must be very proud of it."

"There's no need for pills and medicines here," Carthallow returned. "I never feel better than when we come to Paradise."

Near the end of the headland was a small round building of whitened stone. Mordecai Tremaine stepped over the iron staple driven deep into the ground at the entrance and looked inside.

"Used to be a fisherman's lookout hut," Carthallow explained. "Apparently it was a good vantage point to watch for the shoals of fish that came in at certain seasons."

As they walked back toward the house, the bridge came into view; its frailty, exaggerated by the distance, emphasized their separation from the mainland. Mordecai Tremaine's romantic imagination was stirred into activity.

"It reminds me of a medieval castle," he said. "If you could pull up the bridge like a drawbridge you'd be secure within your walls!"

"Except from the income-tax collector!" returned Carthallow.

He was obviously pleased by his guest's enthusiasm. He made no secret of the fact that the house was his toy.

Although at some places the fall of the cliff was less sheer and for part of its height might be climbed by a determined man, there was no point where it could be scaled all the way from the sea. In addition, the water never receded beyond the jagged rocks that marked the limits of the headland, and when the tide was full it swept under the bridge itself so that the whole place became an island and the illusion of a moated castle was complete.

The house itself was solidly built of squared stone blocks, as befitted a structure so much at the mercy of the elements, but there was nothing about its appearance of the forbidding nature of a castle intended mainly for defense. The millionaire for whom it had been erected had demanded a house that would lend itself to the romanticism of the spot without absorbing the grimness of the cliffs. A long veranda faced seaward, and in the sloping roof were several dormer windows that gave the place the cheerful air of a doll's house.

Four bedrooms and two bathrooms occupied the upper

floor, while the ground floor contained kitchens, dining room, lounge, and a room Carthallow used as a study and library.

Everywhere the furnishings were luxurious. Adrian Carthallow was clearly no friend of austere living. There was a fortune in the deep-piled carpets, the pictures on the walls, and the genuine antiques that were in every room.

The study adjoined the veranda, and its wide window faced the gap in the trees so that it had a clear view out to sea. In front of the window was a kneehole desk. Carthallow said, "Will you excuse me a moment? I promised Lewis I'd look something out for him."

He took a bunch of keys from his pocket, selected one of them, and, after carefully working it loose from the ring, opened one of the drawers of the desk.

"A little habit of mine," he said. "I don't know what made me start it, but I always take the key I want to use off the ring."

Inside the drawer was a small, leather-covered book. Carthallow withdrew it and thumbed through the leaves. He found the page he sought and made an entry. He replaced the book and took a card from a clip at the back of the drawer. He looked at it frowningly for a moment or two and then put it carefully away inside his wallet.

Mordecai Tremaine was standing quite close to him. Carthallow's searching fingers had disturbed the contents of the drawer and had revealed what had been lying underneath the book. It was a revolver.

He pushed his pince-nez back into position with that instinctive movement. Carthallow saw him, understood his unease, and smiled.

"My protection," he said, and patted the butt of the weapon. "After all, this is a fairly lonely spot and you never know what dangerous characters are likely to come wandering about. Besides, one of my—admirers—might take it into his head to pay me a visit!"

There was a gasping sound. Both of them turned to stare at Roberta Fairham. Her pale eyes, sharpened by a sudden fear, were fixed upon Carthallow.

"Adrian—you're not serious?"

He rewarded her anxiety with a lift of his eyebrows.

"Serious?"

"About thinking that someone might want to do you an injury. Do you really believe you might be in danger?"

"Why not?" He locked the drawer and worked the key back on to the ring. He stood facing her, his hands on her shoulders so that he was looking down into her face. "For those who seek to express the truth there is always a price to pay. It is the privilege of any creative worker to suffer for his art."

His attitude was theatrical. Mordecai Tremaine disliked it

and found himself in consequence disliking the man himself. It was too obvious a pose.

But Roberta Fairham did not seem to find it false. She was breathing quickly. She said, "You know, Adrian—you know that if there's ever anything I can do to help you all you need do is to ask for it. Anything."

She emphasized the last word. There was an eagerness in her face, and her lips were moist and parted. Over the lusterless, flatly drawn fair hair, Adrian Carthallow looked at Mordecai Tremaine. He said, "I know, my dear. And *you* know how much I appreciate it."

They went out of the study. At the end of the hall was a doorway beyond which lay a narrow flight of stairs. The stairs wound upward to that part of the house situated above the bedrooms and gave access to a large room that covered most of the area beneath the roof. Its windows were of the dormer type that Tremaine had noticed from the end of the headland. They gave a panoramic view of the surrounding sea, coastline, and countryside.

The place was reminiscent of Carthallow's London studio in its confusion of canvases, easels, brushes, pigments, and other tools of the artist's profession. A number of rough sketches of places Tremaine recognized as being in the near neighborhood were in evidence; he saw the watercolor upon which Carthallow had been engaged when he had encountered him.

Roberta Fairham moved around the studio with the air of a disciple treading upon familiar but hallowed ground. She picked up a small scene in oils of the coast at Trecarne Head.

"I haven't seen this before, Adrian. It's perfect."

He shrugged carelessly.

"Just a trifle, my dear."

She replaced the painting reverently.

"Adrian's so modest about his talent, Mr. Tremaine," she said. "But he can't disguise it. Did you read what sir Roger Barraton said about him in his last book, *Masterpieces of Art*? He said that Adrian was easily the most versatile of modern artists. He said that he had Rembrandt's mastery of light and shadow, a knowledge of how to obtain a luxuriance of color that rivaled Titian's, and Gainsborough's quality of the unexpected and his ability to use oils as a kind of watercolor."

Enthusiasm excited her voice and lent her vitality. The mousiness had all but gone from her. Mordecai Tremaine nodded. He had not read sir Roger Barraton's comments, but he knew that he was regarded as one of the world's experts on matters of art and that his opinions were accepted with deference.

Strangely, Adrian Carthallow was not content to glow in the bright light of Roberta Fairham's flattery. He seemed, in fact, put out by it. He changed the subject deliberately.

"Come and have a look at the view from here, Tremaine," he said, moving toward one of the windows. "The sun isn't quite low enough to show the full effect yet, but in half an hour's time it'll be the kind of thing the public says couldn't possibly be true when you try to paint it."

Tremaine looked out obediently upon the line of gray cliffs running far out to Roscastle Point, the steady curve broken by the breakers at the rough shoulder of Trecarne Head. The sun had been dropping steadily and the red had deepened so that a world of fiery color had come to splendid travail in the clouds, sending incredible reflections across the water. A fisherman's smack was rounding the point and was outlined on the edge of eternity, moving so slowly that it gave the illusion of being poised there forever.

"They wouldn't believe it now," he said. "Have you used this view as one of your subjects?"

"Only in one or two odd things," said Carthallow lightly. He indicated the painting at which Roberta Fairham had been looking. "You can't afford to go in for that sort of picture seriously. If you want to make a name in these days you've got to force the public to sit up. You've got to concentrate on giving them something that will shock them into recognizing that you're in existence."

"You sound cynical," said Mordecai Tremaine regretfully. "I thought it was fatal for an artist to be a cynic."

"It isn't fatal," returned Carthallow. "It's essential. It saves you from having illusions. You know Millet's *Angelus*, of course? It was produced in the States as a cheap print. At first it hung fire, and then the publisher decided to give it a different title. He called it *Burying the Baby* and the sales began to soar!"

Tremaine wondered how much of Adrian Carthallow's air of superior contempt was a pose deliberately assumed and how much reflected the real man. Bombastic, egocentric— and perhaps even something of a sadist—he undoubtedly was, but there was more to him than that. The innumerable sketches and paintings scattered about the studio were a proof that his self-confidence was well founded. His output must be enormous, and his genius was obvious even in the rough black lines of the discarded sketches that had served apparently as the foundation for more ambitious works.

Roberta Fairham's pale face still wore the embarrassing air of the disciple.

"What are you engaged upon now, Adrian?" she asked.

She quivered expectantly, like a faithful household pet, eager for the first sign of recognition from her master and yet too well disciplined to allow that eagerness active rein.

Adrian Carthallow smiled. It was not altogether a pleasant smile. He looked rather like a satisfied, over-corpulent cat about to pounce upon a luckless mouse. Almost he seemed to lick his lips.

He indicated the big easel that stood facing the far wall.

"I've persuaded Helen to sit for me," he said. "It's been a long struggle—she's always held out against me on the score that husbands and wives shouldn't paint each other because they know too much about each other! But now that she *has* agreed I'm going to make the most of my opportunity. It won't be easy to do her justice, but I've told her that if I only manage to come somewhere near it there won't be any doubt about its being the best thing I've ever done."

His face was enthusiastic. If Mordecai Tremaine's mind hadn't been so clouded with nebulous thoughts in which Helen Carthallow's dark beauty was complicated by the existence of Lester Imleyson, he would have looked upon his eagerness as a gratifying example of the pleasures of a happy marriage. As it was, he pondered darkly, but silently, whether Carthallow was justified in setting his wife upon such an obvious pedestal.

Roberta Fairham said, "Oh. I see."

She said it through her teeth in a cold and distant voice. That sudden flame of life had been extinguished, leaving her more insignificant and devoid of personality than ever.

She did not seem to be interested in the studio anymore. They remained a few moments longer while Mordecai Tremaine expressed interest in the oils and pigments neatly labeled at one end of the room in contrast to the general disorder, and then they went back down the narrow stairs.

16

The others had gathered in the lounge. As they went in Tremaine heard Lewis Haldean's booming laugh and Hilda Eveland's infectious chuckle. There certainly appeared to be no constraint between them.

Lester Imleyson was perched on the arm of Helen Carthallow's chair, and she was looking up at him smilingly. Imleyson made no attempt to move, nor did Adrian Carthallow seem to notice anything amiss.

The evening was warm, and the french windows leading to the gardens were open. They could hear the sighing of the sea beneath the headland.

Elton Steele looked up.

"Well, Tremaine," he said, in his slow, friendly way, "what do you think of the eagle's nest?"

Helen Carthallow said, "Elton believes in keeping an eye to business. He looks upon every residence as a desirable property!"

The big man grinned.

"What Helen means," he said, "is that I'm as proud of

Paradise as if it were my own. It was on the firm's books for years before Adrian came along. We'd given up hope of ever getting rid of it. That's why I was so delighted when Adrian made such a good job of putting it back into shape."

"I'm surprised," Mordecai Tremaine said, "that it was allowed to stand empty."

"Falporth hasn't always been so popular," Steele told him. "People who wanted to buy a house stuck out on a particularly inaccessible piece of the Cornish coast weren't too plentiful. Besides, the place was derelict and overgrown—didn't look at all attractive. Not to mention the local ghost stories."

Mordecai Tremaine's eyes glistened.

"Ghost stories?"

"Don't be too optimistic," said Steele. "You know how rumors begin to grow about a house that's left empty for any length of time, and this one had the added advantage of being lonely and in an unusual position. A few winds whistling around it and a few shadows on a gusty night were enough to set the gossips talking."

"It was built by a millionaire, wasn't it?"

"Yes—fellow named Griffiths Guest. Perhaps you've heard of him? He got married when he was over fifty to a woman twenty-five years younger and brought her down here for their honeymoon. One morning she was found dead on the rocks at the foot of the headland—suicide. It was pretty well hushed up at the time, but according to rumor there was a tragic story behind it."

Steele's face looked troubled, as though he found it disturbing to talk about it although it had happened to other people many years previously. His hand caressed the bowl of the pipe he was smoking; he packed the tobacco unnecessarily.

But he reckoned without Mordecai Tremaine, who was never averse to hearing a repetition of a tale he already knew if he thought the telling might reveal an additional item of information or would enable him to study the reactions it produced in different company.

"What *was* the story?" asked that gentleman.

"There was a lover in the case," said Steele slowly. "It seems that she married Guest out of a sense of duty to her family—her father was in a tight corner financially, and she felt she owed it to him. When it came to the pinch she found she couldn't go through with it. She ran out of the house one night and went straight over the edge. There was no doubt that it was deliberate."

"Was Guest *that* much of a brute?"

Steele shook his head.

"No. That's what makes the thing the more tragic. He was genuinely in love with her—would have done anything to make her happy. It broke him when she killed herself. That's why he shut the house up and let it go to ruin. He wouldn't sell it. After his death it did come on the market, but by that time it had deteriorated so badly that it didn't attract any buyers. The winters on this coast don't improve a house."

Lewis Haldean had been listening with obvious interest. He leaned forward.

"Don't you think a house like this always retains something of its atmosphere?" he remarked.

"What on earth do you mean, Lewis?"

It was Helen Carthallow's voice. There was a trace of asperity in it. She looked, thought Mordecai Tremaine, as though she didn't like the way the conversation was tending.

Lewis Haldean seemed unaware of her displeasure. His blue eyes were enthusiastic. He was a suddenly boyish Viking allowing his imagination to run. Mordecai Tremaine warmed toward him.

"When there's been a tragedy of that sort," the blond man went on, "don't you think it leaves an influence behind it? After all, if we don't merely drop into a hole in the ground when we die, if there *is* an immortal soul, it can't mean that we just vanish without any trace at all. There's bound to be some kind of aura. I'm not expressing it very well, but you see what I'm getting at?"

"Yes," said Mordecai Tremaine perversely. "I see what you're getting at."

He had not recovered from the discomfiture of his arrival

when he had suspected Helen Carthallow of laughing at him. After all, if she really was no more than a shameless hussy there was no reason for him to spare her feelings.

"The locals must have some reason for their attitude," went on Haldean. "It can't all be pure moonshine. I've always had a queer feeling about this house—a kind of belief that what that poor unhappy girl did has left an impression that will always be an essential part of it."

There was a vibrant, dramatic quality in his voice that lent a strange earnestness to his words. Lester Imleyson raised an eyebrow.

"Aren't you exaggerating a bit? I can't say *I've* noticed anything of this aura of yours. Have you, Hilda?"

He glanced at Hilda Eveland. She made a gesture of mock despair.

"I'm the wrong person to ask," she said, with her good-natured rolling chuckle. "I'm too solid to have any contact with ghosts!"

"It's a house of tragedy," said Haldean impressively. "That's what the locals think, and I can't help believing they may be right."

"Rubbish," interposed Imleyson. "You'll be saying next that it should be left empty before there's another tragedy."

He was looking at the blond man challengingly. Mordecai Tremaine guessed that the clue to his attitude lay in the fact that Helen Carthallow had shown herself to be displeased. Haldean seemed to become aware at last that he had annoyed her and hastened to retreat from what he now observed to be an exposed position.

"Good lord no," he said. "I wasn't going as far as that. All I really meant was that it gave the place a kind of added interest. I've probably been talking a lot of nonsense, anyway."

"Stick to your guns, Lewis!" said Carthallow protestingly. "A touch of the ghostly atmosphere might work wonders for me. Think of the publicity!"

Hilda Eveland shivered.

"If you're going in for ghosts, Adrian, you can cross me off your visiting list."

She spoke lightly, but she had glanced significantly at Helen Carthallow, and it was the signal for a change in the conversation. Steele promptly asked Haldean what the results of a fishing trip from which he had just returned had proved to be, and the icy fingers that had unaccountably been creeping along Mordecai Tremaine's spine ceased to trouble him.

Their talk settled gradually into a pleasing intimacy and ranged over many subjects, both serious and gay, personal and universal.

"You're a lucky man, Adrian," remarked Haldean, when they were engaged upon a discussion of happiness a chance observation of Hilda Eveland's had begun. "Your art gives you something that's essential to a full life. It gives you purpose. And without purpose you can't even begin to live. You can only exist. Don't you think so, Tremaine?"

That gentleman nodded sagely.

"I agree," he said. "A man without purpose is just going to drift aimlessly and probably end up a neurotic failure."

He enjoyed his evening. Walking back along the cliffs he was in a pleasantly sentimental glow. He felt that he had known them all for a long time and that they were a charming set of people among whom no serious differences could exist.

Elton Steele had asked him to drop in to his club in Falporth for a drink and a game of bridge one evening; Lewis Haldean had pressed him to join him on his next fishing trip. He was, it seemed, in the habit of going into St. Mawgan, where he had a number of acquaintances among the local fishermen, and staying there for a night or two while he made it the base for his operations. Falporth, he said, had become too commercialized.

Even Helen Carthallow had lost her slight air of irony toward him and had asked him to call whenever he wished. The beach in the neighborhood of the headland was too far from the town to be overloaded with visitors, and he was sure of finding a deck chair at the back of one of the caves. She had promised to take him down the next time he came so that he could make himself free of them any time he felt the desire for a nap in solitude.

But it was with Hilda Eveland that he had found the closest affinity. She was so unashamedly content with life; so ready to laugh and so eager to look for the best in people. She was a sentimentalist, too; he had discovered that when Carthallow had brought up the question of popular taste and she had countered his cynicism with a robust defense of the simple folk who believed that virtue was always triumphant.

He had discovered something else. She was a reader of *Romantic Stories*. There was no surer way to Mordecai Tremaine's heart.

17

The next day Jonathan Boyce decided that he preferred a deck chair in the garden to any more vigorous way of spending the morning, and Mordecai Tremaine took his stroll over the cliffs alone. It was therefore inevitable that he should have walked in the direction of Hilda Eveland's house.

It was set back some distance from the edge of the cliff, but there were few other buildings in the near neighborhood, and the view from its windows suffered little while it gained a great deal in shelter from the winds. The gardens were massed with flowers. As Mordecai Tremaine walked up the short graveled drive he thought he saw Hilda Eveland's personality in the riotous colors that blazed happily if haphazardly on either side.

She was obviously pleased to see him. They sat in deck chairs on the lawn with the coffee she had hastened to make and found that their mutual liking of the previous evening was not merely an ephemeral thing and that they had many points of contact.

Within half an hour Tremaine had been given a review of Falporth and its inhabitants—with particular reference to those whom he had met on the previous evening—that was sufficient to give him a working who's who of the district.

Hilda Eveland herself had been a widow for twenty years. Her husband had been killed in a road accident. She had come to Falporth in an attempt to forget that tragedy and had remained ever since. She lived alone except for Matilda Vickery who, it seemed, was an invalid and was confined to her bedroom.

Elton Steele was the senior member of the local firm of estate agents of Steele & Hilliard. He had made Adrian Carthallow's acquaintance when the artist had bought Paradise.

Lester Imleyson, too, was a local product. His father had an interest in a number of hotels in Falporth as well as a flourishing agricultural supplies agency he operated from Wadestow.

"I suppose he helps to run things for his father?" said Mordecai Tremaine tentatively.

"Lester can't seem to make up his mind what he wants to do. He was supposed to be taking up art, but I haven't noticed him doing much in that line."

"Oh, I see. No doubt that's how he came to meet Mr. Carthallow?"

"I think," Hilda Eveland observed, "it was *Mrs.* Carthallow he met."

Mordecai Tremaine looked at her over his pince-nez. He thought her tone was significant. But their friendship was still short. He hesitated to put it to the test so soon.

Instead of posing the question that was on his tongue, he said, "What about Mr. Haldean? He didn't give me the impression of being one of the local people."

"He isn't," she told him. "Lewis has a bungalow down here, but he rarely uses it unless Adrian's at Paradise. I believe they see a good deal of each other in London."

"Yes," Mordecai Tremaine said, the memory of a certain incident in his mind, "I rather thought they did."

Hilda Eveland reached for the tray carrying the now empty coffee cups.

"If you aren't in a hurry to get anywhere," she said, "I'll show you around. In any case I can hardly let you go without introducing you to Matilda. She'd never forgive me. She likes to see every new face, and I try to humor her if I can. It's all she has left, poor dear."

Momentarily there was a new note of seriousness in her voice. It did not last, but it gave a glimpse of another Hilda Eveland, one who did not always find life amusing.

The house did not possess the obvious luxury of Paradise, but it was nevertheless attractively furnished. Hilda Eveland had clearly planned her home with care.

"I like it," said Mordecai Tremaine. "It's so—so restful."

He realized as he said it what had been wrong with Adrian Carthallow's home. It had not enjoyed the calm of this house for all its apparent advantages. There had been an atmosphere of restlessness about it, as though it had been pervaded by Carthallow's own unquiet temperament.

He recalled what Lewis Haldean had said about atmosphere. Maybe the big, blond man, with the Viking beard and the air of drama, had been nearer the truth than he had imagined. Maybe there *was* a quality about Paradise that could not adequately be put into words; something that was an intrinsic part of the house and yet was not wholly of it.

Hilda Eveland knocked lightly on one of the doors on the upper floor and led the way into a big airy room, full of flowers and with a neatness about it that belonged properly to a showroom in which no one stayed for long.

There was a woman propped up against the pillows in the bed that faced the open window. Her hair was gray, and her face was lined both with age and with suffering. Her hands, resting upon the coverlet, were cruelly twisted by the disease that tied her to this one room and would never relax its grip until death came upon her. But her eyes were bright and she regarded her visitor with an eagerness that was unforced.

"This is Mordecai Tremaine," said Hilda Eveland. "We met last night at Helen's. He's on holiday down here."

Tremaine took one of the frail hands gently into his own.

He did not know quite what to say. The sharp brown eyes examined him with the quick intentness of a bird.

"I saw you going in," she said. "I've been wondering who you might be."

"You saw me?" he said, surprised.

A smile came into her face. His reaction had been what was expected of him. Obviously this was her special and personal joke with all newcomers.

"I see everybody," she said. "Nobody escapes old Matilda, even though she is kept in a cage!" And, relishing his bewilderment, she raised her arm—not without a wince of pain she did her best to conceal. "The window," she told him. "That's my spyglass!"

He looked as he was required to do and saw that from her bed she could see out over the cliffs. The path lay clearly in sight, winding its way toward Adrian Carthallow's house. He saw the house itself and its screening trees out on the headland. From this position the bridge leading to it was plainly outlined, a thing of delicate tracery, etched against the sea and the sky.

"You certainly have a wonderful vantage point," he said.

"I didn't know how much there was to see," she said, "until I had to lie here and watch things properly. I don't have to worry about books and cinemas when there's so much to look for just by lying here. There's always the clouds, and the sea, and the birds, and the colors early in the morning and at sunset. And there's people, too," she added, with a sudden wickedness. "You'd be surprised at what I've seen."

"Matilda must have the sharpest eyes in the district," said Hilda Eveland, with her rich laugh. "She sees everybody who goes across that bridge, and I haven't known her make a mistake yet. There'll be no chance of hiding anything as long as she's here."

Mordecai Tremaine patted the drawn fingers that still lay under his own.

"You're a very brave woman," he said softly.

There was a moistness in the brown eyes.

"I'm a lucky one," she told him. "I owe it all to Hilda. She—"

"Nonsense!" said that lady firmly. "Don't you get spinning any more of your fairy tales or else—"

She broke off. Someone had just rung the front-door bell of the house. It had been a distinctive ring. She said, "That sounded like Lester. I told that young gentleman what I thought of him last night for neglecting you so badly."

"Oh, no! You didn't really say anything to him?"

"Nothing he didn't deserve. And nothing you won't be able to put right in two seconds!" Hilda Eveland pressed the invalid's shoulder affectionately. "I'd better go and let him in before he starts climbing up to the window like Romeo!"

Mordecai Tremaine went out of the room with her. As

they went down the stairs she said, "Matilda's known Lester since she used to feed him surreptitious cakes when he was a small boy. He's always been a favorite of hers. She'd do anything for him."

The doorbell was now pealing protestingly. She opened the door hurriedly to reveal a grinning Lester Imleyson holding a parcel in his free hand.

"Morning, Hilda!" he announced cheerfully. "The prodigal has come to report according to orders. How is she?" He caught sight of Mordecai Tremaine and nodded a greeting. "Hullo, Tremaine. Marvelous day!"

"Marvelous," agreed Tremaine to the empty air, for Imleyson had already passed him and gone bounding up the stairs.

He said, slowly, "Last night I thought I knew you, but I see that I was basing my judgment on insufficient evidence. I'm only just beginning to find out how fine a person you really are."

"If you go on like that," said Hilda Eveland, "I shall forbid you the house!"

But her eyes were smiling and Mordecai Tremaine knew that they understood each other. As he went down the path, he heard from the open window above him Lester Imleyson's boisterous tones saying something outrageous and Matilda Vickery's delighted giggle of make-believe protest.

18

So much of interest was packed into the next few days that looking back on them later Mordecai Tremaine was surprised that the period of time involved was so small. The explanation was due partly to a spell of fine weather that made the already long summer days appear even more spacious and partly to the fact that he was engaged upon the stimulating adventure of making new acquaintances.

For instance, there was Charles Penross. The inspector was experiencing a fairly quiet time and as often as his duties permitted he would drop in for a chat with Jonathan Boyce. They were chats Mordecai Tremaine was reluctant to miss; two policemen yarning over past events in the varied fields of crime provided a feast his appetite for detection could not resist.

He enjoyed their sessions the more because Penross treated him as an equal. Thanks to Jonathan Boyce, the dapper little inspector with the booming voice had accepted him from the start on a professional basis. Several times when the discussion turned upon some famous murder case or other in

which an obscure legal point had been at issue, Penross asked
for his opinion and Mordecai Tremaine felt himself growing
in stature.

He talked enthusiastically of ballistics and fingerprints
and medical jurisprudence. His library of criminology was
an extensive one, and he had accumulated a vast store of
technical knowledge. If Penross was at first surprised that
such a mild-looking elderly gentleman should display so
much acquaintance with criminal matters, he soon adjusted
himself to the situation and discoursed as freely as though
Mordecai Tremaine was one of Scotland Yard's professional
man hunters.

And then there was Lewis Haldean. He encountered the
blond man on the cliffs a couple of mornings after the dinner
party at Paradise.

"Are you doing anything special tomorrow?" Haldean
asked him, his dramatic tones automatically implying that
there could in any case be no opposition to what he was about
to suggest. "If not, why not come over to St. Mawgan with
me? We can run over by car. I promise you some good fishing."

Mordecai Tremaine, secretly unwilling to risk his stomach
in a small boat for an unspecified number of hours, tried to
think of a polite reason for declining. But Haldean was breez-
ily insistent. When they parted company a few moments later
Tremaine reflected dazedly that since there was now no hope

of drawing back, his best policy would be to make a discreet breakfast and hope that there would be no drastic change in the weather.

Haldean lived toward the rear of Falporth in a green-roofed bungalow overlooking the public gardens on the outskirts of the town. It was built against the slope of a hill that protected it from the strong winds that blew periodically from the sea. Being a bachelor, he was looked after by an elderly couple who acted as housekeeper and gardener, saw to his general wants, and kept the place tenanted during his absences.

He saw Mordecai Tremaine approaching and, opening the window, hailed him cheerfully.

"Shan't keep you a moment! Come on in and make yourself at home!"

The front door of the house was ajar. Tremaine went inside and found that the room from which the blond man had addressed him was his bedroom. Haldean was putting on his sports jacket. He swept a huddle of shirts and underclothes from a chair and tipped them on to the bed.

"Forgive my bachelor chaos. My housekeeper's always threatening to leave me unless I mend my ways, but fortunately she doesn't mean it."

Mordecai Tremaine smiled and sat down upon the chair that had been cleared.

"You sound like the Bachelor Gay," he observed. "I

wonder no designing female has ever managed to get you into her net!"

"I've had one or two narrow escapes," Haldean said, "but luckily I've been able to save myself at the last moment."

Waiting for the blond man to finish his preparations, Tremaine glanced curiously around him. He saw the book lying on the bedside table and noted its title mechanically. It was a work on metaphysics. Haldean's choice of late-night literature seemed to be on the heavy side.

His eyes roved to the dressing table and arrived by way of hair tonic and fixing cream at a framed photograph. It was the photograph of a girl. Judging by the hairstyle it had been taken many years previously. He studied the delicate round face with the dark, appealing eyes. It was a trustful face. Not perhaps beautiful—the mouth was a shade too large and the nose betrayed rather too pronounced an inclination toward a tilt—but there was a quality of gentleness in it that found an echo in Mordecai Tremaine's sentimental soul. There was something written across the bottom. He adjusted his pince-nez, peering forward in an effort to see more clearly, but he could not read the inscription.

He became suddenly aware that Lewis Haldean was looking at him. He sat back in his chair, his expression apologetic.

"I'm awfully sorry—frightfully rude of me. I was admiring your photograph. The face seems so—so gentle."

Haldean picked up the photograph and stood gazing at it for a moment or two.

"Yes," he said slowly, "she was gentle."

Mordecai Tremaine said, "*Was?*"

Haldean nodded.

"She—died. It was a long time ago. In San Francisco."

"What was her name?"

"Margaret." Haldean lingered over the word, and Mordecai Tremaine, believing him to be in the mood for confidences, was unashamedly curious.

"Your sister?" he asked, thinking it unlikely.

Haldean smiled.

"No," he said. "Not my sister." He replaced the photograph. "Still, you don't want to listen to my reminiscences. I've kept you waiting too long already."

Mordecai Tremaine was disappointed but intrigued nevertheless. Despite the blond man's appearance of lightheartedness he suspected that the photograph meant a great deal to him. Did it, he wondered, carry the explanation of why Haldean had remained a bachelor? He felt the influence of *Romantic Stories* creeping upon him and manfully turned his thoughts into another channel.

Very soon he had other matters to occupy him to the full. Haldean was a good driver, but he believed in speed. Mordecai Tremaine spent the journey to St. Mawgan in a state that was part philosophic resignation and part prayer for deliverance. He experienced a detached wonder at the thought that he was still alive as Haldean slowed down to maneuver the car through the narrow, winding streets of the town.

It was, indeed, hardly more than a fishing village. On the outskirts there were a few hotels and a huddle of small private houses, each of which carried a card in its windows announcing that it specialized in bed and breakfast or full board, but the real St. Mawgan was a picturesque if somewhat untidy collection of whitewashed buildings with slate roofs grouped around the harbor.

Haldean's destination was a pub overlooking the water. It was a low-ceilinged, rambling old place that looked as though it had served as the setting for many a smuggling drama. No doubt its cellars had held more French brandy than the excisemen had been allowed to see.

The blond man was on good terms with the landlord, a burly, weather-beaten Cornishman whose tanned and wrinkled face was a proof that he combined looking after his bar with hauling the nets.

"Sometimes I spend a night or two here," Haldean explained. "Saves me the trouble of going back into Falporth. Besides, Tregarwen here does me well," he added, with a wink. "There's more good whiskey in his bar than the usual visitors suspect, and he has a friend or two among the farmers who see to it that he doesn't starve."

Moored to the stone jetty a few yards from the pub was a motor launch. She was not new, but she was a roomy craft and had obviously been recently overhauled and painted.

"Not bad, is she?" said Haldean, with all the pride of ownership. "She was in pretty bad shape when I bought her, but there isn't much old Tregarwen doesn't know about a boat, and I gave him a free hand to put her in trim."

"He's certainly made a good job of it," observed Mordecai Tremaine approvingly.

Although his stomach was distressingly apt to show resentment at anything approaching a rough sea, he was always stirred by the sight of small craft bobbing at anchor and by the harbor smell of salt and cordage, tar and fish. The small boy in him was still alive to the exhilaration carried on an ocean breeze.

The qualms that had assailed him earlier proved to be without foundation. The sea was smooth, and he thoroughly enjoyed his day. When Haldean brought the launch skillfully through the harbor entrance late in the afternoon, Mordecai Tremaine was feeling like an old salt who had spent his life on the waves and was wondering wolfishly what there would be to eat.

Besides physical well-being the day had also brought him mental stimulation. There was nothing like being isolated on a small boat almost out of sight of land, he reflected, for inducing confidences. He felt now that he had known Haldean for many years.

He had himself introduced the subject of Adrian Carthallow.

"You seem to be on excellent terms."

"Adrian and I understand each other," Haldean had said. "We don't always see eye to eye, of course, but we don't have any serious disagreements. At least—"

He had stopped, and Tremaine had regarded him hopefully. And after a moment or two the blond man had gone on, his eyes on the sea: "I haven't been altogether happy about him just lately. He's been driving himself too hard. A man can't keep up such a pace for ever."

Mordecai Tremaine had thought of the two studios crowded with examples of Carthallow's work.

"His output must be very large. But he doesn't give me the impression of being under a strain. I thought he enjoyed his work."

"He enjoys it all right," Haldean had agreed. "That's part of the danger. A creative artist will go on driving himself—or will go on being driven by his inspiration, whichever you like to choose—until the crack-up comes. One moment he'll seem to be perfectly normal and in the next—pff! Something gives way and it's too late for anything to be done."

"Why don't you try to get him to take things easily?"

Haldean had given a rueful grin.

"I have," he had said. "And nearly had my head bitten off for suggesting it! Adrian isn't the man to take kindly to advice from other people, no matter how tactfully it's offered. Anyway, I've an idea that he doesn't find it easy to slacken off. You see, a man gets used to living up to a certain standard; he tends to spend up to his income without realizing it. Adrian must be doing pretty well, but he likes to feel the benefit of the money he earns, and some of his tastes are inclined to be expensive. There's always the possibility, too, that the market for pictures may strike a bad patch, so that he wants to gather in the harvest while he can. In fact—"

Haldean had broken off abruptly and had pretended to be busy with his line. He had given Mordecai Tremaine the impression that he felt that he had been on the verge of becoming a little more confidential than their newly developed intimacy warranted. He had made no attempt to finish the sentence he had begun, nor had he returned to the subject of Adrian Carthallow. He had displayed, on the contrary, a decided eagerness to talk about every other topic instead.

Nevertheless, Mordecai Tremaine had added one more intriguing note to his mental record. Haldean's remarks had linked up significantly with something Carthallow himself had said to him in response to his joking observation about being secure within the walls of Paradise because of its resemblance to a moated castle.

"*Except from the income-tax collector.*"

That had been Carthallow's reply. At the time Tremaine had looked upon it as being merely humorously meant, but now he was not so certain. He was wondering whether it had sprung out of a deeper concern that was preying upon the artist's mind.

It may have been the reason why he decided the next afternoon to take advantage of Helen Carthallow's invitation to make use of a deck chair on the beach just below Paradise. Unfortunately for his design, Carthallow himself was out. Explaining his errand, he was disconcerted by the look of doubting speculation in Helen Carthallow's dark eyes, but she took him down to the beach and showed him the cave where the chairs were stored.

"It saves bringing them down each time," she explained, "and very few people come as far up the beach as this, so that there isn't much danger of anyone walking off with them."

Mordecai Tremaine expressed his gratitude and looked for a spot where he could obtain the full benefit of the sun and at the same time would be undisturbed by the breeze blowing off the water.

"Forgive my running away from you," she said to him. "I'm expecting someone to call." She brushed back that troublesome lock of hair, and her dark eyes turned full upon him. "It's Lester," she added. "Lester Imleyson. You met him the other night, of course."

"Yes," said Mordecai Tremaine, "I met him the other night. I thought he seemed rather a nice young man."

She smiled at him, but she did not rise to the obvious bait. He watched her as she crossed the sands and went up the winding path, and in a few moments her slim figure went over the bridge leading to the house.

He wished he knew what was going on in her mind. He wished he knew what she thought of her husband and what her husband thought of Lester Imleyson.

It was a pleasant day, and the sun was distinctly soothing. He found it gradually becoming more and more difficult to think, and finally he ceased to think at all.

He awoke with the irregular whisper of the waves in his ears and a crick in his neck where he had been lying awkwardly in the deck chair. He opened his eyes to find himself looking at the rocks fringing the cliffs against which he had taken up his position. Lying on them, fifteen or twenty yards away, were bathing wraps and towels.

He was looking along the beach, and beyond the rocks he could just make out the edge of the surf where the curve of the bay brought it within his line of vision. Two figures were coming toward him, obviously just having left the water.

One was a man and the other a woman. He saw the woman take off her bathing cap, shaking free her hair, and he recognized Helen Carthallow. Her companion was Lester Imleyson. They joined hands and came running up the beach like children in a holiday mood.

Mordecai Tremaine admitted afterward that it was dubious conduct, but he closed his eyes and lay without movement as though he was still asleep. Their voices became clearer. He heard Helen Carthallow say, "I'm sorry, Lester. I really can't."

"But why not?" came Imleyson's persuasive tones. "I've got the car parked in a quiet spot. I'm sure nobody's likely to see us go. We could drive up to the moors and be back in time for dinner."

Helen Carthallow's voice was reluctant but adamant.

"It's no good, Lester. I promised Adrian I'd sit for him for an hour. He'll be here at any moment."

"Why not let him wait for a change? He isn't painting you out of the goodness of his heart. *You* know that." Imleyson sounded sulky. "Anyway, if he must do somebody's portrait, I'll get Roberta to come over. She'll jump at the chance."

"He *is* my husband," she said.

"You needn't rub it in," he returned bitterly. "Why the devil doesn't he have the decency to give you a divorce? The swine's just playing with us both. He—"

Mordecai Tremaine, eyes shut fast, did not see Helen Carthallow's warning gesture, but he knew that she had made it. Imleyson said, in a lower tone, "It's all right. He's asleep."

But there was no more conversation. Mordecai Tremaine fought against an almost intolerable series of desires. His eyelids seemed to be trying to force themselves open. His neck and shoulder were giving him the sensation of being a prisoner in a straight jacket. And, of course, he wanted to sneeze—devastatingly and explosively.

He held on until the strain was impossible to be borne and then opened his eyes wide. He heaved a sigh of relief. The bathing wraps and the towels had gone. Cautiously, like a man coming out of a deep sleep, he straightened himself in his chair. After another moment or two he got to his feet. The path leading up the cliffs was deserted; the bridge over his head was empty.

He folded the chair and replaced it in the cave. The tide was coming in fast, but he thought there would still be time to walk back along the beach before it cut off the next headland in the Falporth direction. He did not think he was likely to meet either Helen Carthallow or Imleyson if he used the cliff path, but he had no desire to take the risk. He was afraid he might betray himself.

Normally he would have explored the caves he passed on the way, but he was in no mood now for any such small boy's pastime. The situation upon which he had just been gazing possessed too adult a flavor for that.

He arrived back at the Tynings' in a mood of unusual depression, and he was glad that his host had reserved seats at the Falporth Follies for that evening. It would serve to rid his mind of the unpleasant thoughts that were crowding upon him.

He was secretly expecting a fourth-rate concert party, with a soprano who had once been passably good-looking but whose voice and whose figure had suffered together from the relentless march of time, and a knockabout comedian whose patter would be a rehash of all the more tested of the hardy annuals. He was agreeably surprised to find a sparkling show in which clever material was neatly put over; in which the chorus work was well-timed; and in which there was even some creditable attempt, despite the limitations of the small stage, at presenting scenes worthy of a far more pretentious revue.

Mordecai Tremaine settled back to enjoy himself and forgot all about Helen Carthallow and the triangle known as eternal.

For precisely thirty-five minutes.

Among the male members of the company was a rather short individual whose dinner jacket gave him a somewhat squat appearance. He took part in the opening number, and it crossed Mordecai Tremaine's mind on first noting him that there was something familiar about him. Thereafter, however, he vanished from the stage, and that fleeting impression was lost in the delight engendered by an exceedingly polished rendering of *My Hero* from the *Chocolate Soldier* by a lady who seemed to be quite young and who was undoubtedly attractive.

But thirty-five minutes from the opening bars from the pianist the squat gentleman made his appearance again. He came down to the footlights and proceeded to give a series of impersonations of well-known film and radio stars. It was a very able performance, and it well merited the prolonged applause he received.

It was applause in which Mordecai Tremaine joined in a very preoccupied manner. For he had recognized the other now, and he was certain that it was the shabby man whom he had seen with Adrian Carthallow in the East End of London. That queer-shaped head was unmistakable.

As soon as the house lights went up he studied his program. It was an easy matter to identify the impressionist, for all the scenes were numbered. He was billed as Morton Westfield. There was a small inset photograph of him on a page set apart for photographs of the various members of the company. The photograph confirmed the recognition.

It was, thought Mordecai Tremaine, a highly curious coincidence. If it *was* a coincidence.

19

Adrian Carthallow, brush held at arm's length, was engaged upon a watercolor of the magnificent fury of surf and spray at Trecarne Head. Seated upon a nearby rock Mordecai Tremaine had watched the quick, confident movements from the first bold charcoal outlines to these final touches of color that were completing a painting vividly alive.

He had encountered the artist coming across the bridge leading from Paradise, and when he had seen the canvas sketching bag the other carried he had thought that his plan to spend the afternoon in an intimate atmosphere that might lead to interesting confidences had headed into an early failure. But to his surprise Carthallow had invited him to go along with him.

"If you won't be bored, of course."

"Good heavens, no," Tremaine had returned, as if the thought was heresy. "You're sure you won't mind my being around while you're working?"

"I'll be delighted to have someone to talk to. The only time

I object to people seeing how the wheels go around is when I'm working on a portrait. I *am* inclined to be difficult then."

Carthallow had fetched his car from the stone-built garage near the entrance to the bridge and had driven them both to Trecarne Head. He had set up his easel at a point where the cliffs dipped steeply to form a valley and from which it was possible to see the full grandeur of the cluster of great rocks below.

Tremaine watched him, fascinated by the apparently effortless way in which the scene came into being under his swiftly moving brush.

"What a marvelous thing color is," he observed, as a broad band of yellow ochre swept across the sky.

Carthallow gave a chuckle.

"You think it's a case of the light that never was on land or sea? " Light red followed the yellow ocher. "I know this isn't the sky you can see at this moment, but I don't believe in turning out a mere photograph. After all, a camera can do that and do it much better. I like to capture the atmosphere of a place and give it warmth and emotion."

Mordecai Tremaine left his rocky seat, and, over Carthallow's shoulder, he studied the painting. From the palette, with its neatly ranged pigments, gray, ultramarine, light red, and raw umber had gone in turn to be transformed into the rocks and cliffs; the sea that boiled around them had not long before been uninspiring patches of gray and ultramarine and emerald green. He stood filled with the layman's admiration before the metamorphosis. It was not Trecarne Head as it now appeared, but it was a Trecarne Head that no one who knew the spot could fail to recognize.

"You've caught it perfectly," he said.

Carthallow warmed visibly under the praise, although he affected a due modesty. Mordecai Tremaine thought that the moment had come. If there *was* anything to hide, surely now, completely off his guard, the other would reveal it.

"By the way," he said, "I saw an acquaintance of yours last night."

"Yes?"

"At the show at the Pavilion," Tremaine went on. "I went last night for the first time and saw him there. It was the fellow with whom you were talking when I ran into you that day in the East End—in one of the streets near the tower."

Adrian Carthallow's hand, neatly touching in a corner of the sky, was quite steady.

"Which fellow?" he said casually.

"Rather a seedy-looking merchant," said Tremaine. "At least, he was at that time. Has a peculiarly shaped head—seems as though it's been flattened."

Carthallow frowned. He studied the painting, inserted a final dab of color, and sat back to study it critically.

"Oh," he said. "*That* one. You say you saw him at the Follies? I shouldn't think so. You must have been mistaken."

"No," persisted Mordecai Tremaine, "I'm sure I wasn't mistaken. It was the same man all right. He's billed as Morton Westfield."

"Is he?" Carthallow removed the painting carefully from the easel and began to pack up. "I don't know his name—he's a chap I thought might sit for me, but it didn't come to anything. It can't possibly be him you saw. *My* man was a typical East Ender—not the sort to be appearing in a show like the Follies here. Maybe there's a certain superficial resemblance. It's surprising how many near doubles there are in the world."

He seemed completely unconcerned, as though the matter had no interest for him. He picked up his sketching bag and led the way back to the car. So that, Mordecai Tremaine told himself, was that.

It was surprising how quickly he had assimilated and been assimilated by the little circle that revolved about the Carthallows. Already he knew their backgrounds and their relationships with each other. The only person about whom he was at all doubtful was Elton Steele. He could not satisfy himself about the big, dark man with his slow manner of speaking and his ability to efface himself and yet seem to be a force to be reckoned with.

Steele always gave him a disconcerting impression of

knowing far more than he revealed. His strong face invariably held an expression that appeared to suggest that although he might not say a great deal, he was capable of taking the lead among them if he so desired.

It rather annoyed Mordecai Tremaine. He disliked strong, silent men who affected a pose of superiority. He preferred ordinary mortals who spoke their minds.

"You're being too hard on Elton," said Hilda Eveland, when he opened his heart to her. "He isn't like that at all. He's the solid, faithful sort. He's probably given you that idea of him because—"

She broke off. Mordecai Tremaine said, "Because?"

"Oh—nothing."

They were on the footpath leading across the fields to Pencran, which lay some two or three miles from Falporth. Hilda Eveland had described Pencran as an attractive little village set behind the sand hills and had said that Mordecai Tremaine ought to see its twelfth-century church, which had recently been restored.

"Suppose you act as my guide?" he had suggested, and the idea had appealed to her.

They could see the scattered roofs of the village in front of them. On a hill to their left was the gray stone church, bleakly exposed to the winds from the sea. They went up the narrow road to explore its cool, dark interior, with its ancient font and exquisitely carved choir screen, and then made their way back down into the village where neatly set out tea gardens waited beguilingly in their path. It was still early when they came out, and it was Hilda Eveland who suggested a walk across the dunes before they caught the bus back into Falporth.

The breeze was strong enough to be pleasantly cooling but not so boisterous that it whipped the sand into their faces. Mordecai Tremaine enjoyed himself strolling along the uneven path with the Atlantic surf sounding musically in his ears. He was reveling so enthusiastically in his surroundings, in fact, that he failed to notice two people who were occupying one of the sheltered hollows between the dunes and almost stumbled over them.

It was obvious that he had interrupted a very intimate scene. The two had been lying with their arms around each other, clearly not expecting to be disturbed in such a secluded spot. Mordecai Tremaine hesitated, uttered a somewhat incoherent apology and hurried on.

Two minutes later, when they were out of earshot, Hilda Eveland said, "You saw who they were, of course."

"Yes," said Mordecai Tremaine. "I'm afraid I did."

"It's an open secret," said Hilda Eveland. "Everybody knows Lester's crazy about her."

Tremaine's mild face was troubled.

"Mr. Carthallow," he said. "Is he—does he—"

"Does Adrian know? Surely you don't think he'd let anything like this escape him?"

"When I first met Mr. Carthallow," said Mordecai Tremaine, "I thought he was very much in love with his wife."

"I don't doubt it," Hilda Eveland returned dryly. "That's Adrian's technique. The smile on the face of the tiger." She studied her companion's distressed expression, and her own features softened. "I know your trouble, Mordecai. You like to believe the best of people. It gives you a blind spot. I don't know your opinion of Adrian, but you can take it from me that the right word for him is louse."

Mordecai Tremaine stopped. Hilda Eveland's face was flushed. The normal good humor had quite gone from her eyes.

"I didn't imagine," he said slowly, "that you felt like that about him. I've heard criticisms of him, of course—that portrait of Miss Neale, for instance, led to a lot of comment. But I put most of it down to the kind of thing any successful man has to contend with."

"Christine Neale's portrait was only one of Adrian's unpleasant little efforts. He painted her like that deliberately to make her squirm—because he likes hurting people. We don't go around talking about it, but we all know what he's really like. We know what he does to Helen. That's why Elton hates him so badly."

"Steele? Hates him?" Mordecai Tremaine looked shocked. "I didn't dream of anything like that."

"I don't suppose you did," she said. "On the surface everything seems to be friendly and normal, but underneath it's a pretty devil's brew." Hilda Eveland's voice took on a sober note. "Sometimes, Mordecai, I frighten myself wondering what's going to come of it."

"If Carthallow knows about Imleyson," said Mordecai Tremaine, searching for something substantial to grasp, "hasn't he taken any steps about it? Surely he doesn't just sit back and let it go on?"

"That's part of the technique. Adrian isn't in love with Helen. He isn't in love with anyone except Adrian. But he won't give her a divorce. He keeps up a pretense that he doesn't think there's anything wrong, knowing all the time that he's torturing her."

"Why did she marry him?" said Mordecai Tremaine.

He thought as soon as the words were out that he had phrased the question brutally, but his companion gave no sign that she had noticed it.

"I suppose she must have been in love with him once," she said. "After all, he's pretty successful with women, although he doesn't seem to want to bother with them. They throw themselves at his head, even now. Take Christine Neale, for instance—or Roberta."

"I must say," he observed, "I feel rather sorry for Miss Fairham. He snubs her so pointedly. And she seems so—so ineffectual."

Hilda Eveland said, "I wouldn't underestimate Roberta. She's deeper than she looks."

They went on in silence for a moment or two, and then Mordecai Tremaine said, "If the situation is as bad as you say, I wonder why Lester Imleyson hasn't tried to do something about it."

"You mean why haven't they gone off together?" Hilda shook her head. "Lester hasn't a real job, and the only money he has is what his father allows him. If he left Falporth the situation wouldn't be too good. Besides, maybe Helen wouldn't go with him. I've known her a long time, but even I wonder whether I really understand her or whether I can be sure of what she'll do next."

Tremaine knew what she meant. It fitted so well with what he had already seen of Helen Carthallow. It was no easy matter to make contact with the real woman who must lie beneath the vivid lips and the overbright manner of the wife of Adrian Carthallow, successful artist who believed in keeping himself news.

They were leaving the sand dunes now and coming back into the village. Hilda Eveland said, "I'm sorry if I've made it all sound very sordid. We're not a very pleasant collection of people, are we?"

"Human beings," said Mordecai Tremaine, a little sententiously, "are such complex organisms that it's inevitable that their relationships should sometimes be difficult to unravel."

He saw that she was looking at him with a twinkle of amusement again and added hastily, "Where does Mr. Haldean come into the picture?"

"If you mean is he in love with Helen," she returned, "the answer is that he isn't. I think he's fond of her, but that's hardly the same thing. You haven't been getting any notions about him, have you?"

"I'm afraid I can't help getting notions about people," said Mordecai Tremaine. "I've allowed it to develop into a kind of habit. But I didn't think Mr. Haldean was in love with Mrs. Carthallow. As a matter of fact, I had rather a different idea about him. It was because of a photograph I saw on his dressing table the other day."

"A photograph?"

"Yes—of an attractive, dark-haired girl with rather a nice face. He called her Margaret. From the way he spoke about her I gathered that she was the reason he had never married. He said that she'd died a long time ago."

"Margaret?" Hilda Eveland frowned. "Lewis usually tells me all about himself, but I don't remember him speaking of anyone of that name."

Mordecai Tremaine did not reply. His thoughts were a

long way off, going back over the years. He believed that he had a common bond with Lewis Haldean, for he himself had remained a bachelor only because the woman he had loved had died tragically soon.

It was a chapter in his life about which few people had ever learned and about which he did not speak. Which was why Hilda Eveland never knew the reason for the depression that was upon him as they made their way back to Falporth.

20

If Mordecai Tremaine had not suspected any undercurrents of feeling before his excursion to Pencran, he would have been on the watch for them after his experience in Hilda Eveland's company. In addition, her candor had caused him to go back over his contacts with Adrian Carthallow, and the results of his mental research had not improved his opinion of the artist. Carthallow's attitude became decidedly suspect in the light of this new interpretation.

It made him judge what he saw and heard in the succeeding days with a degree of cynicism and suspicion he had not previously possessed. He realized that he was now seeing things of which the others had been aware all the time.

He looked at Elton Steele and saw, instead of a detached, placid man, secure in his physical strength, a man in whose dark eyes hate was brooding but whose emotions were being kept rigidly and frighteningly under control. He looked at Adrian Carthallow, and instead of the exuberant, good-natured creative artist, proud of his success, he saw the sardonic amusement of the sadist, delighting to wound in secret, firing verbal darts his victims could not deflect without self-betrayal. He looked at Helen Carthallow, and beneath the gaiety of her voice and her laughter he detected the nervous strain of a woman who was nursing a fear that was steadily overwhelming her.

He thought of what Hilda Eveland had said about being frightened where it was going to end, and the brittleness of Helen Carthallow's manner and the way in which he sometimes caught Elton Steele looking at her made him frightened, too. It was impossible for human beings to go on indefinitely under such an increasing tension. Sooner or later something—or somebody—was going to break.

Even Lewis Haldean was not immune from the atmosphere. His enthusiasms and dramatic poses seemed forced on occasions. Outwardly he was on the best of terms with Carthallow, but signs were not wanting that they frequently did not see eye to eye. Haldean gave the impression of being a man who was trying to preserve a fabric he knew must inevitably come to pieces in his hand; he was, Mordecai Tremaine thought, like an actor striving to maintain a play against a hostile audience and in which even his fellow players were undoing his efforts.

Two days after the Pencran incident there was a swimming and sunbathing party on the beach, and in the early evening they all went back to Paradise at Carthallow's invitation. The conversation was gay, and even Elton Steele had joined in with a greater display of high spirits than was usual with him.

Mordecai Tremaine and Hilda Eveland were the last to climb the steep path up the cliffs. Tremaine said, "A very enjoyable afternoon."

Hilda's plump face regarded him smilingly. She stopped with her hand upon the rail to gain her breath.

"I'm glad," she said. "I was beginning to be afraid, Mordecai, that I'd spoiled everything for you by letting my tongue run away with me the other day."

"Mrs. Carthallow seems in excellent spirits."

She nodded, as they began to climb the steps again.

"For once Adrian's been acting as though he's genuinely fond of her. I hope it's a sign that the tide's going to turn."

But later, when they were in the house, Mordecai Tremaine's optimism began to dwindle. The first sign of discord came when he encountered Haldean and Carthallow as they descended the stairs from the studio. Carthallow was saying, a note of irritation in his voice, "Damn it all, Lewis, I'm not a child! I know what I'm doing! You'll get your money all right."

"You know I'm not worried over the money for its own sake," said Haldean. "It's you I'm thinking of. All this isn't

doing your work any good. And if you break down what's
going to happen then?"

"It'll be *my* worry," snapped Carthallow. "You don't need to
preach so much. D'you think I don't know the mess I'm in?"

And then he saw Mordecai Tremaine, and a sullen resentment smoldered in his eyes. Haldean looked uncomfortable.
Tremaine decided that there was only one thing to do and
effaced himself as though he had heard nothing.

The second incident occurred after dinner. Most of the
company were in the open air, and when Hilda Eveland asked
him if he would fetch her handbag, which she had left in the
lounge, Tremaine did not realize that the room was occupied.
His approach was quite silent, and his hand was on the door
when he heard Helen Carthallow's voice from inside.

"Tell me the truth, Lewis. How much is it?"

Mordecai Tremaine should, of course, have knocked and
gone in at once. He would have been the first to admit that his
conduct in remaining where he was did not qualify for inclu-
sion among the things done in the best circles. But his natural
curiosity had received a stimulus from Hilda Eveland, and it
was momentarily impossible for him to move from the door.

Haldean's vibrant voice sounded unwilling.

"Nothing large enough for you to worry about, my dear."

"How much, Lewis?" she insisted.

"About five thousand."

She gave an exclamation of dismay.

"As much as that—"

Haldean's voice came hastily.

"I'm not a rich man, Helen, but I'm not a poor one either, and you know my wants aren't many. I'm in no hurry. There's no question of my pressing Adrian."

"I know that, Lewis," she said quietly.

"Besides," he went on, "a man in Adrian's position can soon make enough to settle such a comparatively small sum. After all, he's a success. He can command his own prices."

"Do you think so?" she said, and there was a bitterness in her voice. "A lot of people think that Adrian must be a rich man, but if you spend money quicker than you make it you don't accumulate much more than an overdraft. You and I understand each other, Lewis, so there's no need to pretend. Adrian doesn't tell me much about his affairs, but I do know that he's been drawing more checks than he's been paying in. He hasn't had many commissions just lately. His work doesn't sell as well as you might imagine. One or two things haven't made him exactly popular, and it does make a difference."

"I know he's rather inclined to cross swords with people," Haldean agreed, "but, after all, if he paints what he sees he's only being true to himself as an artist."

Her voice was dry.

"You don't need to make excuses for him, Lewis. Not to

me." She laughed. It was not a sound that had any humor in it. "I dare say you're thinking it's odd that I should be showing so much anxiety about Adrian. I suppose it's because I've grown so used to playing the dutiful wife in public that I can't step out of the role too easily."

Mordecai Tremaine was feeling that he had stayed long enough. His conscience was behaving very unpleasantly indeed.

He walked softly back down the hall and then came forward again, ostentatiously clearing his throat. He opened the door and went into the lounge.

"Oh—I beg your pardon," he said. "I didn't realize there was anyone here. Hilda left her bag behind. Ah—there it is."

He picked up the article in question and made his exit. He was relieved when the door had closed behind him. It was disconcerting to know that two pairs of eyes were watching his every movement and that each pair contained both suspicion and conjecture as to just how long he had been waiting outside the door and just how much he had overheard.

21

For so long had Mordecai Tremaine trained himself to arise at 6.30 a.m. that the process was no longer attended by pain. He awoke each morning automatically and, springing from his bed, performed his routine exercises. His sparse, pajama-clad figure did not—and would not now—bear any resemblance to the mighty torsos of the physical culture advertisements, but he was convinced that he derived great benefit from the rapid jerks in which he indulged in front of his open window.

Breathing deeply, like a man well satisfied with life since he was aware that he had, this morning at least, done all those things he ought to have done, he went out on to the cliffs. Normally his pre-breakfast stroll took him over the path leading to Falporth; today, he thought, he would vary his program and would walk along the sands in the opposite direction. They looked flat, clean, and inviting; the air was rich with the tang of seaweed and salt.

His enthusiasm took him further than he had intended. Sometimes walking briskly over the firm, golden beach, sometimes scrambling over the tumbled rocks running out here and there from the main cliff, he went on until a glance at his watch reminded him that unless he took care he would be late for breakfast. And a breakfast prepared by Kate Tyning was something no reasonable man would wish to miss.

He decided that he would go as far as the other side of the outcrop of rocks facing him and would climb the steps he knew lay a few yards beyond so that he could walk back by the upper path.

Out by the low road and back by the high road, he was thinking happily, and then he saw Adrian Carthallow.

There was another man with him. It was the shabby man to whom he had been talking that day in the East End. The man with the curiously shaped head who was now appearing with the Falporth Follies, under the name Morton Westfield. The man whom Carthallow had denied knowing only a day or two before.

Mordecai Tremaine drew quickly back out of sight. It was an instinctive movement, prompted by some inner sense of warning he could not explain. The two were deep in conversation, and he knew they had not seen him. The sand had muffled his approach, and in any case the constant swish of the surf would have prevented any slight sound he might have made from reaching their ears.

At the point where the two were standing the rocks

shielded them from observation. Unless someone approached directly along the sands, as Tremaine had done, they could not be overlooked, and at this comparatively early hour it was unlikely that many people would be astir, particularly so far from the main beaches.

Cautiously Tremaine moved closer. Keeping in the shelter of the rocks he managed to reach a spot no more than a few yards from Carthallow and his companion and yet where he was concealed from their view. The workings of his conscience were faint indeed. Adrian Carthallow had lied about the man who was calling himself Westfield. That significant fact, allied to the knowledge he already possessed concerning the artist, was sufficient to justify an attempt to find out more about the relationship between them.

They were talking in guarded voices, and even the muted noise of the surf was enough to muffle their words. Only a phrase or two could be distinguished. Tremaine heard Westfield say, "Reynolds…Belmont satisfied…get a good figure…"

And then Carthallow's voice, louder, sharpened by anger.

"Damn it, man, d'you think you can turn out these things like sausages?"

The voices were lost again. Tremaine pressed closer to the rock, but it was impossible for him to hear what was being said. Until, so close that it startled him, he heard Carthallow say, "We'd better not meet again down here. It's too risky.

There's an interfering old busybody called Tremaine who saw us in town and recognized you the other night at the Pavilion. If he sees us together he's quite likely to make himself a damned nuisance."

"He doesn't—" began the other quickly, and Carthallow took him up with a laugh.

"Suspect anything? Why the hell should he? I put him off all right—told him that the fellow I met in London was someone I was interested in as a model and that he couldn't possibly be playing in a concert party down here. He thinks he's made a mistake over a chance resemblance. But there's no need to stick our necks out. I'll meet you in Wadestow. I'll be going over to the races. You can tell me then what you want."

Mordecai Tremaine, pressed against a limpet-covered rock, was trying desperately not to breathe more often than was essential to keep the life in his body.

Carthallow and his companion had moved from their original positions; that was why he had heard their voices more clearly. They were apparently about to part company. Which meant that this was the crisis. Upon which way each of them decided to go would depend whether he was discovered. And if he *was* discovered…

He was aware of a distinctly uncomfortable feeling. He had suddenly realized how lonely the beach was and how well the rocks would screen any scene of violence that might be enacted.

He did not dare look to see what was taking place. All he could do was to crouch and hope.

It was an unnerving experience while it lasted, but the fates had decided to be kind to him. When at length he looked about him he saw that Carthallow had gone up the beach in the direction of his house and that Westfield was walking rapidly toward Falporth. Evidently they had not suspected his presence.

Nevertheless he waited until there was no further sign of either of them before he moved from the comforting obscurity of the rocks. He thought that he would prefer to be late for breakfast rather than encounter Adrian Carthallow or the shabby man.

Going back over the sands—he had decided against the cliff path now—he tried to analyze his feelings. After all, Carthallow might have had a perfectly legitimate reason for seeing Westfield at a secluded spot where there would be little prospect of being observed, and he might have had an equally legitimate reason for concealing the fact that he was acquainted with the man.

"Well, he *might*," thought Mordecai Tremaine dubiously. But it was not a theory to which he felt inclined to attach much importance.

By hurrying he managed to get indoors just as breakfast

was being served. Providentially it was a little later than usual.

"Anything doing today, Mordecai?" asked Jonathan Boyce.

The Yard man was looking tanned and fit—much too healthy, as he admitted, to be able to spin out his convalescence much further.

"I think I'll join you in the garden, Jonathan," Mordecai Tremaine returned.

He was hoping that Charles Penross would pay them a call, and he was not disappointed, for at eleven o'clock the inspector appeared at the gate.

"Lucky devils," he said boomingly, as he saw them taking their ease in two deck chairs on the lawn, coffee cups at their side. "It's too hot to go around looking for people who park their cars on the wrong side of the street."

"I take it," Boyce returned, "that that remark means that business is slack?"

"Happily so," said Penross. "The crime graph is pointing nicely downward."

"You're in time for coffee, anyway," said Kate Tyning, who had come out into the garden at that moment. "Sit down, Charles, and I'll fetch you a cup."

When the inspector was comfortably settled in a nearby chair, Mordecai Tremaine seized his opportunity.

"If there isn't much doing," he said, "I wonder whether

you'd make a few inquiries for me? I'm rather interested in one of the people in the Follies show we saw the other night. He's the impressionist."

"Westfield, d'you mean?" queried Penross. "Morton Westfield? Fellow with a funny-shaped head?"

"Yes," Mordecai Tremaine said, with unguarded eagerness. "Do you know anything about him?"

The inspector gave him a look of curiosity.

"Only that he's a member of the company," he said. "Why? *Should* I know anything about him?"

"I couldn't say," replied Tremaine hastily. "It's just that he looks familiar to me. I've a feeling that I've seen him before although not under that name."

"That's quite possible," said Penross. "These theatrical people often use a stage name."

Tremaine felt that the conversation was not going in the required direction.

"That wasn't quite what I meant," he said. "I'm sure I've met him somewhere, but I can't place him."

"Why don't you go down to the Pavilion and ask him?" said the inspector practically.

Jonathan Boyce had been listening to the conversation with a secret smile of understanding.

"You'll have to come clean, Mordecai. Tell Charles what you want, and maybe he'll oblige."

Mordecai Tremaine adjusted his pince-nez a little nervously.

"I want to know all about Morton Westfield. I want to know his real name, where he lives, and what he does when he isn't with the Falporth Follies concert party."

Inspector Penross sipped his coffee reflectively.

"Why?" he said.

"I'm afraid I can't tell you that. I may be completely wrong, and I don't want to involve you in difficulties."

Penross looked from Jonathan Boyce to Mordecai Tremaine and back to Boyce again. The Yard man nodded. Penross said, "You're quite serious about this?"

"Quite."

Penross drained his coffee with relish, replaced the cup upon the tray, and rose to his feet.

"I dare say we can find out the answers for you. May take a little time, of course. We'll have to be discreet about it."

"I understand," said Mordecai Tremaine gratefully.

He strolled along the beach toward Paradise that afternoon with the feeling that he had crossed his personal Rubicon. He had taken a definite step toward elucidating the mystery that appeared to involve Adrian Carthallow, and whether it led to climax or to anticlimax there could be no going back. He had seen enough of Charles Penross to know that beneath the inspector's friendly exterior there was a steely devotion to his job that would not permit him to abandon any line of inquiry until he had found the solution to each and every one of the problems it raised.

He had taken a book with him with the intention of spending a quiet afternoon on the beach, but he did not read a single page. Steele, Haldean, and Roberta Fairham were already there when he arrived, and not long afterward Helen and Adrian Carthallow came down with Hilda Eveland.

Mordecai Tremaine sat in a deck chair and felt like a sultan surrounded by his slaves as he looked down upon the brown bodies sprawled upon wraps and towels all around him.

The conversation dealt mainly with the two-day race meeting due to take place at Wadestow toward the end of the week. Most of them seemed to be planning to attend it. Lewis Haldean said, "Are you going over, Mordecai?"

Tremaine nodded.

"Yes. I like the atmosphere of a racetrack."

"Don't tell me," said Hilda Eveland with a smile, "that you can even sentimentalize over a bookie!"

"Not quite that," he told her. "But I like the excitement and the crowds and all the color of it."

Roberta Fairham, in a two-piece bathing costume that was unwisely daring for her slim figure, was lying next to Adrian Carthallow.

"How's the portrait going, Adrian?" she asked.

Carthallow raised himself on his elbow and surveyed her reflectively.

"Nice of you to take an interest, Roberta," he said. "It's coming along well. Helen's the perfect model."

"I'm glad," she said.

But her face was sullen. It was as though she had not been able to prevent herself from putting the question and yet, paradoxically, could not bear to talk about the portrait.

Adrian Carthallow climbed to his feet. In a swimming costume his corpulence was emphasized. With his thinning hair ruffled by the breeze he looked a good deal older; Tremaine thought he seemed worried and anxious.

"Who's coming in?" he said.

"I'm ready," Roberta Fairham said quickly.

Helen Carthallow gave her a sudden glance. Elton Steele said, "Are you coming, Helen?"

There was a general stirring. Lewis Haldean got up with an air of reluctance.

"*Et tu*, Brute?" he said dramatically to Carthallow, and the artist laughed.

"You're a lazy devil, Lewis."

"Count me out," said Hilda Eveland comfortably. "I'll stay here with Mordecai and watch the rest of you working."

The little party went off down the beach. The tide was coming in fast now, and the long lines of surf were creaming in with an inviting steadiness. Carthallow had brought several surfboards from the house, and Tremaine watched them as they waded into the water, the boards held high above their heads to prevent a premature wave from catching them and sending them sprawling.

Haldean was the first to go under. Tremaine saw him as he caught a rolling wave just as it began to break and followed it down to the beach in a flurry of foaming water. He rode his board with the ease born of experience, making the most of the buoyant drive behind the surf.

It seemed that Carthallow had not acquired the right technique. His timing was faulty, so that he either plunged too soon or too late and instead of riding in to the sands was left floundering some yards out. Nevertheless he was undoubtedly enjoying himself. Mordecai Tremaine wished that he was a few years younger and that he, too, could join in the sport.

Almost facing the spot where he was seated, two lines of surf converged. Due to some trick of the beach or the current they raced one upon the other and intermingled before flooding furiously over the sands. He imagined himself meeting the inspiring challenge of those tumbling waves and sighed regretfully.

Rather to his surprise Roberta Fairham was an expert at using a surfboard. Time after time he saw her come racing in level with Lewis Haldean, and after a while she took Carthallow's board and waded out with him, evidently trying to impart the secret to him.

Hilda Eveland said, suddenly, "It looks as though Roberta's wishing Lester were on the scene to look after Helen and leave her a free hand with Adrian. Surf riding is her strong point."

Mordecai Tremaine looked down at her.

"I was wondering what had happened to Mr. Imleyson."

"He's had a row with Adrian," she told him. "Officially he's out on business this afternoon—calling on some of the local farmers—but the real reason probably is that he thinks it would be wiser to keep away for a while until things have settled down again."

"Why did they quarrel?"

"The obvious reason. Helen. I don't know what precise spark it was that sent up the powder barrel, but Adrian's been edgy lately. He hasn't been able to play Machiavelli quite so easily. According to Elton he went for Lester hot-headed. And, of course, Lester didn't just stand there and take it."

"Mr. Steele was there at the time?"

"Apparently. The fact that he had an audience wouldn't stop Adrian. It would probably encourage him to go further."

They became silent again. Mordecai Tremaine looked out to where the sun was playing on the ceaseless lines of water flooding upon the beach with the dark figures moving through the spray. Inevitably he began to nod.

He did not see exactly what took place. He heard Hilda Eveland give a startled exclamation and saw her raise herself on her arm. He caught a brief glimpse of a scene of spray and confusion, and then he saw the surfboards discarded on the sands and the cluster of people at the water's edge.

"What is it?" he said. "What happened?"

"It's Helen," Hilda told him. "She's hurt."

"An accident?" he said, peering.

"Perhaps." There was a strange note in Hilda Eveland's voice. Her plump, good-humored face was unsmiling. "Helen was coming in on her board when Roberta suddenly shot out of that cross wave and crashed into her. Fortunately Elton saw what was happening and managed to deflect her enough to break the full force of it. Otherwise it might have been more serious. Those boards can give you a nasty blow."

Helen Carthallow came slowly up the beach between her husband and Elton Steele. She was holding her left arm, and she was limping. When she drew level with him Tremaine saw that there was a long, ugly weal on her thigh and that blood was oozing from it.

Gently Steele took the arm she was holding. It, too, was cruelly marked; the board had evidently scraped along her left side.

Roberta Fairham was hovering in the background, a look of contrition on her face.

"I'm terribly sorry, Helen. I didn't see you until it was too late. I wouldn't have come in so fast if I'd known you were there."

Helen Carthallow tried to smile. Her face was drawn, and she was obviously in pain. With her hair scooped away under her bathing cap and with her makeup toned down by the salt water she had lost her overbright, sophisticated air. She looked rather like a lonely and frightened little girl who was in need of protection. Mordecai Tremaine felt his sentimental heart move in compassion.

"It's all right," she said. "It wasn't your fault, Roberta. I should have been keeping a more careful lookout. Anyway, there's no real damage. My arm's a bit numb, but there's nothing broken."

"We'll get you up to the house and make sure about it," said Elton Steele.

His voice was incisive. He seemed to have taken charge of the proceedings, and Carthallow did not attempt to oppose him.

Mordecai Tremaine glanced at Roberta Fairham. He had detected the false note in her voice, and he thought that in her pale eyes he could see mingled triumph and chagrin. He remembered what Hilda Eveland had told him about not underestimating her. *Had* it been an accident? Or had it been an accident only in so far as Elton Steele had deflected that dangerously flying surfboard?

Steele had been examining Helen Carthallow's arm. He stirred and his eyes rested briefly upon the woman who stood behind her. It was only the merest of glances, but Mordecai Tremaine saw the look upon the big man's face, and suddenly he was very glad that he was not Roberta Fairham.

22

The long main street of Falporth was filled with vacationers taking their ease and with energetically foraging landladies. Tradesmen's vans, cars, and motor coaches jammed its narrowest parts. The ubiquitous photographers were busily snapping every potential customer unwary enough to stare inquiringly at their poised cameras.

It was a scene that appealed to Mordecai Tremaine. He reveled in its color and movement. Jonathan Boyce, who was with him, had been amused at his schoolboy zest.

They were retracing their steps toward the house, for they had been given instructions to be back for an early lunch. Afterward Arthur Tyning was to drive them into Wadestow in time for the first race, which was to be run at two o'clock.

Earlier in the morning Tremaine had called at Paradise to inquire after Helen Carthallow and had found her on the point of starting out for Wadestow with her husband. Her arm, she had said, was still a little stiff, but otherwise she had suffered no ill effects.

Her manner had inclined toward coolness. Mordecai Tremaine had not known whether it had been due to any particular antipathy toward himself—he was reasonably certain that she knew he had seen her with Lester Imleyson on the sand dunes near Pencran—or whether it had been because she was not as fully recovered as she had stated.

Adrian Carthallow had been his usual boisterous self. The lines of worry in his face had not been quite so noticeable.

"Dare say we'll see you over there, Tremaine!" he had called and had driven off with a wave of the hand.

Jonathan Boyce stopped to gaze into the window of a bookshop. Tremaine waited with him, and as he was about to go on again a man came out of the entrance with a newspaper under his arm and he had to step to one side to avoid him. As he did so he saw the other full face for an instant.

He was a gray-haired man, with lined but strong features. His shoulders were squared, and he carried himself erect. He had the look of a man who was used both to giving orders and to having them obeyed.

Mordecai Tremaine was a few yards down the street when recognition came to him. He gave an involuntary exclamation.

Jonathan Boyce said, "Anything wrong?"

"No—nothing wrong. At least, I hope not. I've just seen someone I once met by chance. His name's Neale—Colonel Neale."

Jonathan Boyce had an excellent memory. It was only a moment or two before he said, "Wasn't it a Colonel Neale who was involved in an argument with your friend Carthallow over a portrait of his daughter?"

Mordecai Tremaine nodded.

"Yes. I wonder what he's doing in Falporth. Of course, he *could* be down here on holiday."

His voice tailed away. He looked back, but the gray-haired man had been absorbed by the crowd. Unless he went in deliberate pursuit of him it was unlikely that he would see him again.

For an instant or two he even hesitated as to whether he should turn about and try and catch the colonel. The disturbing influence of that scene in Adrian Carthallow's house in London when the gray-haired man had burst in upon the artist had never quite gone. He had often recalled Carthallow's face as he had stood there with the blood trickling from the corner of his lips. And he had recalled Neale's face, too. The face of a man who would not rest until he had exacted full retribution.

Several times he had found himself wondering why the affair seemed to have died a natural death; why he had heard no more of Neale's attempt to force Carthallow to pay for what, rightly or wrongly, he considered the artist had done.

And now Colonel Neale was in Falporth.

But he did not, in the end, go after the other. After all, what was there he could say?

"Excuse me, Colonel, but I saw you at Adrian Carthallow's house the night you hit him in the face. I hope you haven't come to Falporth in order to cause trouble. It won't do any real good, you know."

No, it was quite obvious he couldn't say that.

Jonathan Boyce had been watching him.

"I imagine, Mordecai," he observed, "we shall be seeing your friends over at Wadestow."

"I think most of them will be there," Tremaine agreed. "Except Mrs. Eveland. She doesn't care for racing." He added: "You know, Jonathan, I've been feeling guilty about spending so much time with them. I hope your sister and her husband don't think I've been neglecting them."

"My dear chap, they've been delighted to know that you've had friends so near at hand. It's saved them having to worry about what to do with you! And as far as I've been concerned I've had a glorious laze. *My* chief worry has been that you might have decided to go and spoil things by finding another body!"

"I'm relieved to hear you say that, Jonathan," said Mordecai Tremaine. "I wouldn't like them to think that I haven't appreciated all they've done for me."

A run of forty minutes brought them into Wadestow in ample time for the first race. Owing to the necessity for changing, the journey by train was one of over an hour, but by road the town could be reached much more quickly.

When they arrived at the racetrack Mordecai Tremaine's eyes glistened happily behind the tottering pince-nez. It was the kind of crowded, exciting scene in which he found perfection, and he spent an enthralling afternoon. The smell of the turf, the eager roar of thousands of throats, the drumming of hooves as the horses came into the straight and flashed past the rails where he was standing all merged into an exhilarating kaleidoscope of color and sound.

The fact that he could not see enough of the course to follow the races properly troubled him not at all. He caught, indeed, no more than a brief glimpse of a huddle of horses and jockeys as they came by and the crowd pressed to the rails. But he found his own enjoyment.

He found it in strolling through the enclosure where the bookmakers were calling the odds or performing swift mathematical intricacies upon the boards decorating their stands; in watching the tic-tac man, balanced perilously upon the buildings on the far side of the track and signaling frantically in his mysterious sign language so that he looked like a spidery Catherine wheel.

He found it in searching hurriedly through his card in an attempt to find a likely winner before the next race began; in joining the queues at the tote windows to buy his units; and three times, gleefully, in joining the smaller queues on the far side of the tote buildings to collect his moderate winnings.

Pince-nez awry and several shillings richer as a result of his intricate financial operations in backing favorites each way, he came away from the track after the last race with the air of a man who had drunk his fill of life's headiest wine.

He had seen nothing of Adrian or Helen Carthallow. He had looked for them once or twice, desultorily, without much hope of seeing them in such a milling crowd. He was beginning to think that it was certain he would not encounter them now when he found himself staring straight at them as they stood at the entrance to the car park.

All the others were there with the exception of Hilda Eveland. He saw that Haldean and Steele were standing apart from the rest of the company and that Roberta Fairham was talking animatedly to Carthallow.

It seemed obvious that she had dressed to impress him. She was wearing a flowered hat and a dress that advertised itself as one of the latest exclusive models, but one that had been intended for a creature of bolder curves and coloring than Roberta possessed. She had, Mordecai Tremaine thought, rather overdone it again. She looked like a timid sparrow unsuccessfully disguised as a bird of paradise.

Lester Imleyson was standing very close to Helen Carthallow. His arm, in fact, was half around her waist in a proprietorial fashion, although it was not visible to Carthallow.

Something about the group conveyed a warning to Mordecai Tremaine. Although he was still some yards from them he sensed an atmosphere; there had, he guessed, been a scene of some kind.

He was about to make his presence known to them when Adrian Carthallow turned away from Roberta Fairham and addressed himself to his wife.

"Come along, my dear," he said. "It's time you and I were going."

The words in themselves were innocent enough, but they held a hard emphasis that told Mordecai Tremaine that their meaning went deep. Carthallow held out his arm. He looked like a polite husband making an understandingly intimate gesture toward his partner, but there could be no doubt in the minds of those who knew him that he was in reality cracking the whip of ownership.

Helen Carthallow hesitated a moment or two, and then, without a word, she took the proffered arm. Tremaine saw Lester Imleyson clench his fists; there was a sullen, resentful look in his handsome face. She gave him a desperate, pleading glance, and then Lewis Haldean stepped into the circle.

The blond man was ill at ease. His usually dramatically firm voice was uncertain. It was as though he doubted his ability to prevent an open breach between Imleyson and Carthallow.

"No doubt we'll see you later, Adrian," he said quickly. He had planted himself in Imleyson's path so that the younger man could not reach the artist without pushing him aside. "Maybe at your hotel."

"Maybe," said Carthallow.

He grinned at Imleyson, mockingly and offensively. And then they had separated and had disappeared into the crowds pressing through the entrance to the car park, Lewis Haldean's restraining arm about Lester Imleyson's body as Adrian and Helen Carthallow went off to find their car.

Mordecai Tremaine was relieved that he had not spoken. He was relieved, too, that none of them had noticed him and that Jonathan Boyce and the Tynings had been talking among themselves and had not seen what he himself had seen.

The whole incident had been over in a few moments, but it had left an impression that etched itself upon his mind as he went with his companions toward their own car.

He saw the mocking, flabby features of Adrian Carthallow, flaunting possession of his wife in front of her lover; he saw the white, haunted face of Helen Carthallow, her lips once more a vivid contrasting scarlet against her powder; he saw Imleyson, a murderous, impotent fury in his eyes.

He saw Lewis Haldean, concern large upon him, trying

to prevent a public scene, and behind him the powerful bulk of Elton Steele like some great background force that might come into devastating play when it was least expected. And he saw Roberta Fairham, trying to appear unconcerned but unable to conceal the savage delight in her gray eyes at the discomfiture of the woman she hated.

The memory worried him all the way back to Falporth. It prevented him from sleeping until a late hour, and it was still with him when he awoke the next morning.

He was denied the opportunity of endeavoring to cure himself with the hair of the dog, for the Carthallows were staying in Wadestow for the second day's racing and would in all probability remain until the day after that. Adrian Carthallow had mentioned as much to him, and it had recalled the conversation he had overheard on the beach. The artist had told Westfield that he would see him in Wadestow, and Tremaine was certain that the "business" with which Carthallow was supposed to be dealing in that town was con-nected with his arrangement to meet the shabby man—he still thought of him as that, although Westfield in his new role was by no means ill-dressed.

Lewis Haldean was not attending the second day's race meeting but had gone off to St. Mawgan where he proposed to spend his time fishing. He, too, would probably be away for a few days, for he planned to sleep at the inn there. Elton

Steele was busy with his work in the town, and Roberta Fairham and Lester Imleyson seemed temporarily to have vanished. With Paradise empty, of course, there was nothing to bring them to that part of Falporth.

Mordecai Tremaine spent a great deal of time relaxing in deck chairs, but somehow his mind would persist in coming back to the subject of Adrian Carthallow. Almost he decided to unburden his worries to Hilda Eveland, and then he changed his mind in case she should laugh at him for an imaginative old idiot.

On the afternoon following the second day of the Wadestow meeting, he walked along the beach to the headland upon which Paradise was built and settled himself in a chair he took from the cave. He had brought the daily newspaper with him, not to read but to employ to protect himself from the sun if it beat down too fiercely upon him, and it was his intention to think over the whole involved problem objectively. If, he told himself, he could make a determined effort to define the vague anxieties that were fretting at him he would probably find that they were only phantoms of his imagination after all.

Methodically he began to set his facts in order. It was undoubtedly very warm, and before long he was forced to spread the newspaper over his head. His thoughts began to drift. They became inextricably mixed with the soothing sound of the sea and the shrill voices of the gulls. They ceased to be thoughts at all.

And it was there that Helen Carthallow came down to tell him that she had killed her husband.

PART THREE

EXPOSITION:

FOLLOWING THE CORPSE

23

Inspector Penross came through the gate leading to Arthur Tyning's house.

"A good day," he said, "has been had by all."

He dropped into the vacant deck chair between Mordecai Tremaine and Jonathan Boyce with a long, grateful sigh. Those two gentlemen waited expectantly. After dinner they had taken up their positions on the veranda in front of the house, and although neither had spoken a word to the other, each of them knew perfectly well they were hoping Charles Penross would look in.

Boyce said, "Any news, Charles?"

"I've spent most of the afternoon with Adrian Carthallow's solicitor," the inspector returned. "As far as I can make out, he was well and truly broke."

Boyce took his pipe from his mouth and stared at him.

"Broke?" he said. "I thought he was coining the stuff. What about his pictures?"

"Oh, he was making money all right, but he wasn't

making enough of it. He was running on a permanent over-draft. Apparently his bank manager had been pressing him pretty hard."

"Anything among his papers?"

Penross nodded.

"There was a cash book in his desk where he kept a record of some of the bigger amounts outstanding. He borrowed a lot of money from Lewis Haldean. According to his figures it came to about five thousand pounds."

"Have you spoken to Haldean?"

"Yes. He didn't make any bones about it. Told me he'd always been on good terms with Carthallow and lent him the money purely as a friend because he knew he was going through a bad time financially." Penross rubbed his chin ruminatively. "Just shows you can't be certain about people. From what I've heard about Carthallow, I'd have thought he was the last man to be in a corner for money."

"Being well known isn't the same thing as being well paid," observed Mordecai Tremaine. "Carthallow built up a reputation for himself, but he hadn't been in the public eye long enough to have established a profitable connection. It costs a lot of money to keep up an appearance of being suc-cessful, and until you've managed to draw a few dividends you're quite likely to live on the borderline of bankruptcy. And Carthallow's attempts at getting his name in the news were inclined to play back on him. He wasn't the kind of artist people felt they could safely approach for a portrait. They didn't know what he might turn out, and he wasn't being given too many commissions despite the stir he'd caused."

"Which brings us back to Christine Neale," said Jonathan Boyce.

Penross raised his eyebrows.

"Christine Neale?"

"You probably read something about it at the time. Carthallow painted her portrait. It wasn't exactly—flattering."

"Believe I do remember something about it," said the inspector thoughtfully. "Didn't her father try to make trouble over it? Threatened to take a whip to him if I'm not mistaken. But as far as I recall, it never came to anything."

"It didn't," said Jonathan Boyce. "But Colonel Neale is in Falporth. At least, he was just before Carthallow—died. Mordecai and I happened to spot him in the main street a few days ago."

"Did you now?" Penross's deep voice had a sudden throbbing note of excitement. And then, regretfully, it died again. "I can't see that it gets us anywhere. Nobody went into that house except Mrs. Carthallow and her husband."

"You're accepting Matilda Vickery's evidence that no one else crossed the bridge?"

"It ties up with all the alibis," returned Penross. "And

I must admit the old lady impresses me. I don't think she misses very much. Of course, I'll check up on this Colonel Neale of yours just in case he happened to get in and out without being seen, but I'm not hopeful. He'll probably be able to prove he was nowhere near the place."

Mordecai Tremaine said, "You still think it *was* Helen Carthallow?"

"Somebody," Penross said, "killed Adrian Carthallow. On the face of it, only two people went across that damned bridge, and one of them was Carthallow himself. There isn't much of a choice, is there?"

"That," said Mordecai Tremaine, "is what I'm trying to get at. You've found out that Carthallow's affairs were in a bad way. He had expensive tastes, was heavily in debt and wasn't doing as well out of his painting as everybody imagined."

"Well?"

"Well, maybe there's your motive. Carthallow knew he'd reached the end of his tether and killed himself."

Inspector Penross sighed.

"This is where I came in," he said. "And I *still* don't see how he could have shot himself and not have left his finger-prints on the gun."

"Helen Carthallow might have wiped them off."

"And left her own so that she could sign what might be her own death warrant?"

"Not necessarily her death warrant," Mordecai Tremaine persisted. "After all, Jonathan here suggested a possible solution. Helen Carthallow reached the house some time later than her husband. She went into the study and found that he'd shot himself. She knew the insurance company wouldn't pay out for suicide, so she wiped the gun clean of fingerprints and deliberately handled it herself so that she could tell that first story about her husband having been joking with her and telling her to pull the trigger, not realizing it was loaded.

"She must have known it would be taking a chance, of course, but she may have thought that it was worth it. She must have had a pretty good idea of how little money there was left, and she wanted to make sure she didn't starve. She reasoned perhaps that if she could get away with that story with the police, she'd be able to put it over on the insurance company as well.

"Naturally, finding him dead like that came as a shock to her, and she didn't have time to think the thing out clearly. When you showed her that the explanation she'd given wouldn't fit the evidence, she thought up her second story. It meant putting herself in a more difficult position and pretty well giving herself a motive for murder by admitting that there'd been a quarrel, but having wiped off the fingerprints and having been found out in one set of lies she knew that the truth itself would only look like another lie in any case, so she had nothing to lose by keeping up her attempt to secure the insurance money."

Penross said, "Very cunning. It might even have been true. *If* there'd been any insurance money to get."

Mordecai Tremaine looked crestfallen.

"Oh. So there wasn't a policy?"

"There was not," said Penross. "I've checked with the solicitor, and I've also put it to Mrs. Carthallow herself. They were both quite definite that Carthallow wasn't insured. He's supposed to have been against that sort of thing on principle, but I rather imagine that his real reason was that he objected to paying money so that somebody else could benefit by it. He doesn't seem to have been interested in the endowment type of policy."

"Even if that motive doesn't exist," Mordecai Tremaine went on, after a moment or two, "it still doesn't follow that Carthallow *didn't* commit suicide. His wife may have had another reason we don't yet know about for wanting to prevent its becoming public."

Inspector Penross looked at him.

"Do *you* think he committed suicide?" he asked. "*Do* you?"

Mordecai Tremaine had the grace to look uncomfortable.

"No," he confessed reluctantly. "No, I don't."

The inspector leaned back in his chair.

"That's a blessing, anyway," he remarked. "It's nice to know that somebody else thinks like I do in at least one particular. Carthallow wasn't the suicide type from all I've heard, and in any case there are one or two things I'd like to clear up before coming down on *that* side of the fence. Those forceps, for instance. And the sunglasses. What were *they* doing in the study?"

Mordecai Tremaine's hand went up to his pince-nez.

"Why," he said, "why, now I come to think of it, I don't ever remember seeing Carthallow wearing a pair of sunglasses."

"But Mrs. Carthallow said they belonged to her husband," Penross observed quietly.

"Yes," Tremaine agreed, "she did. And she also said that the forceps must have belonged to him, too, because he was always using patent medicines and various medical gadgets. But when I was talking to Carthallow one day—it was the first time I went to Paradise—he was full of how healthy a place it was and what little need he had of doctors. He didn't talk like a man who was a hypochondriac."

"I must admit," said Penross, "that she wasn't at all certain about the forceps. She said at first that she couldn't explain them, and it's natural enough that if they didn't belong to her she'd imagine they must have been her husband's."

Mordecai Tremaine stared thoughtfully out over the cliffs to where the sun had set in a wind-streaked sky.

"I'd like to know," he said, "just why Carthallow moved that desk of his into the center of the room."

"And *I'd* like to know," said Penross, "just who made such a mess of Mrs. Carthallow's portrait."

There was a silence. The inspector had lit his pipe and was drawing at it steadily. It was clear that he was waiting for something.

"I take it," Mordecai Tremaine said, "that you're wondering how long you'll be able to go before you're compelled to arrest Helen Carthallow?"

Penross said, "I've laid all the facts before the chief constable. He isn't very happy about things. You see, it *looks* as though we ought to arrest her straight away. But he doesn't want to take a step like that until he's absolutely certain we haven't tripped up anywhere. This isn't just a local affair where we might be able to cover up a mistake without too much publicity. It's headline stuff. You've seen what a write-up the newspapers have given it already. If we take Mrs. Carthallow into custody it's going to be on every front page. And if we *have* missed something…"

Jonathan Boyce looked at him with understanding.

"You have visions, Charles, of your head being presented on a charger to appease the howling mob. Is that it?"

"That," said Penross, "is it."

"Besides," interposed Mordecai Tremaine shrewdly, "she's still an attractive young woman. More so now that she isn't laying on the lipstick quite so lavishly. I can see your dilemma. But what are you going to do about it?"

"I'm glad we've managed to get around to it," Penross returned. "That's why I came. I told you I've laid the facts before the chief constable. That includes telling him about you. He doesn't want to call in the Yard—no offense, Jonathan—and he'll be wagging his tail if we can clear the case up from this end. He's prepared to hold back for at least a day or two and deal personally with any awkward questions that might be asked. If—"

He broke off. Tremaine said, "If?"

"You know all these people," Penross went on quickly. "You've had an opportunity of meeting them on intimate terms. They'll talk to you without setting a guard on their tongues. The chief constable knows all about you, of course, and how you've been able to help in other cases in a similar way. He's wondering whether you'd be willing to work in with us now. Naturally, it would be unofficial, but you'd have all the facilities you need."

"I seem to be fated," Mordecai Tremaine observed, "to play the skeleton at the feast."

Nevertheless, his eyes were bright. Chief constables did not issue such invitations casually. There must have been a good deal of discussion before Penross had come upon this mission, and flattering things must have been said about him. He said, "As a matter of fact, Charles, I've been doing quite a bit of thinking, and there are one or two points that puzzle me. I'd be glad of the opportunity of trying to clear them up, and if you think that I can be of help to you at the same time I'll be delighted to keep in touch with you."

Penross looked relieved.

"You've got the background to this thing, and you can tell whether anybody's behaving in a manner different to what you might have expected. You'll be able to spot all sorts of little points, perhaps, that a stranger couldn't hope to notice. In the meantime, of course, we'll be going ahead with the routine."

"I know what you mean, Charles," Mordecai Tremaine observed, rising to his feet. "I'm just as anxious as you are to prove she didn't do it. But apart from suicide—and I still feel we ought to keep open minds about that—the only way to clear her is to find somebody else who could have been in that house."

"It would certainly help," agreed Penross dryly.

Mordecai Tremaine surveyed him thoughtfully. He said, "Matilda Vickery said that the postman called at Paradise twice on the day Carthallow was shot—or shot himself. I imagine you'll be checking up with the postal authorities?"

"Naturally," Penross said. "Why?"

"I'd like to know the results of your inquiries," said Mordecai Tremaine. "I've a feeling they might prove interesting."

He left the inspector staring after him like a man who badly wanted to ask questions but who did not quite know where to begin.

24

When Mordecai Tremaine went into the drawing room it was obvious that a council of war was in progress.

"Helen's upstairs resting," said Hilda Eveland. "We've been putting our heads together trying to decide what to do about her."

"What to do about her?"

"Don't be obtuse, Mordecai," she told him. "You know perfectly well your friend the inspector doesn't believe the explanation she gave him of how Adrian came to be shot. Otherwise, why is he still asking questions and keeping his men at the house?"

Elton Steele looked up, his dark face clouded and grim and his big hand clenched about his pipe.

"She's shielding Imleyson."

Lewis Haldean made a movement of protest.

"That's prejudice, Elton. Be honest and admit it. Imleyson wasn't there. He couldn't have done it."

Roberta Fairham was sitting on a settee close by, her

pale eyes watching them both with an intensity Mordecai Tremaine did not like. She reminded him of a tigress, without movement but savagely bent upon making a kill and determined that her quarry should not escape her. She said, "The inspector knows that Lester couldn't have done it. He didn't go to the house at all."

Steele turned upon her with a gesture that seemed almost threatening.

"Are you trying to say that it *was* Helen?"

She quailed before the look in his eyes, but she would not retract.

"Helen admitted it herself," she countered. "After all, she *told* the police she shot Adrian."

"Accidentally," put in Haldean quickly. "Don't forget that, Roberta."

"There's only her word for it that it *was* an accident."

The words came hurriedly, as though she wanted to make the accusation before anyone could stop her. There were two vivid spots of color in her cheeks. There was a moment's silence. And then Hilda Eveland said, in a voice that was completely unlike her normal cheerful tones: "We all know why you'd like to hang her, Roberta. But I'd be careful not to say too much if I were you."

It was Lewis Haldean who saved the situation. He leaned forward, his blond beard glinting silkily, his voice vibrant.

"Let's admit there's something in what Roberta's said. We don't want to start bickering among ourselves. The thing's too serious. And on the surface it does look bad for Helen."

"*You're* not going back on her, are you, Lewis?" said Hilda Eveland.

"Of course not," he said, sharply for him. "I don't think for one moment she killed Adrian."

"Then how," Mordecai Tremaine said quietly, "do you think he died?"

The blond man turned to face him.

"I think he committed suicide," he said. "I knew Adrian better than anybody except Helen. He could be pretty unpleasant at times, but he never showed his unpleasant side to me, and we didn't get on badly. Sometimes he talked frankly with me, and I know that he was in a tight corner for money. I lent him a fair amount myself. It's no secret now—the police know all about it. He was worried. There's no doubt about that. And he was a creative artist. There's no doubt about that, either. When people of that type are up against it you can never be quite sure what they're going to do. They'll appear to be acting normally, and then without any warning they'll go over the edge."

Steele was obviously impressed by his sincerity.

"And that's what you think happened to Adrian?" he said.

Haldean nodded.

"That's what I think happened to him. There's more to it than that, of course. It's clear that Helen's hiding something. We've got to persuade her to let us know what it is. Once we've found out the reason for her telling the police that she shot Adrian we can start trying to help her in earnest. But there's nothing we can do until she's given us her story."

"She's already given her story," said Hilda Eveland, a frown creasing her plump face. "She's given it to the police."

"But as *you* admitted just now, Hilda, the police don't think it's the right one. That fellow Penross is no fool. If he doesn't believe her it's because he has some reason not to. Something doesn't fit, and if we can get Helen to be frank with us maybe we can help to make Penross change his mind."

There was a resentful look in Elton Steele's brooding face.

"You seem damned certain she hasn't told the whole truth."

"Don't be a fool," said Haldean, without malice. "It's no good refusing to face facts. *That* won't help her."

Roberta Fairham's face was old and shrewish. Malignancy was naked in her pale eyes.

"The facts seem plain enough," she said. "They had a quarrel. Everybody knows why. What about the portrait? How are you going to explain *that* away?"

"Maybe it was Adrian," said Steele slowly. "Maybe he didn't think he was doing her justice."

"No!" she said fiercely. "No! He would never have done a thing like that. He was a great artist. He couldn't produce bad work—it wasn't in him to fail, and he would never have destroyed something he had created!"

Her vehemence silenced them. Tremaine realized that it was because, although they disliked both the woman and what she had said, they knew that she was right.

There was a sound from the doorway. Instinctively all of them turned. Helen Carthallow was there.

Her face was very white, and there was strain in her eyes. She faced them almost challengingly. It was as though her beauty was backed by a quality of hard defiance.

It was plain from her attitude that she knew they had been talking about her. And it was equally plain from their embarrassed reaction to her appearance that they were aware that she knew.

Mordecai Tremaine seized upon his opportunity.

"You're looking tired," he said. "I think a breath of fresh air is what you need. Suppose we take a stroll in the garden?"

He thought as soon as he had spoken them that the words sounded a little too obvious. But there was, after all, no need for camouflage; all of them were too close to the reality of the situation for that. Hilda Eveland said, quickly, "Yes, why don't you, Helen? It will do you good."

Helen Carthallow made no objection. As he went out

of the room with her, Tremaine felt suddenly like an actor playing a part. He knew that they were aware of his friendship with Inspector Penross and that, although no word had been said, they realized that he wanted to speak to Helen Carthallow alone.

As they were going down the path she said, "Did the inspector send you?"

The hardness and the defiance were in her voice. Mordecai Tremaine looked at her over his pince-nez.

"Not exactly. But I do know a little of what he's thinking."

"So do I," she said. "I suppose that as soon as he's managed to find a bit more evidence I can expect the handcuffs. Isn't that it?"

"You must put yourself in Inspector Penross's place," he said quietly. "It's his job to investigate your husband's death. Whatever he may feel personally, he has to judge according to the facts. And the facts are that the explanations you've given him haven't been—frank. You can understand how it must look to him."

He thought from the momentary expression that came into her face that her attitude had softened and that she was going to confide in him. But when she spoke her voice was unyielding. "I can't help how it looks to Inspector Penross," she said. "I've told him what happened, and that's all there is to it."

"Is it?" Mordecai Tremaine put his hand on her arm. "Don't run away with the impression that the inspector wants to trap you. He wants to help you. He *will* help you. *If* you will let him." He waited, but there was no sign of response in her eyes. They remained cold, distant, and bitter. And after a moment or two he said, casually, "It's a good thing Mr. Imleyson wasn't there." She reacted so quickly that he knew that it was what she had been waiting for.

"What do you mean?"

"Isn't it obvious?"

She turned to face him. She was breathing rapidly, and there was a defensive look in her eyes.

"What has Lester to do with it? He wasn't there. The inspector knows he wasn't."

"Does he?"

Mordecai Tremaine displayed a deceptive lack of interest. He thought it might produce results.

Helen Carthallow's hand went to her throat. She could not hide the leaping shadowy fear that came at that moment.

"What—what does he suspect?"

"What *should* he suspect?"

The question brought her to the knowledge that she was betraying herself. The hardness came back into the white face.

"Nothing," she said. "Nothing at all."

They did not remain long in the garden. There could be no hope of any confidences now. They walked back to the house in silence.

There was a tense atmosphere in the room where the others were still gathered. Tremaine felt it as he passed through the doorway, and then he understood the reason for it.

Lester Imleyson was there. He was standing motionless, his eyes on Helen Carthallow.

"Good evening," he said.

Helen Carthallow's lips moved stiffly. She said, "Good evening, Lester."

Mordecai Tremaine pushed back his pince-nez. He looked from one of them to the other. Imleyson's face was unsmiling, with lines of strain about his eyes and a tautness in their depths. He took a step forward and held something out to her.

"I only came over to give you this," he said. "I believe it *is* yours?"

It was a lady's small silk handkerchief. A tiny sound escaped from Helen Carthallow's lips. For a moment there was no mask to conceal her thoughts, and Mordecai Tremaine saw the fear and horror naked in her face. It filled him with dismay and a terrible lurking doubt.

He heard her say in a voice that was a whisper barely under her control: "Yes. Yes, it is mine. Thank you for bringing it, Lester."

"Not at all," he said. His eyes met hers. As he passed over the handkerchief and she took it from him there was no contact between their fingers. "I don't want to disturb you," he added, levelly. "It's been a trying time. You should be resting as much as you can."

"Yes," she said, and now she had recovered herself, and her voice held that hard note. "It's been a trying time."

Lester Imleyson said good night, and she let him go without a further word.

And twenty minutes later, as he strolled slowly back across the cliffs, Mordecai Tremaine wondered uneasily what grim significance had underlain that brief, disturbing scene. For Lester Imleyson was reputed to be in love with Helen Carthallow, and he had seen for himself that rumor had not lied. At this time one would have expected Imleyson to have been at her side, comforting her, protecting her, proving his love.

Two people united against the world. That was the picture his romantic soul had expected to find. And instead they had stared at each other with the hard eyes of strangers.

25

The weather had changed, and a cold wind was playing across beaches upon which only a few well-wrapped souls, deck chairs placed with their backs to the sea, were braving the morning air. Mordecai Tremaine came briskly down the stone steps leading to the miniature promenade upon which was situated the pavilion housing the Falporth Follies, and as he did so he caught a glimpse of Morton Westfield.

The sight of the man's queerly shaped bald head as he went into the building by the stage door started his mind exploring a new channel of thought. He wondered whether Inspector Penross had yet managed to obtain any information on the subject of Westfield's antecedents. No doubt Adrian Carthallow's death had driven all other matters into the background. He would have to mention it the next time they met.

For he had a feeling that the relationship between Morton Westfield and the artist had been an intriguing one; that early morning rendezvous on the beach had not been arranged without reason.

However, it was not Westfield with whom he was immediately concerned. He went on, scanning the faces of the passersby, and climbed the hill leading from the other side of the promenade up to the town. He did not think he would be likely to meet Lester Imleyson at Hilda Eveland's again—not, at least, as long as Helen Carthallow was there—but fortunately in such a small place as Falporth he could be reasonably sure of running into him sooner or later if he kept a sharp watch.

He found him where the road ran toward the harbor, staring moodily over the rails at the fishing craft lying high and dry on the sands uncovered by the retreating tide.

"Hullo, Imleyson. Didn't expect to see you just here."

The other turned from the rails. A frown brought his brows together.

"Sure you haven't been looking for me?" he said.

The blunt challenge in his manner called forth an equal bluntness in Mordecai Tremaine. That gentleman settled his pince-nez more firmly.

"Very well, I *have* been looking for you. I want to talk to you."

"No doubt on behalf of your friend the inspector?"

"What," said Mordecai Tremaine, "makes you afraid that might be the reason?"

"Who said anything about being afraid?" demanded Imleyson with sudden fierceness.

"Nobody," returned Tremaine mildly. "Nobody at all." He moved up to the rails at the other side so that he could talk without fear of being overheard by any third person. "I would have thought," he said, "that you of all people would have been interested in trying to help Mrs. Carthallow."

Imleyson stiffened, and his hands clenched upon the metal.

"What do you mean by that?"

"I think we understand each other well enough."

"Where does that take us? Carthallow's death was an accident."

"You mean Mrs. Carthallow *says* it was."

Imleyson's reply did not come immediately, but when it did the words were deliberate and were underlined by the emphasis he gave them.

"If Mrs. Carthallow says it was an accident, it's quite sufficient for me."

"It's what I would have expected from you," Mordecai Tremaine observed. "Naturally, it's what you *want* to believe. But you can't be certain it is the truth. After all, you weren't there." He added, after the slightest of pauses: "You weren't, were you?"

Imleyson said, "No. I wasn't. But I know Helen—Mrs. Carthallow. I know it couldn't have been anything else but an accident."

"Let me see," Tremaine said musingly. "You were coming

back from Wadestow and your car broke down. That's right, isn't it?"

"Yes, that's right."

"Where did you go when you did get back here? You didn't go to Paradise at all?"

"No," said Imleyson. "I went—"

He broke off. He eyed his companion aggressively. He said, "There's no reason why I should answer all your blasted questions. I'm not on trial, am I?"

"No," said Mordecai Tremaine, "you're not on trial."

But from the manner in which he said it he left Imleyson in no doubt as to what he really meant.

He met Penross half an hour later as the inspector was coming out of the police station, set discreetly in one of the side streets of the town. Penross said, "Hullo. Anything to report?"

"Nothing definite," said Mordecai Tremaine. "I had a talk with Mrs. Carthallow last night, and I've just left Imleyson. I don't feel very happy about them."

"You mean," Penross said, giving him a shrewd glance, "the lovebirds aren't cooing any more?"

Tremaine nodded. The inspector adjusted his pace, and they walked slowly along together.

"I'd already noticed it," he went on. "Doesn't seem to fit, does it? I'd like to know whether it's genuine."

"You think it might be a put-up job between them?"

"Why not? I gather Imleyson's been sweet on Mrs. Carthallow for some time. Normally that would give him a seat in the front row of the suspects, and both of them must be aware of it. It's possible that this apparent coolness between them is an act that's intended to put me off the scent."

Mordecai Tremaine gave his companion a long, reflective look.

"What's on your mind, Charles?"

"Suppose," Penross said, "they did it together? Oh, I know that a lot of things will need explaining. But the motive's there right enough. Carthallow was getting awkward. Didn't seem to be playing the complacent husband quite so willingly. Maybe he threatened to make things so difficult that they decided that the only way out was to kill him. According to Mrs. Carthallow's story, of course, her husband never was so obligingly broad-minded about her association with Imleyson when they were alone, and it was part of his way of hurting her to keep up a pretense in public of being very fond of her. But as far as I can see there's only her word for that. If only," he added, "there was some way of proving that somebody else did get into that house after all."

It was obvious from the inspector's manner that there was more behind his words than he had so far indicated.

"What have you found out?" said Tremaine quietly.

"I've been along to the post office," Penross returned. "You mentioned that an inquiry there might prove interesting. It did." He said, "Did you think there might be anything peculiar about the fact that the postman called at Paradise twice on the day Carthallow was killed?"

Mordecai Tremaine nodded.

"Yes," he said, "I did. And was there?"

"There was. He *didn't* call twice."

"The one call he made being halfway through the morning. Am I right?"

"You are," Penross said. "But how did you know that?"

"I didn't. But I had my suspicions. When I went into the house with Mrs. Carthallow that day there was an envelope lying on the hall table. It was unsealed—the kind of thing that usually contains a circular. Very often they're not sent out until the second delivery. There was no sign of any other letter. It came back to my mind after you'd told me that the postman had made two calls. I realized, of course, that it was quite possible that there *had* been something else delivered that had been dealt with and that the circular had been left on the table because it was obviously unimportant, but neither Adrian Carthallow nor his wife had been in for long—they certainly weren't there when the postman was making his rounds—and I thought that the fact that there hadn't appeared to be anything else about was at least worth looking into."

The inspector gave a murmur of approval.

"It was," he said. "The man who does the Paradise delivery is certain that he made only the one call. There's usually a fair amount of correspondence for Carthallow's place, and a blank day is rare enough to be noticeable. The point is why did Matilda Vickery say she saw him call twice?"

"Because," Mordecai Tremaine said, "she's under the impression that she did. Only the first time she saw the postman go across the bridge it wasn't the postman at all."

"You mean it was someone wearing a postman's uniform?"

"Precisely. You remember Chesterton's story about the man nobody noticed because they took him for granted? In this case the person was seen all right—by Matilda Vickery. But when she saw the postman's uniform she took it for granted that it *was* the postman and didn't pay any more attention."

Penross looked at him expectantly.

"And who," he said, "do you think it *really* was?"

"I think," said Mordecai Tremaine, "it was Roberta Fairham."

26

It was quite obviously not the answer for which the inspector had been waiting. He looked disappointed.

"Roberta Fairham?" he said, slowly, like one who saw his hopes fading in a blaze of unexpected, wilting light. "What makes you pick on *her*?"

"It's guesswork," said Tremaine. "But I think it's sound. I met her once at a fancy dress ball in London. She went as a postman. And when I was thinking about the people who were known to have crossed that bridge, trying to find a loophole somewhere, the incident came back to me. I felt reasonably certain that if there had been anything odd about those two calls the postman was supposed to have made, Roberta Fairham was mixed up in it. She knew about Matilda Vickery being able to see the bridge, and she realized that if she wanted to get into the house without being recognized she'd have to make use of a disguise that wouldn't arouse suspicion. It was a piece of luck for her that there was no early morning post that day and that the official postman didn't have to call until later."

"I'll need to have a talk with Miss Fairham," said Penross grimly. "That young lady is going to find herself with some explaining to do."

Nevertheless there was a reluctance in his manner. Mordecai Tremaine, who thought he understood the reason for it, put a hand on his arm.

"Don't take it to heart, Charles," he said quietly. "This is only the beginning. Maybe something else will come to light soon that will make things look more the way you want them to."

"What d'you mean?" said Penross, a little too quickly.

"I mean Lester Imleyson," Mordecai Tremaine returned. "As you very well know. If you could prove that he *was* in the house you'd be a lot happier."

"It would certainly be tidier," Penross admitted. "It would help to explain that portrait. If anybody had a motive for wanting to destroy it, he certainly did."

They walked on down the road and instinctively turned together in the direction of Hilda Eveland's house. Tremaine said, after a moment or two: "By the way, were you able to find out anything about Westfield?"

Penross wrinkled his brows.

"Westfield? Oh, you mean the chap at the Follies. As a matter of fact I'm expecting a report at any moment." A sharper note came into his voice. He said, "You don't think *he's* mixed up in it, do you?"

"I wouldn't be at all surprised," said Mordecai Tremaine airily. "But then, I'm prepared not to be surprised at anything."

The inspector relapsed into a silence tinged with suspicion. He did not make any further reference to Westfield during the remainder of their journey, but Tremaine knew that he was giving the actor considerable thought.

Hilda Eveland greeted them on their arrival.

"If you want to see Helen, Inspector," she said, "I'm afraid she's out. She's gone into the town, and I doubt if she'll be in before lunch."

"It's all right, Mrs. Eveland," Penross told her. "It's Miss Vickery I'd like to see."

She looked at him with an expression of surprise.

"Matilda? She's here, of course. Would you like to go up?"

Mordecai Tremaine led the way, and they went into Matilda Vickery's room. She was lying back on the pillows so that she could look out of the big window. She turned her head as they came in, and they saw that she was in pain.

"I'm sorry to worry you again, Miss Vickery," Penross said, "but there's a small point I'd like to clear up regarding the people you told me went across the bridge to Paradise on the day Mr. Carthallow was shot."

She drew back against the pillows. There was fear as well as pain in her eyes. Her fingers plucked nervously at the sheet.

"The—the people who went across the bridge?" she said, and it seemed that she could barely utter the words.

"Yes," said Penross. Her agitation had not escaped him. He regarded her curiously. "You told me you saw the postman twice," he went on. "I wonder whether you could give me a little more information about those two occasions?"

The fear in her eyes gave way before a sudden, upsurging relief. She said, as though trying to gain time to face a new situation: "Oh—the postman. Yes, I remember. He did call twice. What is it you want to know, Inspector?"

"What I want to know, Miss Vickery," said Penross, "is whether you're certain it *was* the postman?"

There was nothing strained or false about her reaction.

"Of course I'm certain," she said. "He called once with the early morning delivery, and again later in the day."

"Did you recognize him?"

"I recognized his uniform. I didn't see his face clearly. The bridge isn't near enough for that. But I know the postman who delivers there. It's Jack Roskom. He lives on Carbis Street."

"I know," said Penross. "Are you prepared to swear that it was the same postman who called on each occasion?"

She was looking uncertain now. His insistence had shown her that he believed there was an element of doubt in the statement she had made to him, and she was searching in her memory for some reason for it.

"I don't understand you, Inspector," she said slowly.

"I've seen Jack Roskom," he explained. "He tells me that he made only one call that day. There was no early morning delivery."

"You mean it *wasn't* him?" she said, startled. And, after a moment or two, she went on: "There *was* something different about him that first time. He didn't seem quite so tall, and his walk wasn't the same. But I didn't pay all that much attention although I *do* remember now that I wondered whether there could be a new man on the round."

"The position seems to be," said Penross, "that you took the postman for granted because of the uniform. Is that right?"

She nodded her agreement, and he said, "Can you think of anyone else whom it might have been? Anyone you know. Could it have been, for instance—a woman?"

"A woman?" Clearly the thought was an unexpected one. She leaned back against the pillows, and they could tell that she was desperately anxious to help them. "It *might* have been. But I couldn't be certain. It was too far off."

Mordecai Tremaine said, "Each time the postman called I take it that you saw him go across the bridge and come back again?"

"Yes," she told him.

"On the first occasion was there a considerable interval

between the time you saw him—or her—go over and when he or she returned?"

She thought again for a moment or two, and then she nodded.

"Yes, there was. It was quite a while before he came back. I can remember more about it now. I thought he must have had a registered letter and had been trying to get a reply, not knowing there was no one at the house."

"But he did come back?"

"Oh yes, he came back. I would have noticed if he hadn't."

Mordecai Tremaine looked significantly at the inspector. He saw the chagrin come into his eyes, and he knew that Penross understood what he had tried to convey.

Maybe there *had* been a false postman. Maybe it *had* been Roberta Fairham. But it didn't help. Because she hadn't stayed. She had left again before Adrian Carthallow had returned.

Penross said, "Thank you, Miss Vickery. I think that's all I need to ask you."

"I'm sorry if I haven't been of much assistance," she said.

The inspector was turning to walk toward the door when Mordecai Tremaine said, quietly, "I think you *could* be of assistance, Miss Vickery."

Something in his tone made Penross pause. The fear had come flooding back into Matilda Vickery's eyes. Her voice was unsteady. "What—what do you mean?"

"I mean," Tremaine said, "you could tell us the truth."

The room was so quiet that they could hear the faint sighing sound of her breathing. Penross was quite still, watching her.

"I've—already told you the truth," she said, with an effort.

"I'm afraid," Mordecai Tremaine said, "you haven't. You haven't told us that you saw Mr. Imleyson go across the bridge."

She raised herself from her pillows, facing them with a pitiful defiance.

"No! It isn't true! I didn't see Lester!"

Mordecai Tremaine went across to her. He took one of the crippled hands in his own. He said, gently, "I know you want to shield him. He's always been a favorite of yours, hasn't he? But you can't go on with this. The truth is bound to come out before long, and it's much better that you should tell us of your own free will. After all, if people conceal evidence— even if it's from the best of motives—it looks as though they have something to hide. In the end it only makes things worse for the person they've been trying to help."

"Lester didn't do it," she said. "He didn't kill him!"

"Nobody," he told her, "is saying that Mr. Imleyson killed Mr. Carthallow. But I'm sure you realize that if you persist in withholding important information about his movements the inspector has no choice but to regard him with suspicion. And you *did* see him, didn't you?"

Under his steady gaze her own eyes dropped.

"Yes," she admitted, in a low voice. "I saw him."

Penross made a movement in her direction, but Mordecai Tremaine gestured to him not to speak.

"It was after Mr. Carthallow went in, wasn't it?" he said.

She nodded. Her words were barely audible.

"Mr. Carthallow was first, and then Mrs. Carthallow crossed the bridge. Lester went over a little while afterward."

"When did he come away from the house?"

"It was after Mrs. Carthallow left."

"You mean," said Tremaine, "it was between the time Mrs. Carthallow went down to the beach to fetch me and the time we went back together?"

"Yes," she told him. "That was it."

The distress in her face was painful to see. Mordecai Tremaine's sentimental soul was troubled, but he knew there was nothing else he could have done.

"Don't think," he said, "that we want to try and persecute Mr. Imleyson for any reason. If he's innocent of Mr. Carthallow's death it's the inspector's job to help him and to do his utmost to prove it. You must believe that."

"Of course," said Penross, a little gruffly. "Of course. I shall have to ask you for another statement, Miss Vickery, embodying what you've just said. It's a pity you didn't tell me earlier."

There was a note of irritation in his voice. Mordecai

Tremaine said, quickly, "Technically, you know, you've committed an offense by not telling the whole truth, but, under the circumstances, I think the inspector will be prepared to overlook it. Eh, Inspector?"

Penross still had a disgruntled air. But it was impossible to be sternly official with a woman in Matilda Vickery's pathetic state. He said, "Yes. I'll overlook it. Under the circumstances."

When he was walking away from the house a few moments later, however, he allowed his feelings to find expression.

"Why the devil," he said, "she couldn't have told me all that before, I'm damned if I know."

"Your future looks like being a grim one then, Charles," observed his companion. "Because you *do* know."

"What are you getting at now?" Penross demanded.

"Matilda Vickery has always had a soft corner for young Imleyson," Tremaine said. "He goes to see her quite a lot—takes her little luxuries now and again. She's known him since he was a boy, and she'd do anything for him. Naturally, she knew all about what was going on between Imleyson and Helen Carthallow, and as soon as she heard about Carthallow's death she connected it with the fact that she'd seen Lester Imleyson cross the bridge just about the time he must have been killed. She's an intelligent woman, and she knew perfectly well that her evidence might put a rope around his neck. So she decided she wasn't going to talk."

"I suppose you can't blame her," Penross said, mollified. "I wonder whether Imleyson knew she was going to support his alibi?"

"I doubt it. He probably didn't think of the fact that the bridge could be observed from her window when he said he didn't go to the house. No doubt he took ordinary precautions against being seen and thought he was safe. The interesting thing to my mind is what he's thinking now that he knows Matilda's been perjuring herself for him."

The inspector pulled thoughtfully at his chin.

"Yes," he said, "that *is* interesting. If he killed Carthallow he must be in a pretty jittery state at the moment wondering just when the balloon's going up."

Mordecai Tremaine settled his pince-nez firmly on his nose.

"You were saying not long ago, Charles, that the trouble with this case was that there weren't enough people who could have committed the crime. The field seems to be opening out."

"It's opening right enough," said Penross.

His tone was grim, and it was easy enough to read his thoughts. If Lester Imleyson had crossed the bridge he could have killed Adrian Carthallow. And he could have defaced Helen Carthallow's portrait.

And he had had a perfect motive for doing both.

27

When he was still some distance off, Mordecai Tremaine thought that the man on the seat at the end of the gardens was Lewis Haldean. The blond beard and the Viking profile were too distinct to be mistaken.

The fine weather had given further signs of coming to an end, and a wind was blowing with an unpleasant and unseasonable wintriness through the town. Shielded by a steeply rising hill that served as an ideal windbreak, Valance Gardens provided an obvious refuge, and after leaving Inspector Penross to his official duties Tremaine had made his way there with the intention of settling down to half an hour or so of quiet communion with himself. Several vague but insistent theories were worrying at his mind. The sight of Haldean, however, caused him to alter his plans. It was pleasanter to talk than to think. Besides, although this he tried not to admit, it was much less arduous.

The blond man turned sharply at his hail as he drew nearer.

"Morning, Tremaine. Didn't see you. My mind was miles away."

Mordecai Tremaine sat down at his side.

"You look worried."

"I am worried," Haldean said. "Damned worried. I don't like the way things are going at all. What's that inspector friend of yours up to?"

"Only what you might expect. Trying to find out how Adrian Carthallow was shot."

"Thanks," Haldean returned dryly. "What I'm anxious to find out is what ideas he has on the subject. About Helen, I mean. If I could do something to help her it wouldn't seem so bad, but she won't talk to any of us. It's as though she's built a wall around herself and we're all outside it, unable to get through to her."

"You think she's hiding something?"

"Isn't it obvious she must be?" Haldean said. "There's no need for me to beat about the bush with *you*."

"No," said Mordecai Tremaine, "I don't think there is. I—"

He broke off, his eyes upon a man who had just walked from the shelter of a thatched cottage restaurant some twenty yards away at the edge of the gardens. It was Morton Westfield. He seemed to be in a hurry. Tremaine nudged his companion.

"D'you see that fellow over there? The one with the

unusually shaped head just going past the boating pool. D'you know him?"

Haldean said, reluctantly, "Where? Oh, I see. No, I don't know him. Am I supposed to?"

He seemed put out by the change of subject and disinclined to be drawn after what he considered to be a red herring. Tremaine said, "I thought you might be acquainted with him, that's all. He was on intimate terms with Adrian Carthallow."

"Was he?"

"You've never met him at any time?"

"Not as far as I can remember," said Haldean testily. "I knew a good deal about Adrian's business, but I didn't know everything."

He seemed to realize that he was acting ungraciously, and his manner softened.

"Sorry. I'm afraid I'm a bit on edge and inclined to snap at people. This wretched business and the uncertainty about Helen have been playing on my nerves."

"That's all right," Mordecai Tremaine said. "I know how you feel."

"I wonder if you do?" said Haldean quietly. His face was very serious. He said, after an instant or two: "Who *was* that fellow you pointed out?"

"His name's Westfield. He's in the Follies company at the Pavilion."

"I haven't been to their show yet. You say Adrian knew him well?"

"That was the impression I gained," returned Tremaine. "I saw them together on a couple of occasions, and each time they were talking in a confidential fashion."

"Adrian didn't say anything about him to you?"

"Not," said Mordecai Tremaine carefully, "exactly. Beyond telling me that it couldn't have been Westfield I saw him with the first time."

The blond man frowned. He clasped his hands around his knees, staring over the flower beds.

"Adrian had something on his mind," he said thoughtfully. "He didn't give anything definite away to me, but I'm certain of it from the way he used to act. Perhaps—"

"Perhaps?" Mordecai Tremaine prompted hopefully, but Haldean shook his head.

"No, it's no good. Westfield couldn't have had anything to do with it. Nobody went over that bridge except Helen and Adrian."

Mordecai Tremaine eyed his companion reflectively. And then he said, "Somebody else *did* go over. Lester Imleyson."

"Imleyson!"

Haldean turned a startled face upon him. Consternation echoed in his voice. He said, unsteadily, "You're not—you're not serious?"

"I'm afraid," Mordecai Tremaine said, "I am. He went into the house shortly after Mrs. Carthallow."

The blond man leaned back. He was trying to avoid betraying how much the news had shocked and distressed him, but he had been taken unawares and he was not succeeding too well.

"Does the inspector know?"

Tremaine nodded.

"Yes, he knows."

Haldean made an obvious effort to give the impression that he did not think the incident was so important after all.

"I dare say Imleyson has some reasonable explanation," he said, attempting casualness.

"It's possible," Mordecai Tremaine agreed, dryly. "But it doesn't look too good, does it? There's only one theory Inspector Penross can follow on the face of things."

"What theory's that?" said Haldean, unwillingly, and Mordecai Tremaine pushed back his pince-nez.

"That they did it together," he said, deliberately brutal.

Lewis Haldean's face looked suddenly old and lined.

"It can't be true—it just can't. Not—Helen." With an abrupt movement he put his hand on his companion's shoulder. Tremaine felt his fingers digging into the flesh beneath his coat. "She *couldn't* have had anything to do with it. I tell you, man, I know her too well."

Mordecai Tremaine regarded him steadily.

"Are you in love with her?"

Slowly the blond man's grip relaxed. He turned away.

"What if I am?" he said. "Does it make her innocence any less sure?"

"No. But it helps to explain why you're so anxious to save her. And it's important to see that all the various pieces in the puzzle fit together."

Haldean's toe traced a pattern on the graveled path. He did not look at Tremaine. He said, "I understand. You're working with the inspector, and you've got to make certain where everybody comes in. I'd just like to say this. I've never told anyone else what I've just told you. Certainly I've never told Helen. I'd appreciate it if she didn't learn it now."

"You have my assurance," Mordecai Tremaine said gravely, "that she won't learn it from me."

There was a wry twist to Haldean's lips.

"Don't imagine that I'm being heroic," he said. "It's just that I'm not so blind that I can't see the truth when it's staring me in the face. I know that I don't stand a chance with Helen, and I'm not anxious to have my emotions paraded in public."

"Naturally not," said Mordecai Tremaine, and added: "What's your opinion of Elton Steele?"

"Steele?" The blond man was disconcerted again by this

sudden switching of interest. He echoed the name blankly. "Steele? There isn't any bad blood between us—if that's what you mean."

"He's in love with Mrs. Carthallow, too, isn't he?"

"I believe he is. But we don't exactly go around exchanging intimate details of that description."

"No," Mordecai Tremaine said. "I suppose not. I mentioned Steele because he rather intrigues me. He strikes me as being a man who might be capable of anything under certain circumstances. And if he's in love with Mrs. Carthallow—"

He did not need to finish the sentence. Haldean took him up.

"If *that's* in your mind," he said sharply, "you can forget it. The idea's absurd. I've known Elton Steele for some time, and he isn't the type to go around murdering people."

"Still, there is a motive."

"You couldn't describe Adrian as a popular figure," Haldean said. "If it's motive you want I dare say you could find dozens of people who might have wanted to get at him. But that doesn't prove that one of them did it. They weren't at the house—and neither was Steele."

"True," Mordecai Tremaine observed. "But Lester Imleyson was."

Haldean said, "All right. So you *have* got something. But don't let it lead you into seeing things that aren't there. For pretty obvious reasons I've no cause to try and whitewash Imleyson, but he isn't a murderer any more than Steele. Come to think of it, I don't know any of us who is."

"Nobody," said Mordecai Tremaine, "likes to think they've a murderer among their acquaintances. But it's a thing that *has* happened to quite a lot of people."

The blond man seemed to be thinking something over. He fingered his beard. He said, haltingly, "Look here, it's an open secret that you and the inspector are hand in glove. You know my feelings about things. If there's any way in which I can help to get this frightful business cleared up just tell me and I'll do all I can."

There was a smile on Mordecai Tremaine's lips.

"So far," he said, "your help has consisted of trying to convince me that nobody I've mentioned could have killed Adrian Carthallow. What I'm anxious to find out is who *did*."

Haldean acknowledged the thrust with an apologetic gesture.

"I dare say I have been a bit of a wet blanket from your point of view. But you know where I stand. I still can't get rid of a hunch that it was suicide. Maybe it does look all wrong, but I knew Adrian and I know Helen. If you could get her to talk I'm sure you'd find I'm right."

Tremaine did not debate the question. He extracted his big pocket watch and glanced down at it.

"I must be off," he said. "Getting Mrs. Carthallow to talk," he added, as he rose to his feet, "hasn't been easy so far. Why don't *you* have a try with her? Between ourselves I can tell you this. If you can prove she's innocent there won't be a happier man than Inspector Penross."

He nodded to his companion and set off along the path before Haldean could make any comment. He had an appointment with Charles Penross at Paradise, and it was an appointment for which he did not wish to be late. For the inspector had sent a message to Roberta Fairham that he wished to see her there, and Miss Fairham's reaction to the item of information that was to be laid before her was likely to prove interesting.

Penross was already at the house when he arrived. Mordecai Tremaine crossed the bridge and went up the winding drive to find him in Carthallow's study, staring pensively out through the gap in the trees toward the sea. The inspector turned as he came in.

"She's not here?" said Tremaine. "Good. I was hoping I hadn't missed her. I'm a bit late—stayed talking to Lewis Haldean in Valance Gardens."

Penross nodded abstractedly. Tremaine said, "You look as though there've been developments, Charles."

"Not exactly developments," Penross returned. There was a note of gloom in his voice. "I've been studying the reports on

Colonel Neale. He's still in Falporth all right. And he hasn't what you might call a reliable alibi for the time Carthallow was killed."

"No?"

"No," the inspector said. "He took a stroll along the cliffs—in *this* direction. He didn't see anybody he knew and didn't speak to anybody who might be able to confirm his alibi. We've made a check at his hotel on the times he went out and came back, but there's a sizeable gap in between. And it's the sort of gap that could prove awkward."

"What was your man's impression of him?"

"Favorable enough as far as it went. Neale answered questions without any fuss and didn't make any bones about the fact that he didn't approve of Carthallow."

"But he said he didn't kill him?"

"Of course. I wasn't expecting anything else. But I wish his alibi was a bit tighter. You can never be certain what a man like Neale will do. He's the dyed-in-the-wool Army type—been used to having people running around after him and treating him as a tin god. And by all accounts he took a bad knock over that daughter of his."

"What you mean," said Tremaine, "is that you think he might have regarded himself as quite legitimately able to treat Adrian Carthallow like he might have dealt with an enemy under active service conditions?"

"Something of the sort," Penross agreed. "Anything—odd about it?"

"Not at all. It sounds perfectly logical. But when I first told you about Colonel Neale being here," Mordecai Tremaine observed quietly, "you knew all about *that*. It didn't seem to impress you very much then. What's the reason for the change in your outlook?"

"If anybody knows the answer," Penross said, "*you* do. When this case started only Mrs. Carthallow and her husband were supposed to have been in the house. Now we know that at least two other people came here as well. I'm not taking things for granted anymore, and that's why I'm keeping an open mind about Neale."

"What explanation did Imleyson give you?"

"So far he hasn't given one. He's gone into Wadestow—on business for his father. Apparently it's genuine enough. I've left a message that I'd like to see him as soon as he gets back."

Mordecai Tremaine nodded. He was moving restlessly about the room, as though there was a special problem worrying at his mind. He stopped beneath the point in the picture rail where the bullet that had killed Adrian Carthallow had been embedded. The damaged section of the rail had been neatly cut away.

"You've had the bullet examined, Charles?"

"The whole thing went down to the lab," Penross said.

"The ballistics people got the bullet out and checked it. There's no doubt that it came from Carthallow's gun. The markings tally. There were still five rounds left, and they were able to put it through all the routine tests. We found the cartridge case from the shot that was fired, and the markings on that have been checked as well. Carthallow's fingerprints were found on the bullets that were in the chamber, but all that proves is that he loaded the thing. It doesn't take us any further in telling us who fired it."

"It was a pretty big hole, wasn't it?" said Tremaine. "Did your science people make any special comments?"

"As a matter of fact," said Penross slowly, "there were one or two rather odd features. There was a certain amount of blackening, and they found powder grains in the wood. But you do sometimes get freak results with firearms."

"So I understand," said Mordecai Tremaine thoughtfully.

He did not pursue the matter, and in a moment or two the inspector led the way up to the studio.

"The Fairham woman should be here any time now," he explained, "and I want to make the most of it when she gets here."

Tremaine looked around once more at the crayon sketches, watercolors, and oils scattered about the room.

"She used to make a great fuss about Carthallow's work. The first time I came here she went off into a lyrical outburst about what one of the art critics had written about him. Even Carthallow felt embarrassed. There's no doubt about his versatility though. He could turn his hand to anything. The trouble was he knew it and tried to tell the world about it."

Penross picked up a tube of vermilion and balanced it idly in his hand.

"Art isn't much in my line," he remarked. "I never could understand why people part with thousands of pounds in good money for a painting on canvas."

"Art," said Mordecai Tremaine, "is universal. When a man paints a picture on the rocky walls of a cave he's doing something that will still be understood centuries later by every other man who sees it."

"I dare say," said Penross, unimpressed. He replaced the tube of pigment. "I grant you, though, there are people who seem to be able to do some pretty tricky things with paintings. These restorer fellows, for instance. I remember reading once about two paintings done on panels that were taken right off and put on canvas instead."

"Two by Rubens," Tremaine said. "They're in the Louvre in Paris."

He was about to launch into a dissertation on the subject when they heard the muffled sound of the front-door bell. Penross looked relieved.

"That sounds like our lady now."

In a few moments Roberta Fairham was shown into the studio by the constable who had been posted below. She had cast off some of her finery. Her face was free of makeup, and she was wearing a dark-gray costume severe in style; her role, obviously, was one of tragedy. She was in ostentatious mourning for Adrian Carthallow.

She paused in the entrance to the studio and looked about her as though the place held painful memories. She said, in a voice low with grief, "You wanted to see me, Inspector?"

"That's correct, Miss Fairham," Penross said, impersonally. The pale eyes regarded him reproachfully.

"I've told you all I can," she said, "but of course if there is anything further you wish to know I'll do my best to help you. I'm sorry you felt it necessary to ask me here. This house is too full of Adrian's—Mr. Carthallow's—presence to make it easy for me to enter it."

Penross said, "You were very fond of Mr. Carthallow, weren't you, Miss Fairham?"

Her head went up. The pale, indeterminate face held a consciously proud defiance.

"I'm not ashamed of it. I loved him."

For an instant or two the inspector looked at her. And then his hand went out and with a swift gesture he brought the easel around so that she was staring at the savagely daubed portrait.

"Is that why you did *this*?"

His voice was cold, scornful, and accusing. It whipped the color into her cheeks as though his palm had slapped them stingingly. It came so much without warning that she recoiled, her hand flying to her lips.

"I don't know what you mean," she said unsteadily.

"I think you do, Miss Fairham," he told her. "I'm waiting for your explanation of why you lied to me when you said that you didn't come to this house on the day Mr. Carthallow died."

"I *didn't* lie! I *didn't* come!"

The words were edged with a shrill desperation. Penross heard it and knew that her guard was down.

"I have a witness who saw you," he said remorselessly. "You would be well advised to tell me the truth. You went into the house wearing a postman's uniform."

They saw what confidence was left in her face drain slowly away, leaving it small and viperish, as Mordecai Tremaine had known it once before when she had been speaking of Helen Carthallow. The mask of grief had been stripped from her.

"All right," she said, between her teeth. "If you know so much I *did* come here."

"And you *did* deface this portrait?"

"Yes!" she flung at him. "I did! And I'd do it again!"

She made a movement toward the easel as though she

intended to put her threat into immediate execution, and Mordecai Tremaine stepped instinctively in front of her. It had the effect of drawing her attention upon him. She stared at him fixedly, and he saw the understanding sharpen her eyes and the vixenish hate twist her lips.

"So it was *you*. I might have guessed it, with your poking and prying into other people's affairs. You saw me that night at the Arts Ball."

"Yes," said Mordecai Tremaine, "I saw you that night— wearing the same uniform."

Penross said, "In your own interests, Miss Fairham, I think you'd better tell me exactly what you did."

She turned to face him again.

"I'll tell you! Why shouldn't I? It was just as you said. I wore the postman's uniform under my bathing wrap so that if I'd met anybody on the way they'd have thought I was just going for an early morning swim. When I got to the bridge I took the wrap off and put it in the bushes. I knew that there was no one at the house and that the only danger was that someone might see me from a distance. I was certain that if they did they'd take me for the postman and not pay any more attention to me."

"How did you get into the house?"

"Adrian gave me a key." She saw the inspector's look of surprise, and her voice became harder. "It's true. I understood

Adrian. He didn't always show it in public, but he could be kind and gentle."

"I'm not disputing your word," Penross said. "There was no sign of an entry having been made forcibly. Tell me the rest."

"You know it already. I came up here to the studio. Adrian never let anyone see his work when he was engaged on a portrait, but I knew what he was doing. He was painting—*her*."

She bit out the last word with a savage emphasis. And then her control began to leave her and the sentences came tumbling and disjointed as though they were being forced out of her by some dreadful inner force she could not resist.

"I asked him to paint *my* portrait. He laughed—said he didn't have the time. And then I discovered what he was doing—painting her instead. I couldn't stand it. I wasn't going to let him finish it—I wasn't going to have them all sneering about me, smirking behind my back. *She* didn't love him. She never did. I squeezed out all the tubes I could over the canvas. I rubbed them in. I told myself when I was doing it that it was *her* face I was destroying. It was *her* fine beauty that was under my hands…"

There was a dribble of froth at the corners of her lips; her features were twisted and distorted. Penross said, quietly, "And what then?"

Her fury died away. She looked at him slyly.

"I went back," she said. "I know what you'd like to think,

and it isn't true. I locked up the house again and went away. I wasn't here when Adrian came. I wasn't here when he was killed. If you know about my crossing the bridge you know that, too. *She* did it. *She* killed him so that she could have that fancy man of hers!"

Penross did not say anything. She *had* gone away. Matilda Vickery had confirmed it, and Matilda Vickery had not lied. There was no reason for her to have lied. Not like there had been where Lester Imleyson had been concerned.

At last: "I'd like you to go down to the lounge, Miss Fairham," he told her, "and wait for me there. I must have your statement prepared so that you can sign it."

And when she had descended the narrow stairs and they were once more alone in the studio, he looked at his companion.

"Not a very pretty story," he said grimly.

Mordecai Tremaine nodded. He was thinking of a viciously hurtling surfboard that might have done grievous injury. It wasn't a very pretty story. In fact, it wasn't pretty at all.

28

There was on Lester Imleyson's good-looking face the sullen expression of a man who knew that he was under suspicion but who was determined to give nothing away. Mordecai Tremaine, taking a morning stroll over the cliffs, had encountered him coming from the direction of Trecarne Head. He had not seen Penross since his interview with Roberta Fairham on the previous day, but he was confident that the inspector would by this time have confronted Imleyson with the challenging fact that he had been seen at Paradise. The younger man's attitude made it clear at once that he was in no mood for finesse, and Tremaine went straight to the point.

"I gather there's been a development since I saw you yesterday."

Imleyson's reaction was as aggressive as he had expected it would be.

"I don't doubt that you know all about it. When am I to be shown the handcuffs?"

"*Has* there been any talk about handcuffs?" Mordecai Tremaine said mildly.

"Your friend Penross didn't trouble to hide his opinion."

"But he didn't arrest you."

Imleyson gave him a sharp glance.

"Maybe he thought it wouldn't look so good if he had to release me again because he'd made a mistake."

They were standing near the edge of the cliffs. Mordecai Tremaine stared out over the water, the wind whipping at his cheeks. He said, "When you went into the house that day did you see Adrian Carthallow?"

Imleyson flushed angrily. At first it seemed that he did not intend to reply, and then he said, shortly, "I saw his body."

"Was Mrs. Carthallow there?"

The muscles along Lester Imleyson's jaw tightened perceptibly. He said, "No."

"You didn't see any sign of her at all?"

"No."

"What did you do?"

"I didn't need a doctor to tell that Carthallow was dead. There wasn't anything I could do for him. I left."

"Why?"

"Because," Imleyson said, "I didn't want some stupid idiot accusing me of having killed him."

Mordecai Tremaine gave a gentle cough.

"And you *didn't* kill him?"

"Don't be a fool."

"I see your point. You could hardly be expected to admit it even if you did. So your story is that you went into the house, found Carthallow dead, and went off again without seeing anyone else or trying to notify the police because you were afraid that in view of the known closeness of your association with Mrs. Carthallow you might be accused of murder. Is that right?"

"You seem to have it all tied up," Imleyson said.

It was very lonely on this part of the cliffs, for the weather was not warm enough now to bring many people out. The water and the rocks seemed a long way down. Mordecai Tremaine glanced at his companion's face and took a step backward, away from the edge of the drop. Imleyson smiled sardonically.

"Nervous? Who kills once can kill twice, eh? You needn't panic. I'm not going to pitch you over—not yet."

Mordecai Tremaine put up a hand to his pince-nez. He felt that he was not cutting a very dignified figure. He endeavored to reestablish his hold upon the situation.

"When you saw Carthallow," he said, "just how was his body lying?"

Lester Imleyson drew a deep breath.

"I've told Inspector Penross all I know. If there's anything you want to find out you'd better go and talk to him."

He turned on his heel and strode off toward Falporth. Mordecai Tremaine stared thoughtfully after him, allowing him time to increase the distance between them, and then he, too, began to walk back in the direction of the town.

His destination was Hilda Eveland's house. As he pushed open the iron gate at the entrance to her garden, he saw that she was busy with a pair of hand shears, trimming the edge of the lawn where it bordered the drive.

"Morning, Hilda."

She turned a red and perspiring face upon him, waved him a greeting, and went on clipping.

"Don't stop me, Mordecai. Once I straighten up I'll never be able to get back down again!"

"As a matter of fact," he told her, "it was Helen I really came to see."

"Too late," she said, wielding the shears vigorously. "She's out."

"Did she go alone?"

"No. Elton came for her. He's taken her for a drive."

Mordecai Tremaine said, "Oh." And added: "He's been seeing rather a lot of her, hasn't he?"

Hilda Eveland snipped away the last few blades of grass and stood upright with a sigh of relief.

"Thank goodness that's over. You know the way the wind's blowing, Mordecai. He's in love with her. I don't know when they'll be back. Did you want Helen for anything in particular?"

"No—I just thought I'd like to talk to her. I've been speaking to Lester Imleyson this morning. You know he went to the house, after all, I suppose?"

"Who doesn't?" she said. "What's the inspector going to do about it?"

Mordecai Tremaine made no attempt to answer the question. He said, "Hilda, what's the trouble between Helen Carthallow and Lester Imleyson?"

He thought he saw a shadow cross her face.

"Trouble?" she said, and he took her arm.

"You know perfectly well what I'm talking about. Before Carthallow died they were almost open lovers, and now they're acting as though they're strangers. Penross thinks it might be an act, but I'm not so sure. I've watched them both. They're like people who've something to conceal and who aren't certain whether the other is going to let them down. Imleyson's always truculent and on the defensive, and Helen's hard and cynical. Why do they avoid each other's company? Why is it Steele who's acting as her protector?"

"Aren't you rather imagining things, Mordecai? You shouldn't pay so much attention to *Romantic Stories*," said Hilda Eveland, but she could not keep the note of uncertainty from her voice.

"I'm not doing any imagining," said Mordecai Tremaine soberly. "How long has Steele been in love with her?"

"A year—perhaps more. You can't be certain with a thing like that. Especially with Elton. He doesn't give himself away."

"No," said Mordecai Tremaine. "He doesn't."

Something in his tone made her look at him with a sudden intentness, her eyes filled with foreboding.

"Mordecai, you don't—you don't suspect *Elton*?"

"No more than I suspect anyone else," he told her. "It's just that Elton Steele seems to me to be the kind of man who might do all sorts of unexpected things, and I don't think it would be wise to ignore him." A memory came back to him of Steele's face as he had stared at Roberta Fairham just after the surfing incident. He added, slowly: "I certainly don't think that would be wise."

He remained chatting with Hilda Eveland for several more minutes, but he knew that he had disturbed her, and as soon as he could do so without making it appear too obvious he took his departure. He went out of his way through the town in the hope that he might see Colonel Neale, but he arrived back at Arthur Tyning's home without having encountered anyone he knew.

In the afternoon the clouds lifted over the sea and the sun shone through. It was still too breezy to encourage him down to his usual spot on the beach near Paradise, but he found a sheltered spot in the garden and settled down in a deck chair. Jonathan Boyce had gone down to the harbor, and the Tynings were making several calls in Falporth. His afternoon should be undisturbed.

He had provided himself with the latest copy of *Romantic Stories*, but he did not read more than a few paragraphs, and even these did not convey any meaning to him. His mind was far too preoccupied with the stuff of the drama with which real life had presented him to enable him to take his human relationships secondhand.

His brain was busy calling back scattered impressions from the past, fitting them into a coherent whole.

Anita Lane speaking to him on the telephone. Adrian Carthallow displaying an interest in police work and going out of his way to be pleasant to an elderly gentleman wearing insecurely balanced pince-nez whom he had never seen before. Lewis Haldean sitting in a gently swaying boat and telling him that he was afraid Carthallow might be heading for a nervous breakdown. A newspaper item. An early morning meeting on a lonely beach between Adrian Carthallow and a man whom he had only a short time previously denied that he knew.

Mordecai Tremaine felt truth being dangled tantalizingly in front of him. *Romantic Stories* lay forgotten on his knees. In his mind a fantastic, unbelievable theory was slowly unfolding, and he knew instinctively that the mystery of how Adrian Carthallow had come to die lay almost within his grasp…

It was the click of the gate that aroused him late in the afternoon. He sat up in his chair and saw Inspector Penross coming down the garden path. Penross had the tense, excited air of a man who brought news.

He saw the deck chair and made toward it.

"Well, Mordecai, we're on to something!"

Mordecai Tremaine tried hastily to push *Romantic Stories* out of sight.

"You are?" he said, still not quite adjusted to the shock of the inspector's sudden appearance.

"It's about that chap Westfield. He may be working for his living as an actor, but he has other strings to his bow. The Criminal Records office knows all about him. He's a very shady character—has contacts with all kinds of crooks. In his own particular line he's something of a con man."

Tremaine was fully interested now.

"Have you found any linkup with Carthallow?" he asked eagerly.

"Nothing concrete so far, but there's no doubt that they were hand in glove over something, and judging by Westfield's record it isn't likely to have been legal. They used to meet quite a lot in London—in places where they weren't likely to be seen by anyone who knew Carthallow. The Yard is still making inquiries. They'll let us know, of course, if anything definite turns up."

"Beyond the fact that it confirms that Westfield's past is a murky one," observed Mordecai Tremaine thoughtfully, "I don't see that it takes us anywhere. You've still got to get over Matilda Vickery's evidence that nobody went over the bridge except the people you've already checked. I don't doubt that Westfield has an unbreakable alibi for the time of the shooting."

"Maybe he has," said Penross. "And maybe he hasn't. As soon as the report came through I went along to the Pavilion myself to see him. He wasn't there. He hasn't shown up since last night, and the manager was tearing his hair because he's supposed to be appearing in the matinee performance this afternoon. I promptly checked at his digs, and the landlady told me that he didn't come in last night after the show as he usually did."

"Hmm. What's your opinion of that?"

"I'm not going in for opinions," said Penross cheerfully. "Not just yet. There are too many loose ends to be cleared up. But it looks promising. Let's say that for some reason or other Westfield—his name at the CRO is Galley, by the way—lost his nerve. Maybe he found out we were making inquiries about him—one of his London pals could have tipped him off—so he decided to bolt. And a man who does that has something on his conscience."

"Does that mean that Lester Imleyson isn't under suspicion anymore?"

"It does not." Penross spoke with the emphasis of a man who was considerably more at peace with the world than he had formerly been. "But this case is beginning to break. After going along in a kind of tunnel that left precious little room for development it's getting into open country. I've sent out an all-stations message for Westfield. He's bound to be picked up soon, and my guess is that by then he'll be ripe to talk."

"Maybe." Mordecai Tremaine sounded preoccupied. One part of his brain had been listening to what Penross had been saying; another part was working busily at something else. He said, "You've heard of Warren Belmont?"

"Belmont?" Penross looked at him curiously, seeking an explanation for the apparent change of subject, but he knew that Mordecai Tremaine did not ask questions without a purpose. "Wait a moment—isn't he the millionaire who was over here from the States at the beginning of the year?"

"He came to Europe to buy art treasures," Tremaine said. "Among other things he took back with him a painting by Sir Joshua Reynolds."

"Yes, I did read something about it. Didn't pay much attention, though—not in my line."

"Belmont bought this particular Reynolds from a peer whose name wasn't mentioned but who inherited a lot of paintings—most of them worthless—when he came into the title. The Reynolds was discovered among them. I wonder, Charles, whether you could find out for me the name of the peer and whether there's been any reaction from Belmont?"

"I might." Penross did not sound enthusiastic. "Can't guarantee how long it'll take, though. If Belmont's gone back to the States it'll probably mean putting through a request to the FBI."

"I'd still like to know, Charles. And I've a feeling that *you* might like to know, too."

Mordecai Tremaine settled his pince-nez firmly in position. He had seen enough of Penross to be aware that the inspector was under no illusions that when Westfield—or Galley—was traced, the problem of Adrian Carthallow's death would be solved. There would still remain the tedious, tortuous business of uncovering the motive and proving the opportunity.

The reason for Penross's jubilation lay not in any belief that he had found a murderer but in the knowledge that he had found an alternative. He had found an alternative to Helen Carthallow.

And it was still Helen Carthallow who was the key to the mystery. It was still Helen Carthallow who *said* that she had killed her husband.

29

There were names carved into the spongy turf. Mordecai Tremaine amused himself searching for them. He wondered who Thelma and Ruby were and whether they had married George and Harry or whether theirs had been merely a sea-side acquaintanceship that had faded when the train had left Falporth on a Saturday morning, taking them back to another year of routine. The headland formed one arm of the narrow bay that was a sixpenny bus ride from Falporth and to which he had made his way in a minor spirit of exploration. The theory that had been creeping to steady life in his mind was still a very nebulous thing, with many ragged edges in its outline, but he was convinced that it held the core of truth, and he wanted solitude and the stimulation of the wind from the sea.

Certainly there was nothing lacking as far as stimulation was concerned. He made his way slowly along the uneven but well-marked path that led to the headland's extremity against a wind that blew more stiffly the further he advanced.

He raised his head as he neared the end of the path in order to take in his surroundings and found himself confronting a man who was standing in the shelter of the rocks. He said, "Good morning, Colonel. Enjoying the view?"

Colonel Neale nodded.

"Yes—magnificent, isn't it? But you seem to know who I am. I don't think we've met before, have we?"

"We haven't exactly met," Mordecai Tremaine said. "But we had an acquaintance in common—Adrian Carthallow."

He saw the sudden contraction of the other's eyebrows and saw his hand go up to smooth the gray moustache, trimmed with a military precision. A certain frostiness of manner replaced the friendliness with which he had at first responded to Tremaine's greeting.

"I've placed you now," he said. "You're Tremaine, aren't you? The detective fellow. I saw your name in the newspapers."

At close quarters he looked older than Mordecai Tremaine had imagined him, but he still had the air of a man used to command. It was easy to visualize him as the martinet, determined to stand no nonsense. That night at Carthallow's house he had been out of his element, among people whose ways were alien to him and with whom he possessed nothing in common. He was by no means the ineffectual, rather pathetic figure he had appeared then.

Tremaine thrust his hands deep into the pockets of his

raincoat and tried to assume his most benevolent and disarming expression.

"It always seems to me such a tragedy when a creative artist is cut off in his prime, as it were. The death of a man like Carthallow is a great loss to the world. Don't you think?"

"No," retorted Neale uncompromisingly. "Whoever put that bullet into him did something I'd been wanting to do myself."

Mordecai Tremaine's apparently shocked eyes regarded him over the top of the pince-nez.

"I'm sure you don't mean that," he said. And then, as though the knowledge had only just come to him and he realized that he had made a blunder, he added awkwardly: "Of course—your daughter. I'm so sorry. Carthallow painted her portrait, didn't he?"

"Yes," Colonel Neale said grimly. "Carthallow painted her portrait." His gray eyes searched his companion's face with an intentness that was not friendly and yet was not openly hostile. He said, "I can hardly believe you were unaware of that fact. As I understand it you've a close connection with the local police inspector who's in charge of the case."

"Whatever a man's real feelings might be," Mordecai Tremaine said, evading the question, "it seems to me to be very unwise for him to go around saying that he would like to have killed Adrian Carthallow—particularly if his alibi isn't too strong."

A wintry smile played among the hard lines of the elderly man's face.

"I thought you weren't quite such a harmless fool as you've been trying to pretend. There's no point in my hiding the fact that I think Carthallow was a scoundrel who deserved all that came to him. The police will be able to find plenty of people who've heard me threaten him, and they know all about my daughter. The newspapers gave it enough publicity."

"Why did you come to Falporth?"

"Why does anybody come to Falporth?" the other countered sardonically. "I needed a holiday."

"Did you know Adrian Carthallow was here?"

"It's common knowledge that I've taken an interest in Carthallow's activities for some months past. I couldn't have avoided finding out that he had a house down here and used to spend several months here every summer."

"Were you prepared to kill him if you could?"

"If I could have done it without putting my neck in the noose," the colonel said flatly, "it would have been a pleasure."

He moved away from the rocks against which he had been sheltering and pulled his raincoat around him. He added, "I've talked to you because I know you've some kind of standing with the police, but if you think it will do you any good you're mistaken. I've already had an interview with the inspector. My alibi may not be too strong, but it's strong enough. Nobody can prove I went into that house, and that's the only thing that's going to convince a jury. Good day to you."

Mordecai Tremaine said, mechanically, "Good day."

He watched the colonel's spare figure go striding vigorously along the path. Despite his years the other was still active; he had obviously kept himself fit since his retirement.

Another thought came into his mind as he, too, went back over the headland. Adrian Carthallow had been killed with a weapon of service pattern. And Colonel Neale would know all about service revolvers.

He was glad there was no sign of the other at the bus stop. It would have been an embarrassment to have traveled back with him.

When they pulled up at the terminus in Falporth and he descended from the vehicle, he almost collided with two people who were passing. He looked up with a word of apology and found himself facing Helen Carthallow and Elton Steele.

They greeted him pleasantly enough, but he knew that the meeting was an unwelcome one to them. The gaiety that had been in Helen Carthallow's eyes died away, and her face became defensive and expressionless. It was as though she had told herself she must be on her guard with him.

Elton Steele put his arm around her waist. There was something symbolic in the gesture. Mordecai Tremaine felt that the big, dark man was throwing down a challenge. He left them with the disturbing impression that they felt themselves to be united against a common enemy and that in their minds they had identified that enemy with himself.

He spent the afternoon at the house with Jonathan Boyce. There was a swell running in the bay, and the Yard man had abandoned the cruise he had been proposing to take along the coast to St. Mawgan.

"Judging by the symptoms," Boyce observed, addressing a Mordecai Tremaine who was embedded in an easy chair facing his own, "you're expecting things to happen."

Tremaine took off his pince-nez and began to polish them reflectively.

"The situation," he observed, "is certainly highly interesting."

He did not, however, expect developments quite so soon. It was just after tea when Charles Penross appeared. He arrived in an official patrol car, and his manner left no doubt that his visit was not merely a social one.

"I've got the information you wanted about Warren Belmont, Mordecai," he said, without preliminary. "It didn't take as long as I thought it was going to. Because there'd already been a reaction from him. New York asked the Yard to make certain inquiries a couple of weeks ago. Belmont went to the police over there because he wasn't satisfied with that Reynolds he bought. One of the leading art experts to whom he showed it when he got back told him he thought it was a fake."

Mordecai Tremaine leaned forward, his eyes alight with triumph.

"What about the man who sold it to him?" he said. "The peer whose name wasn't mentioned. Any news about *him*?"

Penross settled himself on the arm of a chair.

"Yes," he said. "And no. The Yard hasn't been able to find any trace of the mysterious owner. It seems that all the negotiations were carried on by an agent. And the description of the agent fits our friend Westfield like the well-known glove."

"In other words," Mordecai Tremaine said, "Warren Belmont was the victim of a confidence trick that succeeded because the supposed painting by Reynolds was sufficiently like the genuine article to deceive more than one expert."

"Westfield obviously must have put over a good story," said Penross, "because Belmont's hardheaded enough as far as his own business is concerned. But at the same time it looks as though whoever painted that picture pulled off a pretty clever piece of work."

"That," said Mordecai Tremaine, "is where Adrian Carthallow comes into the story."

"That," observed Penross, "is what I was hoping you'd say." Jonathan Boyce lowered his pipe. He looked startled.

He said, "You're not suggesting that Carthallow deliberately faked that picture and sold it to Belmont?"

"It's more than a suggestion, Jonathan," Mordecai Tremaine told him. "It's a fact. Carthallow was in deep water. He was spending money faster than he could earn it, and he had to think up a way of bringing down his overdraft. Selling a fake Reynolds to a millionaire probably seemed to offer quite a promising beginning."

Boyce still had an air of doubt.

"I don't know a great deal about old masters," he said slowly, "but it seems to me that there can't be many people about who could fake a painting well enough to fool experienced art critics."

"Whatever else he might have been," Mordecai Tremaine said, "Adrian Carthallow was a genius. Even his enemies admitted that he could paint. And he was versatile. He could paint in different styles. I was telling Charles the other day how Roberta Fairham once quoted a lot of stuff some well-known critic had written about his gifts. He could have gone a long way, but his trouble was that he was living at too fast a rate and couldn't wait to develop his income honestly. He had to find a shortcut. I suppose the way he chose was an obvious one to a man of his attainments. It's been done before, of course. There was a Dutchman named Van Meergeren who made a fortune until he was found out by selling paintings supposed to be by the seventeenth-century painter Vermeer. He couldn't sell his own work, so he painted so-called newly discovered Vermeers that a lot of people thought were better than the master's other pictures."

"I imagine," Jonathan Boyce said, "that there's more to it than the mere fact that Carthallow was short of money and that he was capable of turning out a pretty good imitation of a Reynolds?"

"There is more to it," Mordecai Tremaine agreed. "Some of it doesn't seem very important at first sight, but it all adds up. When I first met Carthallow I thought it was curious that he should be so interested in crime. Most people are to a certain degree, of course, but his interest seemed to have a more personal touch. Besides," he added deprecatingly, "I couldn't help feeling that it was odd that a man in his position and with his reputation should pay so much attention to an insignificant stranger like me—unless there was something behind it he hadn't told me about.

"In the beginning I thought it was merely that he knew he wasn't exactly popular on account of a few of his paintings and was afraid that one day somebody would make an attempt to get at him. I thought that he was clinging to me with a kind of instinct for self-preservation, although naturally I couldn't really have done anything to help him. But looking back I think that all his talk about successful criminals was due to the fact that he couldn't bear the thought of being unable to parade his triumphs.

"I remember talking to him on one occasion about the perfect crime and saying that the whole point of it was that nobody should even suspect there'd been a crime at all; otherwise it wouldn't be perfect. He said that it must be depressing to commit the perfect murder and not be able to take the credit for it. And once he spoke about Thomas Chatterton, the boy poet who couldn't claim his poetry as his own without revealing himself as a fake.

"Carthallow knew that his own fake paintings were good and in some odd, twisted way he resented not being hailed as a genius for producing them. He couldn't tell the world openly, of course, so he used me as a sort of vehicle for unloading his ego."

Penross was looking as though he thought the argument was venturing into realms a little too theoretical for his liking.

"Did he ever mention Belmont to you?" he asked.

"*I* mentioned the name to *him*," Tremaine said, turning to the inspector. "He denied knowing Belmont and didn't seem to want to talk about him. It struck me as being curious because only a short while before a friend of mine who was in a position to be sure of things like that had told me that Belmont was just the sort of person Carthallow would be eager to cultivate."

"I've not heard that he did have any personal contact with Belmont," Penross remarked. "I dare say he took care to keep well away from him so that his name wouldn't be thought of in connection with the Reynolds if anything in the way of suspicion was aroused about the painting—as did happen when Belmont got back to the States. Maybe, too, he was just a bit scared of you, knowing your reputation, and tried to steer you off what might have been a dangerous line of thought."

"If that *was* the case it had the opposite effect. If he'd said he knew Belmont and had passed it off casually I wouldn't have paid any more attention to it. But what it did was to make me wonder whether he had anything to hide. It was the same where Westfield was concerned. I saw him one day in London with Carthallow and recognized him at the Pavilion here. But when I spoke to Carthallow about it, he didn't seem interested and said it couldn't possibly be the same man.

"And then, early one morning, I saw them together on the beach. I don't mind admitting that I did my best to eavesdrop without letting them know I was anywhere about. I wasn't able to hear a great deal, but I did hear a mention of 'Belmont' and 'Reynolds' and then Carthallow made a remark about not being able to turn out things like sausages."

Jonathan Boyce was puffing out clouds of smoke from his pipe, a sure indication that his excitement was mounting.

"It sounds as though Westfield was trying to get him to produce another fake painting. No doubt he believed that in Carthallow he had a valuable accomplice who could provide him with a permanent meal ticket. I wonder, Charles—I wonder! If Westfield's a professional—and you say that Records knows all about him—it's on the cards that he tried to blackmail Carthallow. He knew that Carthallow was in his power since he'd incriminated himself by faking the Reynolds; the threat of exposure could bring him to heel. So he demanded more fake pictures—this time with a bigger share of the profits for himself."

"Could be," Penross said. "Westfield contacted Carthallow when he was in Wadestow and got him to come back to his house to a secret rendezvous. Carthallow wouldn't agree to his terms—you can't imagine him sitting down tamely under blackmail—and there was a quarrel."

"It's shaping, Charles," said Jonathan Boyce. "Either by accident or in self-defense Westfield shot Carthallow and made his getaway. He thought he was safe and was going to sit tight in Falporth, and then he found out that inquiries were being made about him and he developed cold feet and decided to bolt."

"Don't forget," Mordecai Tremaine observed, "there's still the question of how he got into the house and away from it again without being seen."

"I hadn't overlooked that," Boyce replied. "But once you've got your hands on Westfield, Charles, he'll know the game's up and maybe he'll talk."

Penross had been listening with an expression on his face that was hard to define. It was a mixture of satisfaction and chagrin. He said, now: "As far as Westfield's concerned the game *is* up. But he isn't going to talk."

His tone held a note of grimness. Mordecai Tremaine said, "You've been holding out on us, Charles. What is it?"

"Westfield," Penross said, "is dead." He added: "That was one of the things I came to tell you. His body was discovered wedged among the rocks at Trecarne Head at low tide today. One of the local fishermen spotted something unusual and went in as close as he dared. He reported to us as soon as he got back, and we sent out a search party. It was Westfield all right. His body was caught between two rocks that are uncovered at low water; otherwise we'd probably not have discovered him for weeks."

Jonathan Boyce looked at him inquiringly.

"What's the answer? Suicide?"

Penross pursed his lips.

"Difficult to be sure," he said. "It *could* have been an accident. You know what the coast is like just there—it's an unhealthy spot after dark, particularly if you're a stranger to the district. The edge is crumbling, and it wouldn't be difficult to miss your footing and go over."

Mordecai Tremaine thought of the gaunt, unscalable cliff with the black rocks thrusting viciously through the angry surf far below, upon which he had once stood with Adrian Carthallow. He shivered. His mind was seeing a human figure hurtling down through the darkness, and he could hear a wild, despairing cry that was being torn into nothing on the wind.

Penross was saying, "There's a lot to be filled in, of course. But the motive's looking healthy enough. It was a case of rogues falling out—with blackmail at the back of it."

"I'm inclined to agree," Mordecai Tremaine said, "that Westfield was trying his hand at blackmail, but you still have to clear Helen Carthallow."

"Yes," Penross said, "I still have to clear Mrs. Carthallow. And I don't mind admitting that I'm not as confident as I might look. I'm worried about that story of hers."

He added, "Have *you* any ideas?"

"Yes," said Mordecai Tremaine slowly. "Yes, I have."

Jonathan Boyce took out his pipe once more and regarded his friend suspiciously. He had heard that tone before. He had a feeling that Inspector Charles Penross was in for a shock.

30

Mordecai Tremaine was feeling embarrassed. His discomfort was intensified by the fact that he knew he should have been enjoying himself. These people had gathered here on his account. He should have been experiencing a sense of power and exultation.

He glanced around the crowded lounge of Paradise. They were all waiting for him. He pushed his pince-nez into a safer position with that instinctive, nervous gesture. He said, "I believe Inspector Penross has already given you an indication as to why you've been asked to come here, and in any case with the exception of Colonel Neale we all know each other fairly well so that there's no need for me to go into long explanations."

The elderly, military-looking man with the gray moustache who was seated near the window felt the curious eyes being turned upon him at the mention of his name and crossed one leg over its companion with a calm deliberation.

"As the one apparent stranger," he observed, "I must

confess I'm at a loss to understand why you should wish me to be present."

"I'm hoping you may be able to help me, Colonel," Mordecai Tremaine told him. "In any case, I thought it necessary that you should be here in view of your—interest—in Adrian Carthallow."

"I see. Am I to assume that you believe I may be able to tell you who killed him?"

"No, I don't mean that." Mordecai Tremaine paused. And then he said, carefully: "You see, the name of the person who caused Adrian Carthallow's death is already known to me."

His words left a stillness behind them. An unbearable stillness through which there crept an insidious, chilling fear.

Elton Steele's big hands clenched slowly. He looked at Helen Carthallow, sitting rigid in her chair, her face drained of all its color. His glance went beyond her to Inspector Penross, leaning against the door, his slight form curiously expectant and his bright eyes regarding them all in one comprehensive stare.

"All right," he said, tensely. "If you know, what are you waiting for? Aren't you going to arrest anybody?"

Mordecai Tremaine said, mildly, as if he had noticed nothing: "It isn't quite so simple as that. When a man dies his death isn't an isolated fact that you can lift out by itself and put neatly on one side. It's mixed up with all kinds of other things. That's one of the reasons why I asked you to come here. The newspapers have already given a great deal of publicity to Adrian Carthallow's death, and before long they're going to give it a great deal more. It's to be expected, of course. It's a newspaper's job to give its readers the facts. But there's no reason why it should give them a lot of facts that don't really matter."

Roberta Fairham was holding her handbag on her lap. The catch snapped suddenly under the pressure of her fingers. Her lips were tightly compressed. Tremaine glanced at her. He said, "I see that Miss Fairham understands me. The story of how and why Adrian Carthallow came to die will have to be told to the world, but there's no need for every private feeling and emotion to be dragged out. Certain painful matters needn't go beyond the walls of this room—*provided each one of you will tell me the truth.*"

Hilda Eveland said, doubtfully, "I see what you're driving at, Mordecai. None of us wants to see any unnecessary scandal. But surely we've all told you as much as we know?"

"The trouble is," said Mordecai Tremaine, "that you haven't."

He was looking straight at Helen Carthallow. She returned his gaze with a stubborn defiance. Her voice was harsh.

"You said just now that you knew who killed Adrian. There isn't anything remarkable in that. I've already told the police that it was *I* who killed him."

"You told the police, Mrs. Carthallow, that you shot your husband accidentally. You said that he took the gun out of the desk and that there was a struggle between you."

"Well?"

"In the first place, although *your* fingerprints were found on the gun, your husband's were not. In the second place, it was an idiosyncrasy of his that whenever he had occasion to use one of the keys on the bunch he always carried he invariably took off the particular key he wanted and replaced it when he had finished with it. But when you took me into the study the bunch of keys still hung from the lock—*and the key of the drawer in which he kept his gun was with all the others.*"

Her glance flickered away. The lock of hair came down over her eyes.

"Perhaps he didn't take the key off. I don't remember. It doesn't prove anything."

"I think it does," Mordecai Tremaine said. "I think it proves that it *wasn't* your husband who took out that gun. I think it proves that you *didn't* shoot him accidentally."

Lewis Haldean was on his feet. His blond beard was thrust aggressively forward. Indignation was flaming in his face.

"Look here, Tremaine, I'm damned if I'll sit here and listen to your accusations against Helen!"

Elton Steele and Lester Imleyson moved to add their

protests to his. Steele's expression was openly menacing, but in Imleyson's features Tremaine thought he could detect a gnawing fear.

"You were at the house that day, Mr. Imleyson," he said quietly. "I think you're aware that Mrs. Carthallow isn't telling the truth."

Imleyson was silent. He looked like a man who knew that he ought to be voicing a vigorous denial but who dared not speak too hastily lest he betrayed himself. Steele turned toward him. There was a dull suspicion in his dark face.

Helen Carthallow said, metallically, "It was nothing to do with Lester. He had no hand in it."

"He *did* have a hand in it," said Mordecai Tremaine.

For an instant after that no one moved or spoke. But the tension had reached a point at which something must snap. Looking at the three men still facing him, Mordecai Tremaine was aware of it and knew that he had allowed the drama to go far enough.

"Sit down, gentlemen," he said, "and let me tell you what really happened that day."

It was significant that they obeyed him. He waited until they were seated, and said, "Adrian Carthallow had an appointment in Wadestow on the afternoon of the day on which he died and was not expected back here until the time for dinner in the evening. So Mrs. Carthallow arranged to meet Mr. Imleyson here in the belief that since the servants had been given a holiday, they would be unobserved."

He saw her startled movement and addressed himself directly to her.

"I don't need to stress that point, Mrs. Carthallow. The relationship between Mr. Imleyson and yourself was no secret. The situation was growing difficult. Your husband and Mr. Imleyson all but came to blows at the race meeting. It may be that you decided upon a rendezvous here because you wanted to talk the whole matter over—I don't pretend to be certain of your motive, but you *did* agree to meet here in your house. In order to avoid gossip you left Wadestow by train and Mr. Imleyson used his car.

"Unfortunately for your plans your husband changed his mind about staying. He came straight back here, and since he traveled by road it didn't take him as long as it took you to make your rather roundabout train journey. When you arrived at the house he was already here."

"I told the police he was here before me," she said, but her voice was unsteady.

Mordecai Tremaine nodded.

"I know," he said. "*But what you didn't tell them was that he was already dead.*"

The agony in the dark eyes staring from the white face did unpleasant things to Mordecai Tremaine's heart, but he knew that he must go on. He said, steadily, trying to keep all emotion out of his voice: "You knew Mr. Imleyson intended to drive by road from Wadestow, and your first thought was that he had reached the house before you and had unexpectedly encountered your husband. You thought there'd been a quarrel, with yourself as the cause, and that Mr. Imleyson had killed him.

"It must have been a dreadful moment for you when you went into the study and saw your husband's dead body. You had to force yourself to think; to remain calm instead of giving way to hysteria. There was only one thing that mattered. You had to save Mr. Imleyson.

"You picked up the gun and wiped it clean so that his fingerprints wouldn't give him away, and while you were trying to make sure he hadn't left any other traces of his presence you were thinking out your story. At first you thought Mr. Imleyson had somehow obtained your husband's gun and shot him from a distance of several feet, and that was why your first statement to the police said that you were standing on the other side of the room and that your husband had told you to fire. It wasn't a very good story, but it was the best thing you could invent on the spur of the moment that you believed would tally with the evidence.

"When you realized that it *didn't* tally and that your husband had been killed at close range, you pretended you'd decided to tell the truth and said that you'd had a quarrel and a struggle, in the course of which the gun had gone off accidentally. The fact that you told that first improbable story at all was to my mind a proof of one thing—that you didn't believe your husband's death was an accident but that someone had killed him deliberately. Which meant that you knew someone who had a motive for killing him and some-one who had also possessed the opportunity of doing so. *And it was also a proof that that someone was a person for whom you cared a great deal.*

"I don't know whether you looked for Mr. Imleyson or whether you called his name to see if he was still in the house. But it was because you wanted to give him time to get away if he *was* in the neighborhood that you didn't use the telephone. You came all the way down to me on the beach not because you thought I might be able to help you but because it would do two things. It would delay the arrival of the police, and it would produce a witness to testify that Mr. Imleyson wasn't at the house.

"You were ahead of me as we went up the steps from the beach. When we reached the top you made what I thought was the rather odd remark that there was no one there. I didn't realize it then, of course, but you wanted to make sure that if Mr. Imleyson was anywhere near, you would see him first and would be able to warn him to keep out of sight. That remark to me was made partly in relief and partly to encourage me away from thinking there might be someone else in the neighborhood."

Mordecai Tremaine stopped, but Helen Carthallow did not speak. She was sitting very still, as though she was afraid that if she made a movement her self-control would go. He looked at her compassionately.

"I'm afraid this is all very painful to you, Mrs. Carthallow," he said, "but I think it better that what there is to say should be said here among us rather than that it should be left to appear in the newspapers. You thought that Mr. Imleyson had reached the house before you, but in fact he had trouble with his car and was a few minutes late for your appointment. The door was open, and he went into the house because he didn't expect anyone but you to be there. He saw you through the doorway of the study—and he also saw your husband's dead body.

"He didn't say anything to you. I don't doubt that for a moment he was too stunned to speak. When you'd seen your husband lying dead, your immediate reaction had been that Mr. Imleyson had killed him. *His* reaction was that *you* had done so. That was why he didn't make his presence known to you, and you were so engrossed with what you were doing that you didn't suspect that he was watching you.

"Probably he watched you through the narrow space

between the door and the jamb, and what he saw confirmed him in his belief that you had killed your husband and that you were trying to hide the signs of your guilt. Maybe he actually saw you wiping the gun. He didn't dream that you were acting, as you thought, to save *him*.

"After you had left the house he went into the study with the idea of making sure there was nothing left that might incriminate you. He found your handkerchief. In your agitation and your anxiety to see that there was nothing to direct suspicion against Mr. Imleyson, you'd left it behind. You see, you weren't so calm, after all; you weren't thinking and acting so coolly. It's a proof of your innocence that you did leave it behind, just as it's a further proof that for so intelligent a woman you told so thin a story to the police."

Mordecai Tremaine broke off. Lester Imleyson was staring at Helen Carthallow, his face bearing the look of a man to whom revelation had brought utter dismay.

"Helen," he said. "Helen—I didn't know. I thought—" She was quite calm now. The worst for her was past.

"It's too late now, Lester," she said. "Perhaps it was as well for both of us that it happened that way."

There was no bitterness in her voice, none of the hard quality that had marked her attitude in the days that had followed Adrian Carthallow's death. Mordecai Tremaine said, quietly, "I'm going to say this, Mrs. Carthallow, because it helps to explain both your own position and Mr. Imleyson's. You thought you were in love with each other. But when the crisis came neither of you proved able to stand up to it. Each of you believed the other to have been guilty of a dreadful crime. Each of you tried to shield the other, but there was no longer any trust; there was no love, only a torturing fear. That's why you seemed to become so hard and bitter and why Mr. Imleyson, although he wouldn't listen to any accusations against you, wasn't at your side where he might have been expected to be. When he gave you that handkerchief he intended it to be a sign to you that he was aware of what you had done."

"It isn't too late, Helen." Imleyson made an impulsive movement toward her. "We can start again—"

"No, Lester," she said. "It's gone too deep. We can't go back now."

For an instant he stood facing her, and then, slowly, he sat down again in his chair. It was clear from his face that despite that gesture he knew that she was right. Whatever had existed between them was dead, and there could be no recalling it to life.

Mordecai Tremaine watched them uncomfortably. Although, before Adrian Carthallow's death, he had been inclined to condemn his wife and Lester Imleyson because of their liaison, now that he was witnessing the final and public disavowal his sentimental soul was in distress. The romantic streak in him would not allow him to regard it unmoved.

It was Lewis Haldean who saved an awkward moment from becoming also an unbearably painful one. The blond man was sitting forward in his chair, his blue eyes intent.

"You can't leave things there, Tremaine," he said, in his rich, vibrant voice. "If Helen didn't kill Adrian—or, rather, if you've at last decided to admit that she didn't—and if Imleyson didn't do it, who *did* shoot him?"

"I'm coming to that now," said Mordecai Tremaine.

It was his sense of theatre that made him pause. He looked around at them, and it must be admitted that now he was not entirely without satisfaction on account of the power he held over them.

Even Hilda Eveland was showing signs of strain.

"Don't keep us in suspense, Mordecai. Who did kill Adrian?"

Only Colonel Neale appeared unaffected by the tension in the atmosphere. He was leaning back with apparent calm, a faint smile that seemed to hold something of irony upon his lips.

Mordecai Tremaine said, "Men and women don't lead single-track lives. They branch off in a number of different directions. From time to time other people's tracks cut across them or run closely parallel. That's why, in a case of this nature, it isn't easy to pick out the one line that matters and follow it from start to finish so that you can see just who and why and when. The truth you're looking for is obscured by other things that happened to be going on at the same time but that don't really affect *your* line at all, although sometimes they get so mixed up that they cause you to look at the problem from the wrong angle altogether.

"Adrian Carthallow's death was complicated by the presence of several tracks that were connected with his own but that actually belonged to other people. You've already heard how the relationship between Mrs. Carthallow and Mr. Imleyson served to make the problem more confused. There were other things, too. For instance, there was the portrait. Did Mr. Imleyson destroy it in jealous rage? Or did Adrian Carthallow ruin it himself and for the same reason? Either of those two explanations could have served, but fortunately Miss Fairham was able to clear up *that* difficulty."

Roberta Fairham seemed to have shrunk within herself. She looked old and lifeless—and frightened. Her tongue passed over her lips.

"I didn't kill Adrian," she said unsteadily. "I didn't. I didn't!"

It was significant that no one looked at her. Colonel Neale said, "This is all very interesting, but don't you think it would be as well to come to the point of the matter first?"

"Am I taking too long?" Mordecai Tremaine smiled

disarmingly. "I wanted to make sure that we'd disposed of all the secondary matters before dealing with the major question, so that we could see the real problem more clearly."

He glanced at Helen Carthallow. He said, "When you saw the dead body of your husband, Mrs. Carthallow, did you think he might have committed suicide?"

She looked at him in a puzzled manner, and he knew that she was recalling that this was not the first time the possibility of suicide had been put to her. But she shook her head.

"No," she told him. "The thought of suicide never came into my mind."

"Why not?"

"Adrian wasn't the kind of man to kill himself. His reaction to trouble of any kind would have been to disappear. He'd have gone to South America or some other country where it would have been difficult to trace him. He wouldn't have taken his own life. Besides…"

Mordecai Tremaine did not prompt her, and after a moment or two she went on: "It was the revolver. It was on the floor. It was too far away for Adrian to have dropped it. I knew he couldn't have used it against himself."

"Was his body," Tremaine said carefully, "in exactly the same position as it was when I came into the house with you?"

She hesitated. Her eyes flashed momentarily to Lester Imleyson.

"No," she said slowly. "No, it wasn't. Adrian was sitting in his chair, leaning forward across the desk. I—I pushed him so that he fell on the floor. That was how the chair came to be overturned."

"Why did you do that?"

There was distress in her face. The lock of hair came down over her forehead. Mordecai Tremaine said, quietly, "I think I know why. It was because you thought it looked as though someone had murdered him in cold blood as he sat at the desk, and you didn't want the police to gain the same impression."

Her silence was her consent. Mordecai felt a wave of compassion for her. She must have believed that Lester Imleyson had killed her husband not in the heat of passion but deliberately and coolly as he had sat unsuspecting. She must have endured an unspeakable agony of mind.

He did not wish to prolong her torment now. He said, quickly, "Adrian Carthallow was a successful artist. He made a lot of money. But he didn't make as much as he wanted, and he didn't make it quickly enough. He was heavily in debt. He owed Mr. Haldean several thousand pounds, and there were probably other creditors who weren't so ready to wait for settlement. So he looked around for another method of dealing with his difficulties. And he found it. He found it in selling pictures that were supposed to be by famous artists of the past but that he actually painted himself.

"As a painter he was a genius. He had a versatility of style that enabled him to imitate the work of artists like Gainsborough, Reynolds, and Lawrence so well that he could deceive experts. The trouble was, of course, that he couldn't market them himself. He had to find a man who could sell the paintings for him without allowing his name to be mentioned.

"The man he found was called Galley. Just how he met him I don't suppose we shall ever discover, but Carthallow often went into strange places and was acquainted with a great many people of doubtful reputation. He could always explain it by saying that he was searching for copy—trying to find suitable models for his pictures and studying humanity in the raw. Galley was a con man—a smooth-tongued confidence trickster who could negotiate the selling end."

Hilda Eveland's plump face bore an expression of incredulity. "Are you trying to tell us, Mordecai, that Adrian was actually engaged in a conspiracy with this man Galley to sell faked old masters?"

"Precisely," said Mordecai Tremaine. "We know that one picture was definitely sold—a painting purported to be by Reynolds that was bought by Warren Belmont, the American millionaire who was over here a short while ago. It was very cleverly arranged, of course. Belmont was led to believe that he had made a find and was getting a bargain—the picture was supposed to have been discovered among a lot of old paintings stored in the ancestral home of a peer who'd just succeeded to his title and who was only too glad to sell but who didn't want his name mentioned. It was so good a fake that it fooled experts over here, but suspicions were raised in New York and Belmont asked for discreet inquiries to be made. It may be that other pictures will come to light—the investigations are still going on.

"Galley was in Falporth until recently. He was going under the name Morton Westfield and was a member of the Follies concert party at the Pavilion. He was keeping in touch with Carthallow—I saw them myself one morning on the beach. It seemed that he wanted Carthallow to paint more pictures—I imagine he looked upon him as a kind of magic goose that would go on laying golden eggs indefinitely—and Carthallow didn't sound at all happy about it. Perhaps he realized better than his accomplice that to produce too many fakes would be to risk discovery, or perhaps he already knew that Warren Belmont was suspicious about the Reynolds and that inquiries were being made about it. It's true enough, as Mr. Haldean told me, that Carthallow was worried and obviously had something on his mind.

"It's more than probable that Westfield—or Galley, rather—was trying his hand at blackmail. Having painted and sold one fake painting, Carthallow had put himself in the hands of his accomplice. Instead of being the master, paying a small percentage of the profit for the actual work of selling, he may have become the servant, with Galley demanding more pictures as the price of his silence. Carthallow dared not refuse him outright because he knew that if Galley went to the police his own position and reputation would be gone. Galley would be in it, too, of course, but being only a minor instrument and having turned King's evidence, he would be able to hope for a much lighter sentence."

Mordecai Tremaine's pince-nez had been steadily slipping. In the very moment when it seemed that nothing could save them, he settled them back into position.

"Perhaps," he said mildly, "you can already see what I'm suggesting?"

Both Hilda Eveland and Helen Carthallow were looking puzzled, but Elton Steele leaned forward. His voice held a note of eagerness that was foreign to him.

"You mean that this chap Galley—or Westfield, whatever his real name is—might be mixed up in the murder?"

Mordecai Tremaine did not reply. He sat regarding them, doing his utmost to appear inscrutable.

It was Lewis Haldean who took up the point Steele had raised. He gestured excitedly.

"You think it was Galley who brought Adrian back unexpectedly? You think Galley told him he wanted to see him here where they wouldn't be disturbed and that there was a quarrel and that Galley shot him, either accidentally or deliberately? By Heaven, Tremaine, if what you've said about this picture business is true there's a motive there right enough!"

He turned to face Inspector Penross, still standing impassively against the door.

"Have you tackled Galley, Inspector? What's his story? Was he able to give you a decent alibi?"

Penross glanced at Mordecai Tremaine. That gentleman said, "Unfortunately, Galley isn't in a position to give us any kind of information. You see, he's dead."

The enthusiasm faded slowly from Haldean's face.

"Dead?" he echoed. "But how? When did it happen?"

"His body was found yesterday among the rocks at the foot of Trecarne Head. The newspapers were asked to hold the information until further inquiries could be made. It could have been an accident—the cliff edge is dangerous just there, as you probably know—or it could have been suicide."

"Poor devil." It was Elton Steele's voice. He saw their expressions of surprise, looked disconcerted for an instant, and then shrugged. "Sorry. I suppose if he killed Adrian I ought to say good riddance to a murderer. But I never really liked Adrian, and it's no use pretending I did. I think he deserved all he got."

"Elton!"

Helen Carthallow sounded distressed, but her distress was edged with fear. Mordecai Tremaine eyed her reflectively. Steele twisted in his chair so that he was facing her.

"Don't worry, Helen. They can't hang me just for disliking Adrian. They'll have to prove I killed him first."

"Wait a moment," Lewis Haldean said suddenly. "Wait a moment!" He had been hunched in his chair, a look of intense concentration upon his face. "It's beginning to fit. Suppose Galley *did* come here and kill Adrian—not intentionally but after a quarrel in which both their nerves were on edge. Suppose he knew that the police were already taking an interest in the crooked game with the paintings and that sooner or later they were bound to catch up with him. Isn't it possible that he decided to take the easiest way out? After all, Trecarne Head's the obvious place for suicide. If *that* was what happened it clears up the whole thing!"

"It's certainly a nice, tidy theory," Mordecai Tremaine agreed, "but it takes us back to where we started. How did Galley manage to get into the house and then make his escape without being seen? I asked you all to come here today," he added, "because I wondered whether any of you could tell me anything that would give the answers to those questions."

At first there was a silence. And then Elton Steele's breath came in a long sigh.

"So it *was* Galley," he said.

There was a sudden ripple of conversation. A ripple that swelled into a volume of sound that held conjecture and wonder and relief. Above all, relief.

Mordecai Tremaine glanced at Colonel Neale, a distant, aloof gray figure, somehow immeasurably detached from the others.

"You, Colonel," he said. "You were in the neighborhood of the house that day. Did *you* see anything of him?"

Colonel Neale shook his head.

"I didn't notice anyone in particular. I'm afraid I can't help you there."

"He's dead," Mordecai Tremaine said. "I know where your sympathies lie, but it won't harm Galley for you to speak now."

The wintry smile was on the Colonel's lips.

"I still can't tell you I saw him. I just didn't notice anyone."

Hilda Eveland said, "But, Mordecai, even if he *was* in the neighborhood it doesn't prove he came to the house. He would have had to cross the bridge, and Matilda would have seen him. And she wouldn't have had any reason to tell lies about *that*."

"No," Mordecai Tremaine agreed, "she wouldn't. It looks as though we've reached a deadlock, doesn't it?"

"Perhaps," Lewis Haldean said, "he didn't get to the house by using the bridge after all."

"What d'you mean?" queried Elton Steele sharply.

"I mean suppose he came up the cliff?"

"But that's impossible, Lewis," Helen Carthallow said. "No one could climb up that way. It's far too steep."

The blond man stuck to his point.

"I don't think it would be impossible. Helen, do you remember that day a couple of years ago when Adrian wanted to explore the side of the cliff? He saw a cleft in the rock that he thought might be a cave, and we fixed up a rope and lowered him down."

She frowned.

"Yes, I remember," she said. "But I don't see the connection, Lewis."

"Don't you see, Helen? We fastened the rope around an iron staple in the ruined lookout place out on the headland. *And that staple's still there!*"

Mordecai Tremaine said, doubtfully, "Surely it would need a long rope to reach from the lookout hut right down to the beach?"

"There wouldn't be any need to use a rope for the whole distance. The top portion of the cliff is sheer—a fly couldn't hope to climb it—but once you've got past that the rest is fairly easy. An active man could manage it all right."

"It sounds reasonable," Mordecai Tremaine said. "He could have put a double rope around the staple, lowered himself down the cliff until he came to the part where he could use his hands and feet, and then have pulled the rope after him so that nobody could tell he'd gone that way. It shows us how he might have got *away*, but the question is how did he get *in*? Obviously, he couldn't have fixed the rope around the staple in order to climb *up* the cliff."

Haldean looked crestfallen.

"No," he admitted, "I suppose not." And then, after a moment or two, his face cleared again. "I've got it!" he said exultantly. "Matilda Vickery would have seen him if he'd crossed the bridge in daylight, so he must have crossed it hours before Adrian got back—*when it was still dark!*"

"You mean that he waited in the empty house all day for Adrian Carthallow to come?"

"Yes! Don't you see, if Matilda Vickery didn't see him he must have done it, and it was vital from his point of view anyway that nobody should know about his connection with Carthallow."

Roberta Fairham gave a cry. Her face had gone white.

"Then—then he must have been there when I—I—"

Mordecai Tremaine inclined his head.

"That's it, Miss Fairham. If that's what he did he must have been here when you paid *your* visit. You must have been alone with a murderer. Fortunately," he added dryly, "you didn't know it."

Haldean was still shaping his theory, eagerly fitting fresh pieces into the puzzle.

"With that rope to carry," he said, "he knew that he'd be a conspicuous figure. *So he came by sea.* The tide was full at about half past three that morning. There are several caves at the end of the headland. They aren't very wide, but they run well back into the cliff. On a full tide he could have taken his boat well in out of sight and moored it. Then he scrambled over the rocks and worked his way along the headland until he reached the sands and was able to go up to the bridge and cross over in the dark.

"He waited for Adrian to come, killed him, and then used the rope to make his escape down the cliff just before Helen got back. It's pretty deserted on the far side of the headland, and he would have been able to make sure there was nobody about before he started to climb down. By that time the afternoon tide would have been well in, and it would have been a simple job to get his boat out again.

"The murder may not have been premeditated, but he would have had his way of escape ready because of the need to avoid drawing attention to his visit. There wouldn't have been any danger of the boat being noticed during the day because he could have left it far enough inside the cave to prevent anyone seeing it from the sea, and even at low tide there's water covering the end of the headland so that it was unlikely that anybody would come exploring on foot."

The blond man stopped. He was sitting forward expectantly.

"Well," he said, "there you are, Tremaine. What do you think of *that* for an explanation?"

Mordecai Tremaine nodded approvingly.

"Thank you, Mr. Haldean. You've given us a very lucid account."

He added, quietly, "*I thought that must have been the way you did it.*"

31

At first it seemed that none of them had realized what he had said. And then Hilda Eveland's voice came shakily, incredulously: "Mordecai—you don't, you *can't* mean that it was *Lewis* who killed Adrian?"

"I'm afraid," Mordecai Tremaine said, "that is just what I do mean."

Haldean was bolt upright, as though shock had jerked him there. There was indignation in the thrust of his beard and the blaze of his Viking's blue eyes.

"Look here, Tremaine, I'm not in the mood for jokes of this kind."

Mordecai Tremaine said, "No one knows better than yourself that I've no intention of joking."

Slowly the blond man relaxed. He glanced over his shoulder. Inspector Penross was standing a yard away from him, and his attitude was tense and watchful. Haldean smiled.

"I presume," he said, "you have some foundation for this absurd accusation of yours. I think you'd better tell me what it is."

Helen Carthallow was staring at Mordecai Tremaine.

"There must be some mistake," she said. "Some dreadful mistake. It *couldn't* have been Lewis."

"There's no mistake," he told her gravely. "When you came down to me that afternoon on the beach and told me about your husband, I'd been aroused once before—by what I later discovered must have been the sound of a shot, and I'd also been aware of a vague buzzing noise. I didn't pay much attention to it at the time—it was mixed up with the surf and you can't be certain of things when you're neither asleep nor awake. But afterward, when we were faced with the problem of whether anyone could have got into the house without being seen, that vague sound kept recurring to my mind. It worried me. And at last I realized what it had been—*the engine of a motor launch.*

"I knew then how the murderer—assuming it had been someone we hadn't so far suspected—could have made his escape. And having thought of the sea as a means of getting away without crossing the bridge, the next step was to deduce that somehow a rope had been used to get down the steep, upper part of the cliff and that the murderer had then managed to climb the rest of the way. I remembered, too, that when Adrian Carthallow had shown me the lookout hut, I'd noticed a big iron staple in the ground that would have made an ideal support for the rope. It didn't explain, of course, how the murderer had managed to get into the house in the first place, and the only explanation I could think of was that he'd crossed the bridge in darkness and had waited on the premises all day, leaving his boat concealed in one of the caves at the foot of the cliffs."

Lewis Haldean stretched his legs ostentatiously. He had the air of a man who was completely unconcerned.

"I've just told *you* all that," he observed sardonically. "The point is that *I* didn't work the miracle. Galley did."

"Unfortunately for you," Mordecai Tremaine said, "Galley couldn't have worked it. There was a matinée performance of the Follies that day, and he was there for the opening number at half past two. Inspector Penross has made certain of that. You, of course, were officially staying at St. Mawgan, and on the surface you had an alibi. But when the inspector and I went a little deeper into that same alibi we discovered a rather curious thing. According to your host, Mr. Tregarwen, you enjoyed a protracted fishing trip that day—you left the harbor in your boat with the early tide before it was light and you didn't return until the tide came in again late in the afternoon. You were alone. There was no one to say that you didn't go fishing but that you left your boat in a cave under the headland here and spent the day in this house waiting for Adrian Carthallow."

He pushed his pince-nez higher and regarded Lewis Haldean reflectively. He fancied that the blond man had lost something of his composure.

"I'm not certain of your motive, but knowing Adrian Carthallow's attitude toward women I think I can guess. When I called at your bungalow on the day we went to St. Mawgan together, there was the photograph of a woman on your dressing table. It was a photograph you evidently prized highly, and yet it was one that even your closest friends hadn't apparently seen because when I happened to mention it to Mrs. Eveland she told me that although she was on very good terms with you, she'd never heard you speak of a girl called Margaret, and it was obvious that the photograph conveyed nothing to her.

"I think your plan to murder Carthallow must have been developing over a long period of time—which shows that you must have had good reason to hate him. His expensive tastes aided your design. You encouraged him to gamble, and when he was hard-pressed you lent him money to make sure he'd try to get back what he'd already lost and lose more still.

"I saw you together in London, as you will doubtless recall, although you've carefully avoided any reference to it. It was clear then that you were leading him on, and clear, too, that Carthallow was risking more than he could afford, because he couldn't help showing his chagrin when he lost. He wasn't at all happy about my seeing him, which I rather fancy is another proof that he was in deep water and knew it.

"Of course, your role was that of the trusted friend. You

lent him several thousand pounds and didn't press for payment. You pretended to be worried about him and tried to get him to take things easily—knowing perfectly well that he couldn't afford to do it and that you were only making him more determined to go on. You told people like myself that you thought he was under a great strain and heading for a breakdown, in the hope that the idea would spread. You *wanted* it to be thought that Carthallow was living on his nerves. *You were preparing the way for his suicide."*

Lewis Haldean's hand went up to smooth his silken beard. It was intended to be a nonchalant gesture. But his hand was unsteady.

"That was your intention," Tremaine went on. "You weren't going to let Carthallow's death be treated as murder and run any risks over it. Officially he was going to commit suicide. I don't know how much you knew about Carthallow's connection with Galley, but if you did know the full story you must have been highly delighted. Respected artist, up to his eyes in debt, trying to make ends meet by selling fake old masters. What a perfect motive for suicide!

"Carthallow came back unexpectedly from Wadestow because you'd persuaded him to meet you secretly. You told him that you'd come over from St. Mawgan so that you could talk without being disturbed. I don't doubt that you gave him a convincing reason for the meeting.

"You knew he kept a Webley revolver in his desk. You knew its caliber and everything about it. You also knew that there were plenty of service revolvers of a similar pattern to be picked up in London if you contacted the right people—revolvers left over from the war that might be expensive to buy but that wouldn't be registered under the firearms act and that the police wouldn't be able to trace. Carthallow's own gun, in fact, was just that kind of weapon.

"When Carthallow came into the house he didn't suspect that you were already there, so he went into his study and sat waiting for you. The stage was set now, so you made your entrance as though for the first time. I dare say you thought that if you were unlucky enough to be seen leaving the place by some chance visitor to the neighborhood, a pair of dark glasses would help to prevent your being recognized. Anyway, you came provided with a pair, and I think you were wearing them when you went into the study—probably to heighten the illusion that you'd just come in from the sun. You strolled in with your hands in your pockets, and Carthallow, suspecting nothing, didn't realize that it was because you were wearing gloves.

"As you went in, you took off the glasses and dropped them on a chair, and then you stepped up to Carthallow and, before he could grasp what was happening, you'd placed the revolver against his head and fired. You took his keys from his pocket, and while his body was still propped in the chair you went over to the desk by the window and took out his gun. The mistake you made there, of course, was in leaving the entire bunch in the lock instead of only the one key as Carthallow himself would have done.

"Then you dragged the desk across the floor and placed Carthallow's body as it might reasonably look if he'd shot himself. You knew that moving the desk was a weakness that might possibly lead to awkward questions, but you daren't move the body across to the place where it usually stood. You knew that there'd inevitably be traces that the forensic science experts in the police laboratories would be able to find, and once there was any suspicion aroused that the body had been moved after death, the suicide theory would have been ruled out. You had to account for any odd splashes of blood there might have been on the floor around the body, and the only way you could do that was by moving the desk and making it look as though the shooting had actually taken place in the center of the room. The position of the desk might seem puzzling, but there wouldn't appear to be anything directly significant about it.

"After that you turned your attention to the gun. You knew that the police would soon find out that it wasn't Carthallow's revolver that had killed him. It hadn't been fired, and in any case the barrel and breech markings wouldn't tally with the bullet and the ejected cartridge case. You found the spent bullet in the picture rail and managed to extract it with a pair of surgical forceps you'd brought for the purpose. Then, still wearing gloves, you fired a *second* shot, this time with Carthallow's gun and standing as far back as you dared, into the hole made by the first. You realized, of course, that the hole would be larger than that made by a spent bullet and that there might be more blackening and powder grains and destruction around the edges, but you were gambling on an obvious appearance of suicide to prevent too detailed a scientific examination, and in any case firearms can play queer tricks.

"So far everything was working out just as you'd planned. The police were going to find Adrian Carthallow seated at his desk with his gun still in his hand, and when they tested the bullet and the cartridge case they were going to verify that they had come from that particular weapon. If anything had gone wrong and the first bullet had lodged in his skull, you were going to take his gun and the cartridges and leave your own. Since Carthallow wasn't supposed to have the weapon officially and hadn't registered it, you thought you'd be safe. One Webley looks like another, and nobody would be able to swear it *wasn't* Carthallow's gun if any doubt did happen to arise.

"And then the whole scheme went wrong. You'd fired the second shot, collected the first bullet and the cartridge case, checked for anything else that might need attention—*and then you heard someone coming into the house!*

"That must have been a moment of real panic. You hadn't expected anything like that, and you lost your nerve. You'd thought that Mrs. Carthallow was safely in Wadestow and that the servants wouldn't be back until later. You didn't know who was coming in or how many visitors there might be. And, although you hadn't quite completed your arrangements, you dared not stay because if anyone saw you it would mean you were finished. You made sure you'd picked up your own gun and then escaped through the garden. In your hurry you overlooked both the sunglasses and the forceps."

There was a hush upon the room. Each of them was still, listening without sound or movement to the steady, damning indictment that was coming from the mild-looking, elderly man with the pince-nez who sat facing them.

No one looked at Lewis Haldean. The blond man's normal air of vitality had gone, and there were deep lines of strain etched into his cheeks, but otherwise he gave no sign of the havoc that quiet voice must have caused in him.

"When you got back from St. Mawgan that night," Mordecai Tremaine went on, "you must have been a shocked and bewildered man. Not by the news that Adrian Carthallow was dead—that certainly wasn't news to you—but by the fact that Helen Carthallow had told the police that *she* had

killed him. That was a development you hadn't reckoned
with, and it presented you with a problem you had no idea
how to solve. You didn't want someone else to be accused of
the crime you'd committed, and at the same time you were
understandably anxious to avoid being arrested for it yourself.

"From the first I was intrigued by two things—your insistence that Carthallow might have committed suicide and your
championship of Mrs. Carthallow. It seemed so obviously *not*
suicide, and you harped so much on the point that it *was*
that I began to wonder whether you didn't know more than
you'd admitted—something, in fact, that fitted in with the
suicide theory. That brought me to the next stage. Suppose,
I reasoned, it wasn't really suicide, but that somebody had
intended to make a murder look like a suicide. And suppose
that somebody had been interrupted by Mrs. Carthallow's
arrival before he had been able to finish his artistic setting.

"It began to look hopeful. I'll admit that at first I was
inclined to suspect Mr. Imleyson, but then I realized that
there were too many things that didn't fit. For instance, if
Mr. Imleyson had planned to kill Mr. Carthallow, he would
hardly have arranged to meet Mrs. Carthallow on the scene
of the crime—unless they were in it together, which in view of
the apparently elaborate attempt to make it look like suicide
seemed unlikely, since neither of them would have had an
alibi. And if he'd killed him after meeting him unexpectedly

as the guilty lover, then it just didn't explain the desk and the forceps.

"The more I thought it over, the more convinced I became that I'd have to find someone else—a third party, who knew that Carthallow was coming to the house, who'd been interrupted by the arrival of Mrs. Carthallow, and, indirectly, Mr. Imleyson, and who'd made his escape by way of the sea instead of crossing the bridge.

"That made *you* the obvious choice. You'd been on a fishing trip to St. Mawgan, which meant that you could have used a motor launch without arousing comment and could quite easily have come in this direction—it's quite a short journey by water. You knew all about the arrangements Mr. and Mrs. Carthallow had made and knew that the house would be empty. I recalled your strange harping on the suicide theory and how you'd told me that you were worried about Carthallow and wouldn't be surprised if he had a breakdown. I recalled how intimate you'd been with him and how you'd seemed to know a great deal about his financial affairs. All those things gradually began to form a complete picture, but I think it was a lie you told me in Valance Gardens that made me certain you were the man for whom we were searching."

Haldean looked up. There was inquiry in his eyes. Tremaine said, "I imagine you felt you must be under suspicion because of your vigorous denials that Helen Carthallow had killed her husband. As one of her closest friends you would naturally be expected to adopt such an attitude, but I think you realized that you'd been carrying things just a little too far and you wanted to give me a reason that would satisfy me. So you told me you were in love with her.

"I knew it was a lie. Quite apart from the fact that I'd seen that photograph in your room, Mrs. Eveland had told me that you weren't in love with Helen Carthallow, and I was quite sure she wouldn't have made a mistake over a matter of that kind. So you were lying. And if you *were* lying, then it was a sign that you had something on your conscience.

"I don't doubt that you killed Galley. Upon reflection I think you must have known a great deal about his connection with Carthallow, and perhaps he knew a great deal about *you*—too much, in fact. Maybe he thought he could blackmail you as he'd tried to blackmail Carthallow. So you pushed him over the cliffs at Trecarne Head to make sure he kept his mouth shut."

He stopped. He looked at the blond man. Haldean said, without malice: "You're a clever devil. You knew when you brought us all here that Galley couldn't have killed Adrian. All that stuff about his having developed cold feet and gone over the cliff by accident or because he knew the game was up was just bait in the trap."

Mordecai Tremaine inclined his head.

"Yes," he agreed. "It was bait."

"You knew I couldn't let anyone else—least of all Helen—be convicted for something I'd done. But you weren't too sure of yourself, so you decided to call this friendly little gathering and give the impression that the case was as good as closed and that all you needed before you made the thing public was to find out just how Galley had managed to get in and out of the house. You reasoned that I'd be so relieved at finding I was safe, after all, that I'd give you the whole story, thinking I was pinning the job well and truly on to Galley. And it worked. I behaved like a lamb going to the slaughter!"

His voice rose. He glanced toward the window. A tense watchfulness crept into Mordecai Tremaine's manner.

"The game's up, you know."

"Don't worry," Lewis Haldean said. "I'm not going to try anything. I know when I'm beaten." He leaned back in his chair. "What a fool I was to fall for it—what a stupid, unwary fool!"

He began to laugh—quietly and with genuine amusement. He was still laughing when Inspector Penross placed a hand on his shoulder and told him that he was being taken into custody for the willful murder of Adrian Carthallow and that anything he said would be written down and might be used in evidence at a later date.

32

The garden gate was thrust open. Charles Penross came buoyantly down the path and dropped into the vacant deck chair.

"I hear," he said, "that you're going back tomorrow."

Jonathan Boyce took his pipe out of his mouth.

"Yes, Charles, the holiday's over. We're leaving on the nine-thirty."

Penross said, gruffly, "I just wanted to say thanks—for all the help you've given me."

He was looking at Mordecai Tremaine.

"You did all the hard work, Charles," said that gentleman, embarrassed. "It's easy for a spectator to offer advice from the sidelines." He added: "It's all over?"

The inspector nodded.

"Bar the shouting. Haldean's made a full statement. You were right about the motive. It was that girl in the photograph. He admitted he made a mistake there. He used to put it away during the day in case Carthallow saw it and recognized her, but when you called it had slipped his mind and all he could do was to try and pass it off.

"Haldean was engaged to her. She went off to the States with Carthallow just before the date fixed for the wedding. She died in San Francisco—of pneumonia accentuated by undernourishment. By that time Carthallow had grown tired of her and had left her flat. He hadn't troubled to marry her—you know his type."

"I watched him with Roberta Fairham," Tremaine said. "It wasn't pretty. I take it, by the way, that Haldean hasn't been using his real name?"

"No. That was why Carthallow didn't connect him with the man whose girl he'd once run off with. He knew she was engaged, but apparently he'd never met her fiancé. Not that he'd have troubled himself about him in any case.

"Haldean was genuinely in love with the girl, and he didn't forget. He found out after a while that Carthallow had deserted her, and he went over to America to bring her back. He was too late. She'd died a couple of months before.

"After that, his one idea was to get even with Carthallow. He wasn't short of money, so that there was nothing to stop him from devoting himself to the job. When Carthallow came back to this country and began to establish himself as an artist, Haldean got to know him and gradually achieved a position as his most intimate friend.

"He encouraged him to gamble just as you said, although I don't think much encouragement was needed. His plan was to bring Carthallow to the point where his suicide would seem like the act of a man taking the easiest way out of the mess he was in and then he was going to strike.

"He did know all about the fake paintings and about the linkup between Carthallow and Galley. He knew that if he wanted to he could give Carthallow away, ruin him and get him a term in jail, but he wanted more than that. He wanted to take a personal revenge, and nothing less than murder would satisfy him.

"It was his knowledge about the Reynolds deal with Warren Belmont that enabled him to persuade Carthallow to meet him secretly at the house. He told him that he knew that things were getting dangerous and that he wanted to get together with him where they wouldn't be disturbed to try and find a way out. Carthallow fell for the guardian angel act and arranged the meeting *before* he went to Wadestow. He never did intend to stay in the town until the evening, although he told his wife and everybody else that he did.

"Of course, Galley was interested in Carthallow's friends for obvious reasons, and I think Carthallow must have told him something about Haldean's being afraid there was trouble coming. Anyway, he'd been keeping an eye on Haldean, and after the murder he put two and two together. Carthallow had been a useful meal ticket, and you can imagine that he didn't take kindly to the thought of losing him. He tackled Haldean, told him he knew what had happened and that he expected to be well paid if he was to keep his mouth shut.

"Naturally, Haldean wasn't anxious to spend the rest of his life paying out blackmail, but he knew that he couldn't take the risk of turning Galley down flat. He pretended to go to pieces and arranged to meet him at an old hut near Trecarne Head to talk about terms. He said that with inquiries still going on he didn't want to chance being seen in Galley's company anywhere in the town. It seemed reasonable enough, and since Haldean put up a convincing show of a man who'd lost his nerve, Galley agreed to the meeting. Which was just too bad for him. Haldean was there first, laid in wait for him, and knocked him out with a handy chunk of rock and then dragged his body to the edge of the cliff in the dark and threw him over."

The inspector heaved a sigh. He said, "Well, that's it. I don't mind admitting, though, that I had some pretty bad moments when you were working up to your final curtain at Paradise. You amateurs can sail near the wind and get away with it, but we professionals have to be above reproach. I was having all sorts of unpleasant thoughts about the Judges' Rules and the admissibility of evidence. Fortunately, Haldean seems to have taken it for granted that he was done for, and when I got him down to the station after I'd cautioned him, he gave his statement without any trouble."

Mordecai Tremaine nodded thoughtfully.

"It certainly prevents any awkwardness, Charles. What's Haldean's attitude?"

"It's as though he's resigned himself to take what's coming," Penross said. "He's just not interested—acts as if now that he's done the job he wanted to do he doesn't care what happens. It may not last, of course. When he realizes just where he is he may change his tune."

"Right now," said Mordecai Tremaine slowly, "I think he feels that he's a man who has fulfilled his destiny and hasn't any need to go on living."

"He must have been in love with that girl of his."

"He *was* in love with her. But I'm pretty certain that for a long time now she's been only an excuse in his mind. His real love has been a desire for revenge. He allowed the thought of getting even with Carthallow to become an obsession. That's why he didn't do the obvious thing and go to the police when he found out about Carthallow and Galley. As you said just now, he wanted something more. He wanted a life for a life, and he wanted the self-glorification of believing that *he* was the chosen instrument for taking it."

Penross said, "I can't help feeling sorry for the poor devil. He must have gone through a bad time when that girl died, and from all accounts Carthallow isn't any great loss—despite his pictures."

"But he had the right to live, Charles," Mordecai Tremaine said slowly. "*You* know that. No man can take the law into his own hands."

His hand went up to his pince-nez. There was a troubled look in his eyes.

"Perhaps I should have seen it sooner. I might have been able to do something. I knew that there was trouble of some kind, but I was too slow. I couldn't put my finger on it. If only I'd taken pains with Haldean he might have talked to me. I heard him say once that without purpose a man couldn't begin to live. It occurred to me that it was an odd thing to come from a man who didn't seem to have any purpose himself, but I let it go, Charles. I didn't follow it up as I should have done."

Penross placed a hand on his shoulder.

"I know how you feel," he said quietly. "I've been in this game a long time, and I still don't like it when I have to put a man inside unless he's just plain crooked. You couldn't have done any more than you did. Haldean wouldn't have talked. If he could stick close to Carthallow for so long without letting him suspect anything, he wouldn't have given himself away to you, a comparative stranger."

"Maybe not," Mordecai Tremaine said. "But you see,

Charles, right from my first meeting with him I had a strange feeling where Adrian Carthallow was concerned. It was as though our lives were fated to come together. It was probably just my imagination. I dare say the reason he went out of his way to be friendly toward me when he found out I was here was that he had a guilty conscience and wanted to make sure that my visit was purely an innocent one and that I hadn't come to keep an eye on him.

"That afternoon on the beach, when Helen Carthallow came down to me, I'd been thinking things over because I knew that the situation was beginning to look dangerous, but I didn't dream that it was going to come to a head so soon or so violently. The shot I heard, of course, must have been the second that Haldean fired. What probably happened was that the first shot, although I don't recall it, disturbed my nap so that when the second report came I was already half awake and heard it distinctly. If only I'd taken the trouble to notice the time, we might have been able to clear things up sooner."

"It hasn't turned out so badly," Penross said. "Maybe," he added, "it was a good thing for somebody that Haldean acted when he did."

Tremaine gave him an inquiring glance.

"You mean Colonel Neale?"

"I mean Colonel Neale," his companion agreed. "He didn't come to Falporth merely for his health."

"You think he intended to do something about Carthallow?" Mordecai Tremaine pursed his lips. "I don't know, Charles," he said doubtfully. "There's a big difference between a man who'd like to murder someone and a man who's actually prepared to do it. Still, whether Neale came here with any definite purpose in his mind is merely an academic question. He's cleared now."

"Yes," Penross said, "he's cleared now."

Both of them were silent, and then, after a moment or two, Mordecai Tremaine said, "You won't be—too hard on her, Charles? She's been through a great deal, you know."

There was understanding in the inspector's eyes.

"Don't worry," he said. "I'm not anxious to wash any more dirty linen in public than is absolutely necessary, and Haldean's confession will help to keep the questions down."

After Penross had gone Mordecai Tremaine went out onto the cliffs. This was the time he dreaded. The time of black reaction when the excitement of the pursuit and the exhilaration of the problem were over and he was left with the ashes of despair.

All the romanticism and the idealism within him seemed to be threatened by an engulfing darkness. He wanted to believe in an ordered, happy world in which cheating and lying and dreadful murder had no part. He wanted there always to be a happy ending. And instead he could see only ruined lives and ugly, twisted passions.

He walked slowly along the cliff path, the evening breeze blowing about him and the sound of the surf in his ears, and tried to tell himself that it was no use nursing regrets for what was past. You had to keep your eyes on the future; you had to forget the heartache and the disillusion of what had gone before.

He glanced down to the beach and saw two figures where the waves were still breaking white in that ceaseless flood of cleansing water. One of them was Elton Steele, and the big man's arm was around his companion's waist, holding her closely to him.

Mordecai Tremaine found that his eyes were misty. He took off his pince-nez and began to polish them. The sentimental glow began to creep to hesitant life again in his heart.

He thought that for Helen Carthallow there was going to be a happy ending after all.

ABOUT THE AUTHOR

Francis Duncan knows how to write a good murder mystery, and from the 1930s through the 1950s, his whodunits captivated readers. His character, Mordecai Tremaine, was the best at unraveling a narrative. However, there was one mystery that went unsolved: Who exactly *was* Francis Duncan?

When Vintage Books, an imprint of Random House UK, decided to bring back Duncan's *Murder for Christmas* in December 2015, questions still loomed around the author's unknown identity. In fact, there wasn't a trace of biographical information about the author to be found, and Vintage republished the book without solving the puzzle. Francis Duncan remained a man of mystery.

That is until January 2016 when, after seeing *Murder for Christmas* on shelf at a Waterstones bookstore, Duncan's daughter came forward to the publishers, revealing that Francis Duncan is actually a pseudonym for her own father, William Underhill, who was born in 1918. He lived virtually all his life in Bristol and was a "scholarship boy" boarder at

Queen Elizabeth's Hospital school. Due to family circumstances he was unable to go to university and started work in the Housing Department of Bristol City Council. Writing was always important to him, and very early on he published articles in newspapers and magazines. His first detective story was published in 1936.

In 1938 he married Sylvia Henly. Although a conscientious objector, he served in the Royal Army Medical Corps in World War II, landing in France shortly after D-Day. After the war, he trained as a teacher and spent the rest of his life in education, first as a primary school teacher and then as a lecturer in a college of further education. In the 1950s he studied for an external economics degree from London University. No mean feat with a family to support; his daughter, Kathryn, was born in 1943, and his son, Derek, in 1949.

Throughout much of this time he continued to write detective fiction from "sheer inner necessity," but also to supplement a modest income. He enjoyed foreign travel, particularly to France, and took up golf on retirement. He died of a heart attack shortly after celebrating his fiftieth wedding anniversary in 1988.

Catch up on Mordecai Tremaine's sleuthing in

A MORDECAI TREMAINE MYSTERY

MURDER for CHRISTMAS

FRANCIS DUNCAN

PROLOGUE

No one could have foretold how it was going to end. Not even the murderer.

It is not to say that the crime was hastily conceived and clumsily executed. The majority of murderers are anxious to live to savor the fruits of their villainies. They realize that one slip may deliver them to the hangman. They know that to be careless is to be lost. And in this case, the murderer possessed both desire to profit and the knowledge of how perilously thin the dividing line is between safety and disaster.

But no human plan, however devilish its ingenuity, can be depended upon to follow in practice the exact lines of its careful theory. Somewhere along the route, incalculable and unforeseeable will lie the unexpected, the unknown factor.

The moon was like a spotlight playing over the stage of a theater. Or, like a camera tracking over a studio floor and alternately presenting its audience with close-up and long shot, sharply outlined image and somber obscurity.

The snow had stopped, but the sky had not yet cleared.

The clouds were drifting sullenly, as if reluctant to leave a prey freed only with difficulty from their grip. Sometimes they would gather menacingly upon one another and would crowd over an earth grown dark and full of fear; and then it would seem that they were thrust impotently apart and the white light would flood down, cold and revealing, and not to be turned aside.

And in the moonlight, every detail would be there in hard relief. The black-and-white roofs of the village under the hill; the thin, bare arms of the trees along the roadway; the smooth white downs rolling up to the sky; the big house with its old gray stones; and the white tracery where the snow clung to the creeper.

From the village came the sound of a bell. When the darkness was triumphant, it was a strange and mournful echo that could not be located and that held a note of menace. Imagination needed little encouragement to liken the sound to the tolling of doom.

But when the scene lay exposed under the moon, the fear and the mystery were driven back. The bell was no longer sinister. It was a glad sound of music that carried trium-phantly across the snow, ringing out from the square tower of the ancient church.

The landscape was a Christmas card in three dimensions. There would have been no incongruity if a sleigh drawn by reindeer had come sweeping over the brow of the downs. It did not, in fact, seem fantastic that the red-robed figure of Father Christmas was outlined in the moonlight, moving quickly along the terrace of the big house. It was, after all, Christmas Eve, when such things—particularly in such a setting—were to be expected.

Although it was late, the occupants of the house were not all in their beds. High up in one wing, a light still burned. At intervals, a figure crossed the illuminated frame that was the window.

There were other signs of activity that were not quite so apparent. But if one watched carefully, it was sometimes possible, especially when the moon was obscured, to see a faint glow behind the windows of the ground floor. It was a glow that changed its position, as though it owed its origin to a flashlight carried by someone who moved stealthily within the house.

And outside in the snow and the shadows there were muffled, hidden figures. Concealed from the house and from each other, they watched intently—and waited upon opportunity.

The atmosphere was brooding, tense with foreboding. Fantasy and mystery, violence and death were abroad. It seemed that time was moving reluctantly and with an ever more tightly coiled dread toward some terrible climax.

And at last the climax came.

It came when the bell had stopped. It came when the moonlight, searching again through the clouds, swept softly across the white lawns, revealing the ragged line of footprints. It came when the cold light flooded up to the half-open french doors and, tracing the moisture on the polished floor, came to rest upon the red thing of horror that was Father Christmas, stark and sprawled upon its face in front of the despoiled Christmas tree.

It came with a woman's scream—desperate, high-pitched, and raw with terror.

Look for more books in Francis Duncan's classic Mordecai Tremaine series

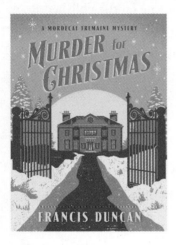

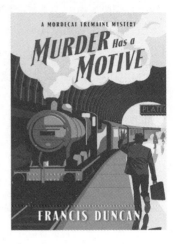